SANCTUARY

by

I. Beacham

2009

SANCTUARY

ISBN 10: 1-60282-055-4
ISBN 13: 978-1-60282-055-5

This Trade Paperback Original Is Published By
Bold Strokes Books, Inc.
P.O. Box 249
Valley Falls, NY 12185

First Edition: April 2009

CREDITS
Editor: Jennifer Knight
Production Design: Stacia Seaman
Cover Design By Sheri (graphicartist2020@hotmail.com)

Acknowledgments

To write is the key to the cage that grants freedom and lets dreams soar. I heartily thank Radclyffe, Jennifer Knight, and the entire wonderful team at BSB for handing me that key and then helping me to fly, in this, my first book.

Dedication

To Anita, To Jan,
Two irreplaceable Australian friends without whom this book
would never have seen the light. Thank you both.

Cursed, the bright angel fell, and as it plummeted, its wings grew dark and tarnished.

Upon the ground, tired and damaged, it tried to stand and ascend again, but there was no sunlight to feed it and the mud and grime lay too heavy on its wings.

For the longest time, it struggled valiantly to shake its burden and to soar once more, but the mire could not be moved, and in time, with too little to sustain it, the angel grew weary and could do no more.

Spirit broken, it wrapped its wings around itself for warmth, and alone in its dark place, it grew wretched.

CHAPTER ONE

New York Fashion Week

It had been a grand banquet hall once. A place adorned by beautiful cornices and marbled pillars which, not so long ago, had been no stranger to elegant gentry waltzing to the popular music of the day. A majestic room then, but no more. The once imposing hall had fallen upon hard times and was no different from the rest of the neglected hotel to which it belonged, all now subjected to the humiliation of modern day.

Today, its chambers debased, it was flooded with psychedelic strobe lights, mind-blowing music that pulsated with an undercurrent of heavy beat, and some four hundred audience members comprised of fashion designers, their cohorts, the media, and the public. Fashion models snaked around the floor, their runway performance over, slithering amidst eager onlookers, promoting the latest outfits they were paid to wear. As usual, these events seemed surreal but were one of the best ways for design houses to show off their latest collections to customers eager to part with money, and retailers hungry to cash in on every trend.

Bernard Bressinger, the fashion editor of *Nouveau Rich* magazine, and occasional fashion correspondent for the large national newspapers, always felt just a little jaded at these functions, but tonight he couldn't believe his luck. For the first time ever, two of the most talented names in female fashion were actually present at the same show. Barely able to contain himself, he looked over at tall, blond Dita Newton, a woman with eyes like a Siberian timber wolf, intense and ice blue. Though the color might suggest a cold nature, she had a reputation for being generous, graceful, and genuine. Bernard was certain she would grant him an interview. All he had to do was drag her away from his rivals in the fashion press.

He knew exactly what they were saying, word for gushy word. The sycophantic flattery and pandering, the demands for exclusive comments about what had made her choose particular designs and fabrics, her divine color scheme, and so on. Dita Newton was a rising star of the fashion world and the hit of tonight's show. She was both designer and manager of Seraphim, a long-established, but until recently, not very successful small Boston fashion house. However, since Newton had taken over its management six years ago, the business had blossomed under her clever direction and stunningly refreshing designs. Tonight's outstanding collection heralded her arrival as an immense talent.

Bernard planned an interview with a slightly different slant, maybe something more personal about her being thirty, slow success, the hard road, but the wait being worth the magnificence and quality of her designs. He decided to wait before he approached her, and to let some of the hangers-on drop off. In the meantime he couldn't help but notice the other designer who interested him. Cate Canton, the publicity-shy owner of competing fashion house, Zabor. This was one of the designers he liked, professionally, admiring the way she remained true to her fashion ideals and had not been caught up in building her own myth as so many fashion gurus were. Bernard couldn't imagine Canton turning bohemian and promoting the most garish, outlandish styles in order to impress an adoring public. No, she had stuck to the classic principles of "less is more," and her understated design values had turned Zabor into one of the fastest growing fashion houses in the U.S.

Despite her status, Canton stood alone on the periphery of the crowd, her attention focused solely on her rival, Dita Newton, a strange, unreadable expression on her slightly flushed face. Bernard found himself taking a deeper breath than usual as he cast an appreciative eye over her. Not stunningly good looking, but most definitely attractive, she was one of those women a man could enjoy looking at.

Her shiny shoulder-length auburn hair caught the light, which picked out the fine, fairer streaks. She was hardly a tall woman, but slim and immaculately dressed, exuding an air of quiet, classic sophistication. Everything about her spoke restraint, from the simple pearl earrings and matching necklace, to the plain but flattering black and white dress. Unable to stop his base tendencies, he took in the shapely lean legs beneath the fine hosiery and the beautifully manicured nails on the delicate fingers of her equally slender hands. If Canton had dressed to be inconspicuous, she was not, but at the same time she possessed a quality that warned others to be wary. She was beautiful, but also predatory and dangerous.

Bernard saw such women as a challenge and, but for the fact he'd heard she was gay, he might have tried to get to know her better. Perhaps her social leanings explained why she remained aloof from her admiring public, dismissive of their insatiable curiosity. In all the many years he'd attended these shows, the mysterious Cate Canton never put in a physical appearance, leaving her front man, Saul de Charlier, to handle things. To say she was reclusive was an understatement. There was more information out there on the Yeti.

He wondered why she was here tonight, for equally unusual, this year for the first time she had not promoted Zabor's collection at the show. Normally, this was where her latest designs were unveiled, frequently undermining those of her rivals. This event wasn't at the top end of the business, or bristling with international names. It was a show place for smaller designers who had cornered a lucrative segment of the ready-to-wear market, customers who demanded quality, style, and chic at an affordable price. Dita Newton and Cate Canton were the leaders of this particular pack, and Bernard couldn't believe for one minute that Canton was skipping the show because her insuperable talent had run dry.

Something had brought her here, but what? He suspected, as did many in the fashion circle, that the unpleasant business rivalry between her and Dita Newton was a factor in her isolation. There were all manner of rumors about the circumstances of their falling-out, but neither had ever commented publicly on the rift. Bernard could smell a juicy story, if only he could persuade one of the two to go on the record. Like every other fashion journalist looking for a front page headline, he had done some digging but all he'd managed to turn up was the old news that Dita Newton was at the helm of the fashion house built by Cate's family because William Canton had placed her there. No one was sure of his reasons. There was speculation about the traffic accident that had killed Cate's sister, but who could say? The response from the

Canton people to that particular line of questioning was invariably "no comment." Interrupted from his thoughts, Bernard saw an opportunity to get Cate's attention. "Miss Canton. What a pleasure."

The woman slowly turned her head, the chin rising in question. Her sharp dark blue eyes focused on him.

Bernard bestowed his most charming smile. "Miss Canton, I'm Bernard Bress—"

"I know who you are." The response was bereft of warmth.

This was one interview unlikely to fall easily into his lap. Refusing to be put off, Bernard widened his smile and mustered his charm. Attempting suave nonchalance, he said, "I see my reputation precedes me."

The deadpan expression remained. Cate was clearly unimpressed. He occasionally came across people who arrogantly thought themselves above giving interviews to the press they expected to publicize their work. Then there were those who were simply uncomfortable talking about themselves. He suspected Canton was one of the latter, which could explain why she shied away from the public. This behavior was unusual in the fashion world, but not entirely unknown. No matter how talented some people were, it didn't necessarily follow that they would be engaging and charming too.

"I just wanted to ask you a few—"

"I don't do interviews, Mr. Bressinger, as you know. Please put your questions to Saul de Charlier. He'll be happy to address them."

Bernard knew hornets' nests that were more approachable than Cate Canton, but he wasn't going to be put off. He hadn't made it to his managing editor position by being restrained and submissive. As Cate started to walk away, he altered the direction of his questioning. "I merely wondered what you thought of Dita Newton's new collection."

Success! The reluctant interviewee turned back to look at him, her face now cast in a more contemplative mood, the cold eyes warmer. She hesitated for a moment and then spoke, this time not in a hurried, curt manner, but with a softness and richness to the husky timbre of her voice.

As if she was suddenly transported miles away, she said, "A wonderful collection. Very innovative, very…creative. It's a winning collection from an inspired designer." She paused and something wistful entered her expression. "Beautiful clothes from a beautiful woman."

There was no cynicism or animosity in her reply, in fact she seemed to have a genuine appreciation and respect for the other designer. Bernard had expected quite a different tone. Weren't these two women supposed to be ruthless business opponents? He wondered if he'd allowed himself to buy into rumors of a catfight because the alternative was pretty boring. If Cate Canton and Dita Newton were nothing more than business rivals seeking to outdo each other, what would he write about in the succulent exposé feature he was planning? Before he could dig deeper, Canton excused herself and walked away, cutting across the floor toward Dita Newton, who had just finished talking to a group of journalists.

Dita almost intuitively sensed Cate Canton's approach. Her stomach churned. She'd been shocked to learn that her adversary was actually in the audience and had been preparing herself ever since she arrived for the unpleasantness bound to take place. Determined not to let Cate spoil the day she'd waited so long for, she mentally composed herself and inwardly chanted the mantra, *Control. Control. Control.* She would be calm and restrained when she greeted Cate, not like the last time, when she'd let her self-control slip.

"Canton," she said, coolly acknowledging the unwanted presence.

Cate merely responded with a half-smile. As she came to a graceful halt before Dita, they both took a while to study each other. Dita found it difficult to interpret Cate's seemingly affable smile and unguarded stance, but that was nothing new. She didn't need to seek out what lay beneath the veneer. She already knew Cate's treachery and was more than prepared.

"You look well," Cate said.

"I am." Dita would have accepted the comment as genuine from anyone else, but nothing Cate said could be taken at face value. Why was she here? What sordid little trick was she up to this time? Dita wanted this encounter over, and fast. The last thing she needed was stress or strain, and the fatally alluring woman in front of her who had once drawn her like a magnetic compass, could deliver both in bucket loads.

"Recovered completely?" Cate's eyes roamed over her with an odd mixture of compassion and desperation.

"Unfortunately for you," Dita chipped back edgily. The cutting response removed Cate's smile. "They say I'm doing exceptionally well, better than expected and ready to meet the challenges again. *All* of them."

Cate nodded slowly and looked down at her feet, anything to avoid the intense glacial blue gaze. Dita's eyes seemed locked onto her like the stare from one of those museum portraits, unnervingly following her no matter where she went in the room.

"Hopefully, you'll encounter fewer problems than you expect," she said quietly.

"Somehow I doubt it." Dita couldn't keep the bitterness from her voice and it drew Cate's eyes back up to hers. Surprisingly, she heard herself say, "I see you haven't entered anything for the show."

Dita wondered why she'd brought it up; she wasn't the slightest bit interested in the answer. Nothing about this woman interested her anymore. She considered how strangely reticent Canton's behavior seemed this evening. It was the way she looked at her, as if Cate wanted to lay everything on the line to save something…something that seemed to mean everything to her. But Dita wasn't fooled for one minute. *Trust her at your peril.*

"I've been busy," Cate replied.

"Yes, on an unscrupulous business venture that didn't pay off." Dita referred directly to Cate's failed attempt to mercilessly interfere and block the success of Seraphim.

"Oh, I got something out of it," Cate said candidly.

She found herself fighting an unpleasant backwash of memories, all of which reminded her of what she'd recently learnt and at what personal cost. She allowed her gaze to rest on Dita's taller and willowy form, soaking in her natural beauty. She was too thin, and despite declaring her good health, she looked pale. Perhaps she had returned to work too soon. The strain of this show must have placed an enormous burden on her.

"I doubt that. You're not used to failure."

"Failure?"

"Not getting what you want," Dita clarified. "But then I've always believed success shouldn't favor the wicked. I find it gratifying that someone like you, born into privilege, can't assume life owes you anything. What matters is how a person uses an initial advantage they were born to. Of course, you wouldn't know what I'm talking about."

If the stinging remark hit home, Cate didn't show the effects, except in the slight pursing of satin soft lips. "I only came to see the show and to wish you success, but I don't think you're going to need it."

"Not from you."

Cate was silent for several seconds. "There was a time when things didn't look good for you, when I thought—"

"When you thought you were going to get everything you wanted."

Haunted interrogative eyes stared back at her. "No." The denial was fast and adamant. "No, I *never* thought that. I'm glad you're better, feeling well again and that things look…good for you."

She sounded so sincere, Dita almost laughed, having learned first hand what Cate was capable of. She let her unveiled skepticism show. "If you'll excuse me, I'm busy and have better places to be, more important things to do."

Not waiting for any acknowledgment, she marched away toward Bernard Bressinger, who hovered patiently nearby to interview her. Cate called out to her by name, and something in her voice brought Dita to a halt. She looked back for a second before steeling herself and continuing on.

Unforgiving as the gaze had been, that one last look had meant everything to Cate. It was probably her last opportunity to commit the beautiful woman's image to memory, a last look she would cherish forever as she watched Dita Newton disappear into the crowd. If their paths were to cross again, it would be by accident, no longer orchestrated, and would always be something unwanted by Dita, who had made her feelings for Cate crystal clear. But then, what could Cate expect after everything she had done?

Moving back into the crowd, Cate spotted Marcus Abner, Dita Newton's marketing director, who for some reason had arrived late and was now trying to push his way through the mill of people to reach his boss. Cate intercepted him.

"Marcus, wait."

The slightly stooped, gray-haired man in his mid-fifties had worked for Seraphim long before Dita Newton took over, and knew Cate's mother before she died. He immediately stopped. Though clearly busy, he was one of life's intrinsic gentlemen who always made time for people. This, coupled with his staid appearance and behavior, made him an anathema in the fashion world. But Marcus's talent lay behind the scenes, where he kept the accounts and marketing focused. He was one of the reasons Seraphim hadn't folded years ago. Smiling warmly, he reached out to shake Cate's hand. Well, at least someone still liked her!

Not wasting any time, she thrust an envelope into his hand. "Marcus, good to see you again, but I can't stay, and I think Dita needs your help." Sensing his confusion, she said, "I need you to give her this. Leave it for a little while, but…make sure she gets it. Please."

"Why don't you give it to her now? She's over—"

"I know where she is." Cate smiled at him and affectionately straightened his tie. In all the years she'd known him, he'd never been able to tie a decent knot. "We've already spoken…sort of, and it didn't go well." She smiled again, more for Marcus's benefit than her own. "I came here to give her that letter, but I chickened out. So, please give it to her when things are quieter. Okay?"

For a moment, they merely eyed each other, communicating so much more than words. Then Cate snatched the envelope back. In a fraction of a second, it had dawned on her that the contents would never be understood and would not even partially heal the rift—the chasm— that lay between her and Dita. Perhaps her words would only inflame the whole wretched situation. Why not just acknowledge that all was lost and move on? She met Marcus's bewildered gaze.

"Sorry, change of plan. It was a silly idea, anyway. Maybe some things are better left unsaid." Unable to smile anymore, Cate feigned indifference as she tapped his arm gently. "Go give the poor woman a hand." She shoved him into the crowd before he could object. "Oh, and Marcus? Look after her."

As he walked away, Cate could barely control a wave of emotion that rose like a colossal wave battering a harbor wall. She covered her mouth to halt an involuntary sob. Damn it. Where was the exit? She had to get out of here and fast if she was going to avoid breaking down in a room full of photographers. She hadn't cried in years and she wasn't going to start now, in public.

She quickly retrieved her coat and, still clutching the letter, ran out into the street. The winter wind that should have left months ago still whispered the promise of more heavy snow. She pulled her coat around her tightly as crystal white flecks stuck to her face and hair.

Moving through the light flurries toward a sidewalk trash can, she dropped the unopened envelope inside. People bustled past her, well-wrapped New Yorkers accustomed to the climatic vagaries of February. Lingering, she stared down into the grimy receptacle. Guilt settled on her shoulders for the thousandth time. There was so much she wanted to say but never would, because Dita was not going to listen, and she only had herself to blame for that.

She raised her hand above her head and hailed a taxi. "I'm sorry, Dita," she whispered. "So very sorry."

CHAPTER TWO

It was late when Dita finally returned to her apartment near Dorchester in the southern district of Boston, tired and exhausted after the fashion week parties and company celebrations to mark her incredible success. This should have been a wonderful moment. Her new Fall collection had been received with the acclaim long overdue from the fashion press and her contemporaries, not to mention the queue of buyers making their pitches to promote the Seraphim range. But all she could think about was Cate Canton standing in front of her, pretending to wish her good fortune. The blatant nerve of the woman!

Dita threw her bags down onto the couch with such force that one bounced onto the floor, its contents spilling out. Cursing, she stormed over to the window of her not-so-spectacular apartment in a not-so-inspiring part of Boston. Lights illuminated the world beyond the confines of her home. The outlook was more appealing now than it would be in a few hours' time, when daylight revealed a dirty, run-down neighborhood. Normally, this night view did wonders for her karma, but not now. Unbuttoning her coat and removing the scarf from her neck, she stared unseeingly at the building on the opposite side of her street.

She had promised herself that she would never let Cate Canton under her skin again, but that woman could play her like a musical instrument. Dita hated feeling like this, angry and uncompromising. It wasn't her true nature to judge others harshly, but betrayal hurt, and those who suffered it either toughened up or gave in, and Dita would never allow Cate that victory.

A slight pain stabbed her chest, reminding her that, though recovered, she still needed to be kind to her body and should perhaps sit and rest, given all the excitement of the evening. She had promised her cardiologist that she'd take things easy for a while.

Dita regarded her reflection in the window. God, she looked tired. But then, she'd been on her feet since before the start of the show two days earlier and hadn't had a break since. She was glad she'd told Marcus she wouldn't go into the office tomorrow. She needed to rest. Success could wait a day. Dita frowned as she let the air rush from her lungs. It bothered her that Cate hadn't unveiled her own new collection. Why? She'd stolen the show for the past three years. Why would she have held back, this time? What devious plan was she hatching? Clearly, she had appeared simply to mock Dita and remind her she was still out there, waiting for her moment to strike. So beautiful and yet, so deadly—a woman of composite combinations, a toxic mix.

Regardless, the absence had played into Dita's hands and she'd been able to usurp Cate, ejecting her from her usual pinnacle as the new diva of fashion, the Donna Karan of tomorrow. Since her adversary had not produced anything for the show, the market was wide open for Dita, and she hadn't hesitated to fill the gap.

Her thoughts bounced around like pinballs. Maybe now she'd be able to reward the loyal, hardworking staff who had done so much for her. Her team worked long hours, often for little payment because their belief in her was so strong. She owed them everything and she was determined that her success would also be theirs. Hopefully, this much-needed triumph would bring all of them the financial security they desperately needed.

Would it bring the opportunity to stop working all hours of the day and for her designs to become part of a recognized fashion label? All these years she'd strived for this; how wonderful that it seemed within her reach at last. Maybe she'd also be able to move and find somewhere to live that was better than this place.

Moving toward the couch, she dropped exhausted into its soft welcoming comfort. I love this sofa, she thought, as she kicked the shoes from her feet. Another thought immediately ran through her head, a cold and merciless possibility that she would normally dismiss, but she let it rest there awhile. Would success put her in a position where she could give Canton a touch of her own medicine? Something warm inside her arose at this notion. Wouldn't she like to get even? Did she owe herself that satisfaction?

She could easily understand the poignancy of the sentiment, "Revenge is sweet." Sitting back and kicking her long, slim legs out in front of her, she considered the tempting possibility of getting her own back. But then she stopped. She wasn't like Cate, a spoiled brat who'd been born into everything and who had proved herself the bad seed.

Dita pushed ideas of revenge away. She had integrity and moral strength, and would never lower herself to Cate's level. She wanted to be able to look at herself in the mirror each morning. So far, she'd accomplished almost all she'd hoped for, and had done so with honor. Dita closed her eyes and let herself relax. There was no reason to change her standards now. She finally had some real power, and she planned to use it positively, not to be dragged down and consumed by a past she couldn't change.

No, Dita thought, senseless revenge was not an option. She would nurture her dream and become a successful designer, let time take away the memories of all those setbacks in her youth. She warmed as she thought of how she was repaying William Canton's trust and faith in her—the man who had given her this chance. She smiled. It was her last movement as sleep swept over her.

The next thing she was aware of was of someone rapping heavily on her door. Opening her eyes she realized she was still on the couch and that it was now light outside. Stiffly, she struggled up and hurried to the door. She found Marcus on the other side, his arms full of newspapers.

Absentmindedly, he walked into her apartment. "Yes, yes, I know, you're not working today, but I had to bring these over for you to see. The reviews. They're staggering. You have to see what they say about Seraphim, your designs…the collection." He stopped talking, his face beaming. "You've done it, Dita. You've really done it."

Standing there in her bare feet, the cold of the linoleum floor creeping up her legs, she smiled at his unbridled enthusiasm. This was quiet, unassuming Marcus Abner, who had just pushed his way into her apartment and was grinning like a demented idiot. Dita had never seen him so animated and his excitement was contagious.

"*Please* come in," she said, grinning back at him. "I don't think I've ever seen you like this."

"Nor I you." Marcus frowned. "Have you been to bed at all?"

Dita saw the concern in his eyes and realized what she must look like. Taking a quick glance at herself in the hallway mirror, she winced. Her usually immaculate hair was all over the place, her lipstick gone, mascara was smudged around her eyes, and her silk blouse sat at a skewed, unattractive angle on her body. Not pretty.

"I fell asleep on the couch. Honestly, Marcus, I'm okay. Now get comfortable." She pointed to a chair. "I'll put some coffee on, have a quick shower, and then we can look at what the press has to say about us."

Less than twenty minutes later, they sat together studying the reviews, a pot of coffee between them.

"Listen to this one," Marcus said. "'Put this woman up there with fashion royalty…inspirational…bold designs…the creator of the dream wardrobe.' You couldn't have done better if you'd drugged them. And Bernard Bressinger, no less. 'I have seldom been so excited by a new collection.'"

"I drugged him." Dita remarked dryly. She took the paper from him and read out quietly, "'Sensually feminine, beautifully crafted pieces. This talented designer has come of age and is destined for great heights, but don't just take it from me, note the words of another gifted designer, the usually reclusive Cate…'" She stopped abruptly, catching her breath. The rest of the words passed like acid across her lips. "'Cate Canton, who says this is a winning collection from an inspired designer. *Very innovative, a wonderful collection. Beautiful clothes from a beautiful woman.*'"

Silence hammered the room and bounced off the walls as they sat there surrounded by a mess of newspapers. Marcus knew enough not to say anything. For the next few minutes, they continued to sift through other articles, but somehow their heady delight had evaporated, and eventually Marcus made some excuse and chose to leave.

As Dita walked him to the door, he hesitated. "If I asked you to do something for me, would you?"

She looked at him quizzically and with a light smile, tried to lift the heaviness she felt she'd caused. "I think so, as long as it's nothing criminal or indecent." She laughed a little.

Marcus reached inside his jacket pocket and withdrew an envelope. He seemed nervous. "This was meant for you, but it never got delivered." He watched her eyes fall to the object in his hand. "She was going to give you this the night of our show, but for whatever reason, she changed her mind and threw it away."

Dita didn't need to ask who *she* was, knowing instantly who the letter was from. "How did you come by it?"

Calmly and with purpose, Marcus said, "You're going to have to forgive me for this, but when she left, I followed her outside." He paused. "I was worried, we'd spoken earlier and I felt she was trying to…" He seemed to realize Dita didn't want to hear how he'd been taken in by Cate's acting skills. "I saw her throw this away before she got into a taxi and I retrieved it. It was addressed to you and I thought you ought to have it."

"The letter isn't yours to give, Marcus." Dita was dismissive.

"Yes, and I won't give it to you unless you promise me you'll read it."

"You've already said it has my name on it, so it's mine to do with as I wish."

Marcus shook his head.

"Then take it. I want nothing of hers."

"Very well." Marcus called her bluff and calmly replaced the envelope inside his jacket.

Before he could leave, Dita held out her hand. "All right. I promise." She almost spat the words.

With a perfunctory "Good-bye," she closed the door after him and marched into the kitchen, holding the envelope in both hands as if it contained some deadly virus. She leaned with her back against the counter and for a while studied the four simple letters on the front that spelt "Dita." She ran a finger over the writing, feeling the slightest indentation of the word, aware that only a short while ago, Cate Canton had held this envelope, her hands upon it as she wrote. Lifting it to her face, Dita thought she could detect the slightest scent of perfume.

Then, with a determined stride, she moved over to the pedal bin and using her foot to open it, she slowly ripped the letter in half before throwing it into the receptacle—where it belonged with all the other trash.

"Damn you, Marcus. Damn you to hell."

❖

Earlier, when Cate finally escaped from the last party, she'd tried to sit back and relax in the taxi as it sped her away from Manhattan and toward the airport.

Glancing out of the window, she watched a cardboard box being tossed high into the air across the other side of the road by an unexpected gust of wind, and acknowledged that this was a miserable night to be out in, the weather turning harsh. Closing her eyes, she considered it was a miserable night, period. The outcome of the evening had done nothing to lift the unpleasant heaviness that accompanied her these days.

She sighed and stared out of the window again at the passing city lights and the brave pedestrians who hurriedly tried to get to their destinations, away from the clutches of the developing storm. Cate felt sorry for them.

Her somber thoughts were sharply pushed aside as her taxi drew to an abrupt halt. Cate saw a sea of red and orange vehicle brake lights, accompanied by a cacophony of car horns. They were at a standstill, the result of road works.

"It's always the same," she heard the disgruntled cabbie mutter. "If they ain't diggin' up the pipes, then it's the cables." He continued complaining about the amount of road construction en route to the airport and Cate realized that she had a native born American driver instead of the usual foreigner who could barely speak the language.

"You'd think they'd get it right, wouldn't ya?" he droned on.

"How so?" She forced herself to pay attention.

"Y'know, dig up the road jus' once and fix everythin' at the same time."

"Wouldn't that put them out of business?"

The cab driver laughed good-naturedly. "Yeah, I guess so."

Less than a minute later, the taxi moved again and veered off the main road in favor of some side route he knew, away from the congestion. The city lights started to disappear behind them, but the driver still grumbled. "Y'know, one day they'll come up with a system where ya don't have to dig up the roads. Maybe send some automated little robot down the line that can detect the fault, diagnose it, then fix it. No road works, no queues. Good idea, yeah?"

"You should market it," she said politely.

"Yeah, maybe I should. I'd make more money than I do now and the hours would sure be better, but I guess I ain't the guy with the brains. If I was, I wouldn't be drivin' no friggin' cab in weather like this."

Cate leaned back in an attempt to distance herself from the unwanted conversation; it was late and she was tired. Closing her eyes, she couldn't tune out the cabbie's continuous rants. He was determined to speak his mind this evening, and she wondered if maybe he'd had a miserable day too.

She rubbed at a knot in her right shoulder, digging her fingers into the tight little spot where the muscles were tense. It didn't help and she gave up. Instead she cross-examined herself. How on earth had she got to this point in her life, continually dredging the anger and bitterness from her past into her future and with such disastrous consequences? She could never hope to justify her actions to Dita, for there was little to excuse her—unless of course, one looked at her past. Might that offer some mitigating evidence in her defense? A moot point because it didn't matter anymore. Cate's life was a mess, and only now did she realize it was all her own fault.

Like a wave pulling back from the shore, sucking the moisture from the sand, the years faded and the past seemed as if it was only yesterday. She stared at the reflection in her window, but the face she saw wasn't her own. It was Dita's.

CHAPTER THREE

Six Years Earlier

Dita Newton sat outside William Canton's downtown office in Boston, nervously fingering the small portfolio she'd brought with her. The job advertisement had sought someone capable of running a small fashion house in Boston, who had proven managerial experience plus a "sharp design focus in a competing industry." She had the latter in bucket loads. Wasn't that why she'd lost her last job? Dita had never meant to be pushy, that really wasn't her style, but her previous employer produced awful clothing and had claimed fresh, new ideas were needed. Talk was one thing, acceptance another. He took umbrage at Dita's unflattering opinion of the range and her suggestions on the direction she thought the company should take. Being sacked was an inopportune moment to discover she wasn't big on tact.

The job before that one had been better. She'd been part of a friendly environment but, again, working on other people's designs. It had not been what she'd wanted, but the less than favorable salary had at least kept her refrigerator stocked. Unfortunately the firm had gone bust and she'd ended up working for another man with an ego she was supposed to prop up. Not her strong suit. And here she was, out of work, broke, and getting thinner by the day. She'd already been mistaken for a model at a couple of interviews, which annoyed the hell out of her...the story of her life.

Being beautiful didn't bother her. Whatever celestial power existed, she had been blessed, and it wasn't enough to be blond, tall, and willowy. Oh, no. Divine intervention had bestowed exquisite skin, the lithe elegance of a cheetah, and of course, her eyes. Even as a young teenager, when she'd played with a pack of tomboys, she'd stuck out like a daffodil among dandelions.

As an adult, what infuriated her was that people were quick to define her by her beauty alone. She was more than that. She was intelligent, creative, and a damn hard worker. She was a fashion designer and she had talent. All she needed was that first break. It would have been easy to give up and become the model she was constantly mistaken for. But she had faith in her designs and capabilities. Was that arrogance? No. Arrogance played no part in who she was. Her belief was founded simply in her destiny. Fish swim; Dita designed.

She ran her fingers through her hair and hoped she hadn't messed it. Yet again, she cast an eye over what she was wearing. The outfit was one of her own designs, a black dress with cream piping around a half-crested neckline, repeated above the small show pockets on either hip. A strawberry pink waist-length jacket completed the ensemble. Dita felt confident that she conveyed the right message. Fashionable. Smart. Businesslike.

Business.

She felt the nerves bubble up as she swallowed awkwardly. Talent notwithstanding, she wondered again how she'd made it to the interview, for she'd been honest in her résumé, admitting her lack of managerial experience but stating that she felt she had design abilities that compensated. A bolt of panic surged through her as she realized she'd been somewhat economical with the truth. It wasn't that she lacked the required level of managerial experience—she had none at all. But she was desperate enough to do anything to get an interview. She just hoped her potential employer would see that her fashion sense and original ideas far outweighed her shortcomings in some areas. Anyone competent could build their management skills on the job, but creativity was a gift.

Dita's anxiety climbed as she pondered her relative lack of formal study. She had only a two-year basic design course behind her, completed at a New York art and design school. Though she'd done well, achieving best student of her class, she hadn't been able to expand her studies and complete the four-year retail management and fashion merchandising program. She felt sure Mr. Canton would question her minimal qualifications, but further study had been impossible. She was already struggling with debt and her grandmother's illness only made the situation worse.

Dita contemplated her past with a mixture of pain and joy. She was an only child. Her parents had divorced when she was still a baby and her father had lost his fight for custody. It was almost unheard of for a court to separate a mother and baby, so Dita had ended up living with her mother. She didn't know why her mother had decided to have her in the first place. She didn't seem to love her, and had resented the struggle of rearing a baby alone.

Dita's father died of pneumonia when she was six, and with the end of his child support payments, her mother seemed even angrier. Not long after that, a new man came into her mother's life. He was well off and wanted to marry her but he refused to accept another man's child. Dita's mother had handed her over to be raised by her paternal grandmother, Amelia Newton. From that moment on, Dita knew only love, kindness, and generosity. She vaguely remembered occasional visits from her mother, but they were rare, and after a few years she never saw or heard from her again. In hindsight, she suspected her grandmother had engineered the outings, trying to foster the mother-daughter bond for Dita's sake. It was a wasted effort. Even then, Dita knew her mother didn't love her and the visits only served to remind her of that. She was glad when they stopped.

Biting too hard on her lip, Dita was jolted back to the present by the taste of blood. She could feel her confidence slipping and worried that her neediness would show. Try as she might, she couldn't stop thinking of how she would spend her first month's pay *if* she got the job. Food. Yes, food was the winning contender. If her fridge got any emptier she could use it to store her shoes. She sighed. What would she do if she didn't get the job? She could find something temporary that would pay the bills, but every time she began another go-nowhere job her chances of breaking into fashion design diminished. Her grandmother had always said nothing worth having came easily. Setbacks meant you took the blows, stood up, dusted yourself down, and tried again. But Dita was getting vertigo with all the up and down movement, and she knew she couldn't sustain too many more knocks.

"Ms. Newton?" An austere-looking woman, presumably the secretary, announced, "Mr. Canton will see you now."

Dita breathed in deeply, assumed her professional stance,

straightened her dress, and hoped she cut an appropriate figure for the job. It didn't help her nerves when she partially walked into the door frame of Canton's office.

Despite her quick recovery, as she managed to get into the room, her hopes instantly evaporated. Sitting behind an impressive antique mahogany desk was a serious-looking businessman, far older than she'd expected, and not one who appeared particularly fashionable. Sharp-eyed, he looked every bit the big business guru and she could just tell he was looking for someone with similar qualities. This was not someone she thought she was going to be able to talk to on a fashion level, her strength—her only strength.

My poor fridge, she thought as the secretary closed the door behind her.

❖

William studied the tall, golden-haired woman who hesitated just inside his office door. Her expression was filled with apprehension, as though she expected to be informed of her inadequate abilities, a failing applicant doomed to be sacked before she was offered the job. She went pale as soon as her eyes met his and almost seemed to have second thoughts about taking the seat he indicated.

Moving from behind his desk to join her, he knew he cut an imposing figure, some said intimidating, but her reaction completely shocked him. Her brow rose as he moved closer, as if she was surprised that he was bothering to conduct the interview at all. Did she view him as some kind of tyrant, or just a boring middle-aged man? He hoped not and mused that he still had a good head of hair and a waistline.

Maybe it was because he didn't like this train of thought that he made an effort to relax Dita Newton. He sat opposite her and asked a few easy questions about her journey to the interview, then he commented on the beautiful weather for the time of year.

"People are always happy when the sun shines," came her offbeat answer.

"Yes, they are," he replied, smiling.

"Yes."

He caught something in her eyes, a recognition that her conversational skills weren't cutting it. Paradoxically, he thought how the sun shone, but she wasn't happy. "Before we get down to the usual questions," he said pleasantly, "tell me, what made you apply for the job, Miss Newton?"

She studied his central ceiling light before answering. "I suppose the obvious answer is that I believe I have the skills you are seeking. I hope you liked the designs I sent you."

William glanced toward the folder on his desk.

It had been one of many to arrive from those who aspired to the post and at first he had despaired of the task before him. Methodically, he had studied each varied form of portfolio searching for something indefinable that would reach out to him like a signal man's light and shine forth his next director. Overwhelming as the task had seemed, the moment he had set eyes of Dita Newton's designs, he sensed a welcomed beam of brightness.

Her work was crisp and her designs sharp with no superfluous frills and plumage. They were thematic, a strong vision of imagery running consistently through her art that evoked a sense of remembering something in the past. In one of her collections, he had strongly felt a 1920s art nouveau connection. Yet her color schemes and shapes had been unrelated. Another batch of designs had a distinctive renaissance feel to them. It was as if she was subconsciously pulling history into the present and reshaping it; taking something good but old and modernizing it. Even her appearance today, the blackness of the dress with its cream piping, then matched with a pink vibrant jacket—the simplicity of the effect was stunning.

"They're quite unique," he commented.

She nodded. "Well, the ad said you were looking for something completely different. I like that, Mr. Canton. To me, that's forward looking. Fashion has to move with the times, smart designers have to lead trends, not follow them. And yet Seraphim hasn't done that...not yet. I've studied your recent fashion lines and there's nothing new or unique, nothing that makes a potential customer want to become a loyal one."

William noted the passion, and the lack of subtlety. She was fearless in her opinions and yet there was a strange contradiction between her courage and her uncertainty in herself. It reminded him of his late wife. Helena had been just like this at the beginning when she'd started Seraphim. She had been so confident in her fashion acumen and yet anxious about taking that first step into the commercial world. All she'd needed was a gentle shove in the right direction and some cooing encouragement. He wondered if his wife might be observing the similarities before him...whether she might approve of Dita Newton. Something deep within him whispered she might.

Miss Newton continued her frank assessment. "You don't offer anything really exclusive...distinctive. I see Seraphim as one of many average fashion houses, but with so much more potential." She steepled her fingers together. "I applied for this job because, if you like my designs, this could be a marriage of interests. Seraphim gets a face-lift and I get the challenge, the chance to show my designs and to grow. Mutually beneficial for us both."

"I see you've only done one professional course." He caught a look of acknowledgment in her eyes, as though she'd been expecting the question. A tense smile tugged at lips that shone like red patent leather.

"Yes, but I've built on that with practical experience in three very diverse fashion businesses. I've been able to hone my creative design skills in a real world work environment. I feel those experiences taught me far more than classroom theory."

William smiled back. He knew the answer had been rehearsed. "There also seems to be a gap between where you left school and started work...as a stock girl for a clothing store." Glancing up from the paperwork in his hand, he eyed her over his half-moon glasses. "This, I assume, is one of your three diverse fashion businesses."

Dita Newton blushed and William felt a little guilty that he had called her experience into question so bluntly. But she held his gaze, meeting his challenge as she drew breath. "I suppose at face value, working as a stock girl may not seem very impressive, but I think if you really want to see how an industry functions, you should work at the bottom for a while."

He nodded. "So that was part of your plan?"

She laughed. "No. The gap you noticed, between my leaving school and starting work...I should have put it on the résumé. I won a scholarship to the University of Rhode Island, but my grandmother became ill." She shrugged. "She raised me and since there were just the two of us and no money coming in, I needed to get a job. The stock position was an answer to my prayers. It was near home and didn't require any experience."

"And your grandmother?"

"She passed away about eight months later."

"I'm sorry." He could see the loss in her eyes.

"Me, too. We were very close. She was my best friend."

William felt impelled to ask her more but didn't. That would be stepping out of the realms of decency and invading her privacy. The objective of this interview was to see if she measured up, and so far that seemed doubtful. She didn't have the experience and training he had hoped for. However, Dita Newton intrigued him. He sensed she was a woman of integrity. It took strength of character to give up a promising start in life to care for a loved one. Strangely, he liked that she'd omitted this from her résumé, not wishing to play a "poor me" card. There was honor in that.

She began to open up when he asked her to show him some more of her designs. Her ice blue eyes danced like an electric storm. She radiated confidence when she spoke of her love of fashion, and of the creative ideas that constantly buzzed in her head.

Pushing a sketch before him, Dita Newton, seemingly from nowhere, produced a piece of fabric that she thrust into his hands.

"Feel that, Mr. Canton. Experience the way the texture crosses your fingertips, the way it plays with your senses. No matter how you crunch it up, it remains without creases. You can see how perfect it is for this design."

She looked at him with eager expectation, seeking his tacit agreement. But William was at a loss. He hadn't a clue what she was talking about; he was a city man and fashion was simply not his forte. That had been the territory of his deceased wife, Helena. Feeling inadequate, he wished he could have fed Newton's enthusiasm with... something relevant. A fleeting memory distracted him; his younger daughter Cate used to make him feel like this.

He clutched the cloth tightly in one hand as if hoping it would suddenly reveal its mystery, and maybe then he would understand why he was hiring yet another stranger to step into Helena's shoes and run Seraphim when it should have been Cate. She was the one who had always been destined to take over from her mother, the one with the strong creative streak and a mania for fashion. But of course, that hadn't happened, for like the fabric, he had been unable to decipher his offspring.

The opposite of her older and composed sister, Caroline, Cate had responded to the death of her mother by becoming a complicated emotional teenager, and William had been ill equipped to cope with her. He was an undemonstrative man and at a time when he should have shown compassion, he was heavy-handed and inflexible. A rift developed between them, and, like a stubborn fool, he made no attempt to reach out. The downward spiral of their relationship became unstoppable after Caroline's car accident. Cate was sixteen then, and whatever her mistakes, he now saw them in a broader context. She was young, lost without her mother, and alienated by him. He shouldn't have been shocked by her rebelliousness, he should have sought better solutions. Instead he'd insisted on having his own way, ignoring her wishes completely, and as soon as she could, Cate had walked out of his life.

Ten years had passed since then and he'd long ago stopped pretending that she would return once she ran out of money. He had successfully tracked her down in Italy a few months after she left. The first time he visited, he had expected a chagrined daughter who would beg to be taken home. But Cate refused to see him or accept his phone calls and he'd decided to let her stew. A year later he tried again, this time intending to offer study fees if she seemed to be working toward a goal. But Cate had refused to have anything to do with him, all but closing the door in his face. Why? Because he had stupidly tried to tell her he was willing to forgive her. Bad words. Wrong words. She had had nothing to be forgiven for. He was to blame with his own stupid, unfeeling behavior.

She'd told him then that she never wanted to see him again, and he'd respected her wishes, hoping she would one day change her mind and contact him. William dolefully handed the material back to Miss Newton, comparing her slender feminine hands with his masculine heavy ones. He knew she found him lacking, incapable of seeing the creative promise of material, so evident to her but lost to him—the fashion Neanderthal.

"Maybe not," Her tone was dry. "No matter, you'll just have to believe me, Mr. Canton, the two blend together splendidly."

"Right."

He couldn't deny that her portfolio was impressive, displaying a sensibility and new direction that was colorful and vibrant, something Seraphim had lost after Helena died. He had fought to keep the business afloat. He had thrown money at it—he wasn't short of that—but the artistic talent? That was not so easy to find, and he had a string of former directors as evidence.

Helena had always intended that Cate would study fashion and then work with her before eventually taking over. The plan had been foiled when Helena went into town one morning and never made it to the store. She had collapsed and died as she'd stepped from her car in the parking lot. According to the autopsy report, she'd been born with a congenital heart defect that had gone unobserved all her life. One minute her heart had been beating—and then it wasn't.

Cate was just twelve years old and William had kept Seraphim for her, expecting her to still go on to study fashion and return to run the business. But his failure as a parent had ruined those plans. And yet he still held on to the business, unable to betray his wife's legacy and determined that Cate would ultimately inherit what was rightly hers. There was another reason, too. While he kept the business, a bond with Cate still existed. If he sold Seraphim or allowed it to fail, that connection would be severed, and all hope of reconciliation would be extinguished. William couldn't make that choice.

He heard a gentle cough. Dita Newton was focusing his attention back to the interview. He asked her what she knew regarding Seraphim's financial status.

"I know that it's been a failing business for years and that you've been propping it up with injections of cash."

"And you obviously think you could do something about that," he challenged.

"I do. Seraphim is losing money because of the fashion direction. You are turning out a quality product, but you can't sell in any volume because your styles are hideously outdated." Barefaced, she continued, "If you want to stay in business with your current stock, you should start supplying clothing for television and movie period dramas."

William watched her flinch the moment she'd said that, regretting her words, but the comments made him laugh. People were never so direct with him and he appreciated the nerve it took. She had no way of knowing how her honesty would affect her chances of employment. Perhaps, he reflected with interest, she simply had nothing to lose.

With slightly more diplomacy, his critic suggested, "Seraphim needs a radical face-lift if it's going to survive. Fashion is about staying ahead of the curve. Seraphim needs to re-brand, just as Burberry is doing. They were flatlining before they hired Rose Marie Bravo."

"Ms. Bravo is a brilliant CEO with a long track record," William said. "I notice you don't have much managerial experience. It would be unrealistic to expect it, of course. You are only twenty-six."

"I'm sure your last few directors were much older and were paid well for their work experience. I'm surprised Seraphim is still in difficulties after being run by people of such…expertise."

William smiled. In the past, he'd hired what he had thought were the right people, and all he'd gotten was a string of disasters, age and experience notwithstanding. "Point taken. So, are you the person to turn this business around, Miss Newton?"

"I have the creative designs, Mr. Canton, and the enthusiasm. With the right staff and your support, I'll die trying."

"That won't be necessary…*if* you get the position."

Instinct made him hire her. It was true, she lacked experience and managerial ability, but William was ready to try someone different, and Miss Newton *was* different. She had that "eye of the tiger" and a hunger for the opportunity to show what she could do, if given a chance. Her passion reminded him in so many ways of Cate…the way Cate had been before he let her down, the daughter who'd once adored him.

William walked Dita Newton out to the reception office and shook her hand. He suspected they both knew she had the job. That same day, he signed and dispatched a letter congratulating her on her new appointment.

❖

Cate Canton set her hairbrush on her dressing table and picked up a little pottery angel. Memories came flooding back as she ran a fingertip along one wing. She was five years old when her mother, after a business trip, gave her the tiny bright blue and gold winged cherub, the first of many in a collection she'd left behind when she walked away from her father's home ten years earlier.

She could see her mother again, leaning down over her, a beautifully manicured hand pushing hair away from her face, as she smiled. *"Caty, this is for you. A gift for my own little angel."* And then her mother had knelt down and held her close.

Feeling the sting of tears bite, Cate quickly cast a last glance around the room she'd become accustomed to. The angel was an artifact of a past that seemed remote, a world occupied by her younger, innocent self. She would never be that girl again. The day she left her Massachusetts home, the one she'd grown up in on the coast, south of Boston, she didn't even bother to say good-bye to her father. She could think of nothing to say. She took very little with her, a few clothes, a savings account, some books, and two photos. One was of her sister Caroline and herself laughing as they'd played on the family yacht. They had been celebrating her sister's fifteenth birthday. She had been eleven. The other was of her sitting by her mother in a Boston park, taken six months before she died.

Cate wondered what her mother would think about everything that had happened. The terrible accident. Cate's problems at high school. Her father's unfairness, forcing her to take a job at his engineering company instead of going to college. In the packing department, of all places, boring work he knew she would hate. Cate still couldn't understand why he'd humiliated her so badly. It felt like a punishment, and maybe that's what he'd intended. He'd blamed her for everything, so he'd tried to destroy her dreams.

Cate took a long look at her mother's photograph. Helena Canton stared back with eyes that challenged her. They had all thought it would be her stunningly beautiful sister who would look most like Helena and that Cate would favor her father, remaining shorter and stockier in build. But as she grew into adulthood, the puppy fat had disappeared and she had assumed her mother's graceful, lean, and classic looks. Though never as tall—Cate was only five feet six whilst Helena had been a good four inches taller—she had similar facial features and the same intense blue eyes. Even their hair was the same now. It hadn't always been. Cate had spent much of her youth trying to control her wayward auburn tresses and wondering if she would always look like she lived next to a wind machine. Time had tamed the problem and her hair now fell in the same soft, attractive waves her mother favored.

Closing the bedroom door quietly, she descended the dark stairs into the bracing cold air of a raw winter's evening in Ferrara. The Via Borgo di Sotto was jammed with bicycles. Hundreds of riders of all ages chaotically cycled the street, on their way to or from the New Year's Eve festivities. Ferrara wasn't called the city of bicycles for nothing and despite the frenzy before her, Cate thought how they enhanced the renaissance charm of the place. Taking her life in her hands, she bobbed and weaved in between wheels and pedals, then crossed a small square and fought another lethal enemy, the Italian driver. Driving was never good in Italy, but at this time of the year it was appalling. It came as a relief when she jogged safely into a courtyard, surrounded by high city walls, and stopped in sight of her final destination.

L'Istituto di Bello Disegno was one of Italy's oldest schools of fashion. Though small, it was highly acclaimed and ran collaborative programs with the best fashion colleges in both London and New York. Cate's mother had studied there, too.

As she approached the eighteenth-century building, Cate hastened her step. Hopefully she wasn't too late. After studying at L'Istituto for three years, she missed her mentor, Madeleine Zobbio, and didn't want to begin the new year tomorrow without sharing a celebratory glass of wine with her. They hadn't seen each other for almost six months. Cate had returned to Ferrara as often as she could while she completed her master's degree in Milan, but it was difficult to get away. To finance her part-time studies and advance her practical knowledge, she'd been working for a couple of different fashion houses there, and seldom had time off, and Signora Zobbio didn't travel much these days.

Cate entered the familiar dark oak doors that had been stained by time and paused in the empty lobby. Her footsteps echoed on the cold marble flooring. The petite, elderly director emerged from a passageway just beyond the main entrance. It was as if she had seen Cate coming. "You are here, at last."

Always exquisitely dressed, she wore an aubergine-colored silk two-piece suit, the jacket styled with a mandarin collar and delicate lacing at the cuffs. The skirt rested slightly above the knee and was arguably too short for someone of Zobbio's age. But, though probably in her late seventies, she still had a captivating trim figure and an abundant measure of imperious confidence the equal of a woman far younger than herself. Zobbio was talented and successful, and accustomed to the attention of others. Even at her age, she was not a flower waiting for a wall. With her zest and energy for life, plus her sharp intellect, no one ever questioned her decision to remain in her position instead of retiring.

Madeleine Zobbio had a shock of thick snow white hair always neatly tied back in a French twist. She was a lucky woman, for life had bestowed on her a flawless complexion, still bereft of significant lines, and the deepest of brown eyes. But time was catching up and Cate noticed her back seemed a little more bowed, the widow's hump slightly more obvious. She smiled inwardly. Zobbio might pass for a sweet, harmless old lady. However, God help the fool who believed that.

They embraced at a polite distance and Cate bent so that they could exchange air kisses on each cheek. "I can't believe I'm finally back in Ferrara for good. I've only just finishing unpacking."

Signora Zobbio removed her eyeglasses. "You know, when I said I wanted you to work hard, I did not mean for you to kill yourself. You are allowed to have fun sometimes, yes?"

Cate smiled. "I know, Signora, but I wanted to see your work on Sophia Rossani's wedding dress. They were raving about it in Milan."

This compliment earned a flippant shrug of the shoulders, but Zobbio's dark eyes darted to a room off to their left. She waved Cate to follow her through a narrow archway into one of the cutting rooms where a shrouded model stood in center place.

"Is that it?" Cate asked eagerly.

"Of course." Zobbio casually inspected the nails on her right hand.

Cate loved the nonchalant response. She knew her mentor was *dying* to show off her latest work.

"May I?" Without waiting for an answer, Cate lifted the sheeting that rested over the model. One sweeping movement and the covering was gone, revealing a resplendent, cream and white colored wedding dress.

"It's stunning." Cate oozed praise.

"You like it?" The director's question implied humbleness but the eyes twinkled with pride.

"Like it?" Cate drew breath, her eyes locked on the dress. "It is everything people are talking about, and more."

She moved around the model, stalking it like a bird of prey, studying every minute part of the silk taffeta gown. "I don't know how you do it. You've been in this business for so long, come up with so many original designs…I would have thought you'd run dry of ideas. But this is so incredible." She touched the intricate embroidery that covered the upper half of the dress. "It's like latticework." Standing back she observed, "The sleeves are cut on a cross."

"Straight lines bore me. I sought something new…inspirational."

Cate acknowledged the wry response with a smile. "New it may be, but it has your signature all over it, your hallmark touches."

"It does?"

"Of course. You can't hide the overall style, it's got you stamped on it. It's the way you stitch things, your little finishing touches. The small bows here, for instance." Cate fingered two minute butterfly bows on each cuff that hid fasteners. "Such attention to detail. Anyone who knows your work wouldn't have to bother looking for the label. You're a genius."

Madeleine moved her head to the side like a silent Hollywood movie star, affecting casual disinterest, but Cate saw the small grin of satisfaction, and it pleased her. It pleased her even more when Zobbio suddenly said, "It means a lot to have such praise from one of my most gifted students."

Touched by the unexpected comment, Cate could only nod. She tried to deflect the commendation by grabbing a paper and pencil and starting to sketch the lines of the design.

Zobbio immediately snatched the pencil away. "No, no, no. It is New Year's Eve, child." She waved her hands as though to shoo Cate out of the room. "Why aren't you out there, enjoying the festivities?" There was a slight maternal trace in the voice of the usually plain speaking director. Her words were slow and precise, tinged by the attractiveness of a heavy Italian accent.

"I could ask you the same thing," Cate parried.

"Ah, I am too old for these wild parties, I have seen too many. I now prefer to meet the next year on my terms with some grace. Usually, I sit in my conservatory with a fine glass of wine and listen to the revelers in the streets below as the fireworks explode above me. Civilized, don't you think?" She didn't wait for Cate's answer as she moved toward the wrought iron staircase that led to her apartment.

"Why don't you come join me for a drink? Perhaps two or three, that is, if you don't mind spending it with an old lady who is of the age to be your grandmama."

❖

They spent the remainder of the evening in the comfort of Zobbio's conservatory, drinking wine, talking, and observing the fireworks overhead. Being so old, the apartment was spacious with high walls and vaulted ceilings. It also had an enviable view, partly overlooking a private, well-tended garden, and a quiet street normally occupied by business folk during the day and the occasional resident by night. However, this evening the street brimmed with party people.

Cate had been here on only a few other occasions, when Zobbio invited her to dinner when she visited from Milan. Things had certainly changed, especially her relationship with the director. When Cate first arrived in Ferrara and applied to the institute, she'd been an angry young woman who had felt hurt and betrayed. Intense and deeply private, her sole objective had been to get into the school her mother had attended and to show everyone that she really did have talent and wasn't a waste of time. Beyond basic, civil politeness, she'd kept very much to herself, shunning friendships that might have diverted her from her mission, and throwing herself into a ruthless cycle of study and work.

She'd been desperately short of funds then, and Madeleine Zobbio had found her part-time work in a small tailoring business as a machinist. With that employment, and an educational grant from the institute itself, Cate had managed to put herself through the challenging course and attain the high standards that Zobbio insisted on.

The relationship then had been purely teacher and student. The Signora had been ruthless, pushing her to her limits and demanding work to the best of Cate's abilities, which she obviously perceived as higher than her contemporaries. It had been no easy ride, no sailing through on natural talents, and at times Cate had wondered if she would make it. Perhaps her father had been right after all in shutting her out of her mother's fashion house.

He had once told her of his bitter disappointment in her, how she had failed to live up to his expectations, and that he'd been wrong about her. She was not the bright, gifted, effervescent daughter he had thought but a lazy, irresponsible, untrustworthy child who seemed content to live off her privileged background and get by with minimal effort.

Cate winced at the memory of that conversation, one of many in which she was unfavorably compared with her older sister. They'd once been a happy family full of laughter and love, but all that had changed after her mother died. Her father became distant and unapproachable, and he continually contrasted Caroline's academic rigor with Cate's sloppy inattentiveness. It didn't stop there. Caroline's friends met his unquestioning approval, but Cate's were unacceptable—troublemakers, drug users, and a bad influence. He constantly questioned her judgment and even failed to believe her pleas of innocence when the school had suggested she was taking drugs. On that occasion he'd called her deceitful and a liar.

The friction between them escalated to intolerable levels after the car accident that had killed Caroline. Cate had been driving and blinding lights had dazzled her on a dangerous bend. She didn't remember the accident, only that her injuries had been minor. Her sister wasn't so lucky, and Cate still couldn't forgive herself for the choices she'd made that night. She still missed Caroline terribly, even more so having lost her mother as well. Cate had been close to Helena Canton, sharing her passion for all things fashion. She couldn't remember a time when she wasn't sketching designs that continually flowed in her head. There had never been any question about her future; she would follow in her mother's footsteps, first studying fashion in Europe, then working in Seraphim.

Her older sister had different plans and passions. Caroline had been more like their father, studious and serious. She'd wanted to be a doctor and would have been wonderful in that profession. Cate hated that she was denied the opportunity to live the life she'd talked about all through their childhood. Though the police report had confirmed the car crash was a tragic accident, Cate knew her father blamed her for Caroline's loss. He never said anything but she could see it in his eyes. And of course, that was why he punished her.

Only weeks after the accident, he withdrew her from her school, stating that it was a place of distinction and excellence, and was wasted on her. He thought the high intellectual standards the school demanded had placed her under stress, causing her to become rebellious. At the local high school he placed her in, Cate was viewed as a spoilt rich kid and made no friends. Somehow she'd endured two miserable years there, focusing on the future she could look forward to.

After graduation she'd expected to go to Europe to study fashion at the same institute her mother had, but her father quashed her dreams, saying she didn't have what it would take—she needed constant watching, was unreliable and dishonest. So that he could keep an eye on her, he sent her to work in the packing department at one of his local small engineering firms. She could still hear his words.

"You will work with good people who make the most of what they have—unlike you. You've wanted for nothing, been educated at the best schools, and had the world at your fingertips. I want you to experience the other end of the spectrum."

Cate wasn't sure which shocked her more, her father's actions or his lack of faith in her. She hated that he viewed her as someone who would never amount to anything, and worse, that he'd decided to destroy her dream of working in fashion, of running Seraphim. She was determined to prove him wrong, whatever it took, and so far it had taken all her willpower and Zobbio's unwavering support.

Cate had grown to respect the director who tested and pushed her, but who never let her fall. The more she learned of her daunting teacher, the more she admired her. Apart from her role at the institute, Madeleine Zobbio ran a charitable organization that took destitute young people off the streets and placed them in halfway houses, before finding them employment. She was a woman of invariable heart and social conscience, and Cate had much to thank her for.

It was after she left the institute to commence her master's program that their relationship shifted. It became clear that neither of them wanted to lose contact with the other, so they spoke regularly on the phone and exchanged occasional letters. Cate found her respect for Zobbio turning into something far deeper. Trust. That subtle change enabled Zobbio to turn from teacher to mentor, and Cate slowly opened up and shared more of herself.

Being invited here again this evening made her feel very special, something she hadn't felt in a long time. Brought back to the present, she realized Zobbio had been talking about her husband, who had died six years ago.

"I feel his ghost here all the time."

"Do you get lonely?" Cate asked.

"We were very happy together and I suppose I would miss him more if it wasn't for my work and my charitable projects. His ghost is far less demanding and much tidier than he was when he was alive. He was a disorganized man, an artist with his paints and drawings everywhere, and his mind always in the clouds."

"Is Guido still overseas?" Zobbio's only son served in the Italian army and had been deployed with NATO forces in Europe not long after Cate left the Istituto di Bello Disegno.

"He is, and I shall rejoice the day he returns." Zobbio topped their glasses up. Cate moved to stop her but received the sternest look, all fake. "Oh, enjoy the wine. You do not have to drive anywhere."

Cate allowed herself a rare laugh and relaxed back into her chair. "I have to walk home. That'll be quite a challenge if I drink any more."

"Tell me what your news is. Have you met the love of your life?"

Cate was a little startled by the direct question. In the ten years they'd known each other, Signora Zobbio had never pressed her on personal matters. Cautiously, she replied, "I haven't had time."

"Now that you have graduated, what is your plan? Are you finally going to return to your country?"

Instantly uncomfortable, Cate said, "No. I'm happy here." She felt self-conscious as Zobbio cast a quick, perceptive eye over her. "There's no reason for me to go back. Not yet, anyway."

One day she would be ready, and she would let nothing stand in her way to obtain what was rightfully hers. One day, she would own Seraphim and run the fashion house the way her mother would have wanted—and damn anyone who tried to stop her. For now, she was content to bide her time and learn her trade.

"It's been a long time. More than ten years," Zobbio angled.

"I'm not ready." Cate immediately regretted the sharp edge in her voice.

"And if you wanted me to know why, you would tell me." Zobbio sighed. "No matter, everyone has their secrets and a part of themselves they wish to keep hidden. You are no different. Though," she smiled sagely, "perhaps you have too many secrets for one so young?"

"I thought I'd continue to live here," Cate said quickly, softening her tone. "I've seen a small shop I want to buy. It's very run down but it's a good price and I can live above it. I've been selling my own designs for several years now, as you know. I already have quite a few regular customers."

"You do know that Ermanno Nardini wants you to work for him? You might not do so badly to be his assistant."

"I know that, but…" Cate realized it was an exceptional opportunity to be asked to work with someone like Nardini, an internationally recognized designer with his own successful fashion house. She didn't want to seem ungrateful.

"But you are in a hurry," Zobbio finished the sentence.

"I'll be thirty soon." Cate was all too aware that she had some ground to make up. She was older than most new designers coming out of their studies, but she had spent ten years learning from the best and she'd already built a reputation for her dedication and designs. "You think I'm making a mistake?"

It was rare that Cate ever asked anyone's opinion regarding personal matters, despite the attempts of fellow students to chip away at her hard exterior. She didn't want their friendship, only their respect. But she felt differently about Zobbio, aware of the singular relationship between them, and the age and increasing frailty of her mentor. She hated to think that at almost any time Zobbio could be lost to her. Her instinct told her to keep her distance for that very reason, yet another part of her resisted her self-imposed isolation.

"If I thought you were trying to run before you could walk, maybe. But you have the talent and the ideas." Zobbio paused for a long while, then added, "And, my dear, you are very much your mother's daughter."

Cate froze. Her cheeks felt chilled as the blood swept out of them.

Zobbio placed a hand over hers. "You think I wouldn't know? This young American turns up at the Istituto all those years ago, *desperate* to attend and refusing to go elsewhere. So, I ask myself, why? What is this unspoken link? Of course, there is a clue. Your name is Morgan and you are the image of your mother. Those blue eyes, they gave you away. I only have ever seen such color in one other…Helena Morgan."

"You never said anything," Cate whispered. Morgan was her mother's maiden name. She'd been using it ever since she left Boston, hoping to make it harder for her father to find her, if he was looking.

With the small arch of an eyebrow, Zobbio replied, "You chose not to declare this."

Cate had the impression this fact had won the director's respect even before she could prove herself as a hardworking apprentice. "And you never wondered why?"

"Of course, but you felt, for whatever reason, that you had to hide your past. I respect your decision." Zobbio moved her hand away and picked up her glass of wine. "I think you should continue with your plans, but it would be nice if you might sometimes feel the need to ask this old woman for advice occasionally, or simply to stay in touch when you leave here."

Cate hesitated before she spoke again, ever cautious in case she gave too much of herself away. Finally, she said, "I think I would be a fool to let someone so important slip away."

Zobbio said nothing, but held Cate's gaze. No words were necessary to convey what emotion ran between them.

With touching sincerity and gentle humor, Zobbio added warmly, "Perhaps the maestro and the talented student can become friends?"

Self-possession and a sense of calm returned to Cate, who with equal sincerity responded, "Perhaps they already are."

The two women clinked their glasses together in bonhomie.

CHAPTER FOUR

In her three years at Seraphim Dita had never seen the normally reserved and calm William Canton look so out of place.

"You're not at all comfortable with this, are you?" she asked, a pulse away from breaking into laughter.

"It's a long way from the boardroom," he said, looking around him at the swath of activity.

They were at the February Atelier New York Fashion Week. It was a show that allowed the smaller, mid-market designers to canvass their work. The place was overflowing with potential buyers, the media and public.

A half-naked model walked past William in something slinky. William nervously fidgeted with his tie.

"Don't worry, that's not one of my outfits," Dita whispered in his ear.

"Glad to hear it. Why anyone would pay that much money for less than a foot of material, I'll never know."

"Your problem, William, is that you aren't hip enough. You need to get in the scene." Dita loved playing with him and saw his responsive eyes narrow in her direction.

"Not at my age, and certainly not with my back," he grumbled. "What in the name of blue blazes am I doing here, Dita?"

She placed an arm through his and fondly tugged it, pulling them both closer to the wall so they'd be less likely to be trampled down by the flow of the crowd. "I wanted you to be part of Seraphim's success. God knows it's been slow in coming, and every time I think we're beginning to get somewhere, we get setbacks. But after yesterday's show, I wanted to drag you out here to see what's happening. We've already had some good orders. If we get any more, we could be in danger of slipping into black." She laughed, but her tone was hollow.

William turned serious. "I can't understand why that hasn't happened already. In the last three years you've turned out some impressive collections." He arched his brows and shrugged. "I still wouldn't know a hot design if it burnt me. But I've never known anyone to work so hard." He gazed at her affectionately. "You do know you're the best fashion director I've employed, don't you?"

Dita tugged his arm again. "Thank you. I just want you to see Seraphim rise again. I know we're going to get back to the success formula we had when Helena ran the company."

Marcus Abner, Seraphim's marketing director, chose that moment to rush up to them, panting. "Can't stop. Two more buyers want the whole range. Things are looking up." He'd gone almost before he'd got there.

"Looks like that success might have arrived." William patted the hand she had resting on his arm.

"We're not there yet," Dita said. "But we're moving in the right direction. Once the orders for this collection are sorted then I'll have the breathing space to sit down and really work on my new designs... but I'm excited."

Unexpectedly, the debonair, well-groomed image of Bernard Bressinger came to a halt before them. Smiling suavely, he said, "Miss Newton, I'm—"

"Bernard Bressinger of *Nouveau Rich*." Dita released William's arm.

Bressinger fawned indulgently in recognition of his fame and notoriety, smoothing his tie. "Your house seems to be having a measure of success, and I think my readers would like to know a little more about Seraphim. The brand has been around for a long time, but I don't recall seeing anything quite as harmonious as your new collection for years. You seem quite prominent among the smaller houses this year. A runway show, no less."

"We're pleased," Dita said cautiously.

Bressinger ran his hand across the top of his balding head. "Miss Newton, as designer and driving force behind Seraphim, how do you view this change of fortune?"

Dita drew breath. "Well, thank you for recognizing the changes, and of course, that's what everyone in the house has been working toward...a change of direction, a new design focus. Obviously I'm pleased that we're attracting a second look these days, but I can't take all the credit. If you're looking at the driving force behind the house, you really should talk to the owner, William Canton." She drew Bressinger's attention to William, who had started edging away stiffly. Not taking her eyes off Bressinger, Dita reached back and grabbed her boss's arm, pulling him forward. "Without his dedication the company would have folded years ago. You may remember it was his late wife, Helena, who started Seraphim."

Dita could have sworn she saw the on light flash over Bressinger's bald head as he targeted an angle for his article. His attention was now fixed on William like a homing missile. "Hmm. So Seraphim is more a family business?" His intensity notched higher. "Tell me, Mr. Canton, when did Seraphim start? Was it your wife's vision or something you both shared?"

Dita stepped back and deliberately ignored the killer glance William threw in her direction. It would do him good to be lauded by the media after all those years of being in the wilderness, running a less than profitable business. It would show those who had accused him of foolish sentimentality that they were wrong. Too many had said, and far too openly, that as a successful industrialist who owned impressive amounts of real estate on both sides of the Atlantic Ocean, he should have known better than to continually prop up a dead wife's flagging business. This was payback time for William.

From a safer distance, she watched the two men talking for a while, wanting to make sure she hadn't dropped William in out of his depth. But she could see he seemed to be talking at ease with Bressinger, who was busily taking notes.

Satisfied she could leave, Dita stepped out of the room and into the adjacent auditorium. She needed a short break. She was tired. Her time at Seraphim had been tough, but a combination of hard work and ridiculous hours had kept the ailing fashion business afloat. Three years of relentless slog had taken their toll. It wasn't that she didn't enjoy being Seraphim's fashion director. She adored her job and loved having the freedom to create her designs, designs that had buzzed around her head since she was old enough to remember. So far, this job had been the culmination of all her dreams, but she couldn't deny that she was a little burned out. Things were getting better, but there was still so much to be done and sometimes she felt daunted as she balanced her time between creation and management.

Sipping a glass of unimpressive cheap champagne, she watched a model wander through the crowd and execute a turn with limp grace. The organizers paid some of their most striking runway models to ornament the room in this manner. This one looked bored, or perhaps her languor was the result of not eating. Dita reflected that she could never have been a model.

Lost in the moment, she laughed to herself as she thought back to the snide comments she'd borne from the fashion community since taking over the directorship of Seraphim. Many had openly speculated that she was too old to make the break as a designer of any influence.

That comment had hurt. Yes, fashion design was predominantly a young person's arena, that's when rising stars first attracted attention. They soon moved up to big fashion houses as assistants to important designers. A few went on to establish their own labels, then aged, often with Bohemian disgrace, and became icons. So now, at twenty-nine, she was behind the curve...but too old?

No. She would show them. They would soon see that she was only getting started. Today she could smell success just around the corner. The breeze had shifted direction and fortune. She couldn't wait for the winter fashion shows. Once she presented the designs she was working on now, no one would dare write her off again.

"Ah, there you are." William's soft lyrical tones drew her attention.

She couldn't help noticing how smart he looked in his crisp white shirt, dark charcoal suit, and brogue laced shoes. He really was the epitome of a gentleman.

"How was the interview?" she asked.

"I think he was happy, though I suspect he would have been happier if you'd talked to him." William gave a quirky smile.

"Rubbish. He wanted the personal angle and you *are* the owner. Hopefully, there'll be plenty of opportunity for the fashion slant later." Dita rubbed the bridge of her nose to conceal a yawn.

"You look tired." William said.

"It's been a busy few months."

"Yes, it has." He eyed her with concern. "You know, I don't think you've had a real break since I hired you, which is way too long."

"Oh, I'll take some time off soon. Once the orders are filled and we've sold through our overstock."

His eyes roamed her face. "When?"

"I'm not sure."

"Seriously, you need a break, everyone does. You'll have a sharper focus after a rest."

She smiled indulgently. "Are you pushing me, Mr. Canton?"

"Yes, Miss Newton."

They exchanged smiles.

"Well, I can't do anything until this season is put to bed so no time soon." She pondered a while. "But I could take a break in August. I'll be finalizing my Spring designs by then, so I can do that anywhere."

"And aren't you planning to go to Italy?"

"Yes, to purchase new fabrics." She could see where he was headed and had to admit the idea was appealing. "I suppose I could tie the buying trip in with some vacation time, maybe stay over…a sort of working holiday."

"Have you ever been to Amalfi?"

Dita shook her head.

"You ought to go. It's quite beautiful." William's expression became introspective, almost wistful. "Italy is lovely in late summer."

❖

William had almost forgotten the interview when Dita stepped into his office, several months after the New York show, and dropped a magazine on his desk.

"You were far too flattering," she said, opening to a page with a photograph of her at the top.

William studied the image. "That's a lousy picture."

"One of the assistants said I look like Madonna after a hard workout in the gym. I took that as a compliment."

William laughed. As time had progressed, he'd grown accustomed to Dita's dry humor and self-effacing comments. He'd also gotten to know her better, which wasn't easy. She was a quiet woman, a little on the reserved side. She worked diligently and was always on time and well-prepared for their weekly meetings. William had spent the past two years poring over detailed presentations of short- and long-term business objectives, production plans, and cost analyses. Dita did what her predecessors didn't: she never hesitated to ask his guidance or opinions on matters of management. This was a new concept for him; those who'd gone before her had never bothered.

"What have you got for me today?" William asked.

"The textiles budget for next year's Spring collection." Dita slapped a spreadsheet in front of him and pointed at a row of figures. She was always serious and hyper-focused during their meetings. It was only when their conversations turned to matters that hinged around actual fashion design that the *creative monster* appeared.

"Volume up by forty percent," William noted, a little shocked.

"That's my realistic projection," Dita said. "I've been over the numbers several times. I want to be conservative, but at the same time we can't shoot ourselves in the foot by underestimating growth."

At risk of sounding like a wet blanket, William remarked, "Some economists are saying we're in a bubble and these retail conditions won't last. If there's a downturn we don't want to be caught with half our capital tied up in unsold inventory."

"I agree, but we don't have a huge business infrastructure to support, so if market conditions change we can react more quickly. Right now, we need to take advantage of the climate we're in. We're scoring with evening wear. Our business clothing competes on price point and quality, and our Fashion Ethics range is a sellout. We can hardly keep up."

William wasn't much into the apparel business, for it had been his wife's dream, but he could still tell the "crap from the classic" and he also had a well-developed sense of broad market trends. After only a short while, he could see Dita's design concepts were sound and had given her the autonomy to see them through. Truth be told, there was also something about her enthusiasm for fashion that reminded him a lot of Cate. When she'd talked about developing a line that plugged into increasing social concerns around fair trade, animal welfare, and the climate crisis, he thought the suggestion was one Cate might have made.

He'd immediately seen the potential, and Dita had cemented the line with several designs that were picked up by young, politically aware celebrities. Almost overnight, countless new stores became customers, wanting to stock these "hot" items. Many of these stores had since expanded their purchases to include other ranges, a factor in Seraphim's rapid growth.

William studied the sheets before him for several minutes, running through the numbers. She was right; her projections were not at all far-fetched. "This looks realistic," he said. "I'm in full support."

"Excellent." Dita folded the spreadsheet and set it aside. "I've made my travel arrangements for Italy."

"Including vacation time," William prompted.

As he'd expected, Dita vacillated. "We're so busy, I'm starting to think it would make more sense if I wait till next year. As soon as I've finished in Milan, I want to get back so I can oversee the samples for the Spring collection."

"No," William said flatly. "You can delegate for a change. You've hired competent people. Give them a chance to prove themselves."

Dita looked a little startled and he realized he'd spoken more adamantly than he'd intended, and that he'd also struck a nerve. Dita was well aware that he'd given her a chance to show what she was capable of, and she prided herself on giving their staff opportunities to do the same. Frowning, she said, "I guess I'm not used to our expansion yet. So far I've supervised *everything*."

"And you've done a spectacular job. But you're not superhuman." William adopted an argument he knew would work. "You have to be fresh for next year. If we're going to break through, you need to be at the top of your game."

Immediately, the mantle of her reserve fell away and William could see in her glittering eyes the burning ambition that fueled her. He'd often wondered where that side of her personality came from. As they'd started to get comfortable with each other, William had occasionally asked about her past: what had brought her to be raised by her grandmother, where she was from, who her parents were, and whether she had brothers and sisters. Her answers were always evasive, leaving him in no doubt she didn't like talking about her background. He quickly realized that she had a fragile underbelly and did not easily trust.

She seemed to lack an appropriate support structure of friends and family, and knowing this, William did something unusual. He allowed friendship to enter the employer-employee equation. Her vulnerability brought out a protective instinct in him, and though slowly at first, Dita began to warm correspondingly, though she never once overstepped the subtle boundaries of their working affiliation. It pleased him that at last he'd found someone capable of hearing the heartbeat of Seraphim, and not only that but an ally, a person he truly liked. If anyone was capable of turning the business around, it would be this young woman.

"You're right," Dita conceded with quiet intensity. "I have to be at my very best."

She finally sat down in the leather armchair opposite the desk and stretched her limbs out like a cat might before it softened and turned tranquil. Easing herself into the worn comfort of the chair, she momentarily played with the pleats on her polka dot dress before calmly placing her hands in her lap. Her expression relaxed into pensiveness, and her light blue eyes were suddenly untroubled. Her gaze seemed inward, as though fixed on a vista in her mind's eye, a beautiful place that invited her to leave her cares behind.

Feeling like an intruder on her private landscape, William said, "There's a hotel in Amalfi my wife used to talk about. She went there when she was studying in Europe. I'll give you the details. It's supposed to be charming."

Dita's focus changed and he had her full attention once more. "A charming hotel in Amalfi. I like the sound of that." She smiled at him. "You're very good to me, William. I promise, I won't let you down."

❖

Cate threw the magazine across her hotel room and watched it flop pathetically against the back of the couch. She was fuming, her arms down at her sides, fists clenched as her heart beat wildly. She'd just showered and started dressing for tonight's party when she'd taken a phone call from her senior assistant in Ferrara. They were cut off after five minutes and she'd had to wait for reconnection. She'd picked up one of the fashion magazines in her suite and was leafing through when she saw the name Seraphim.

"Damn it," she cursed, staring at the harmless pages that had ignited her rage.

The article had been unexpected. She had scanned the cover teasers without a second thought. "Counted Out but Coming Back: New Life for an Old Name?" could have referred to anything. The font was small and the header was one of several flagging the minor articles inside this month's edition. *Nouveau Rich* had obviously considered the item fairly unimportant.

Not to her.

There on a single page lay an interview with her father, who spoke of hope for the rising fortunes of Seraphim, and how their recent successes were due to the talents of the current fashion director, Dita Newton. He'd talked of how incredibly lucky he was to have eventually found someone so perfect for the job, especially after a series of uninspiring predecessors. The article described Newton as "beauty with brains," a virtual unknown with much promise who seemed to be reading the market with increasing adeptness.

"Beauty with brains." Cate spat the words. She snatched the magazine up off the floor and looked to see what gushing idiot had written that piece of pathetic prose. Bernard Bressinger. There was a name to remember. Not that Cate gave interviews, but if she was ever tempted, hell would freeze over before she gave one to him.

She studied the small photograph of Dita Newton. It was a head and shoulder shot of someone blond and rather Nordic in appearance. It wasn't a good picture and Cate instantly labeled her as well presented, rather than attractive. Beauty with brains? A typical male assessment. She continued studying the photo for several minutes before ripping it from the article and placing it at the back of her organizer.

So this was her competition? The woman running her mother's business and, if her father was to be believed, shoring up its flagging fortunes? No matter. To hell with what he thought. When she was ready, Seraphim would be hers and God help anyone who tried to stand in her way.

❖

A hand swooshed across and plucked a glass of white wine from the tray of drinks that was circulating. The attached body then pushed through the party revelers in the Cellar Bar at the chic Bryant Park Hotel in New York City, cutting a path to the woman who had just walked down the stairs.

A rich Scottish accent boomed out. "Caty, darling. I thought you were never going to make it. You aren't even fashionably late…you're beyond that. It's almost tomorrow."

Cate Canton found herself looking at the grinning face of Jeremy McKay, owner of Suba Q, a fashion chain on both sides of the Atlantic. He thrust the glass into her hand almost before she'd parted with her coat, and then challenged her to maintain balance whilst he gripped her in a tight bear hug.

Cate liked this man. She hadn't seen him in almost a year but he never seemed to change. He was stockily built, about the same height as her, with a head of flame red hair and the most amazing long eyelashes above soft hazel eyes. He never veered from being openly friendly and hospitable, his contagious sense of humor setting both colleagues and strangers instantly at ease.

"I was trying to get here sooner," Cate said with genuine regret. Jeremy's parties were legendary. "I was just running through a few final things at the shop before I fly back to Italy tomorrow."

"Och, how's it feel to be planning your second U.S. store, and in Manhattan no less?"

Cate took a greedy swig of her wine. It was like nectar to her senses. She'd been on her feet all day and this drink was very welcome. "Pretty good," she said with pride.

"Aye, I bet it does. I remember how I felt when Alison and I opened our first Suba Q here. We were so excited, neither of us slept for a month. Here we were in New York City…we kept pacing up and down in front of the store taking photos. Christ, we could have opened a photo gallery with the hundreds of pics we took." He smiled warmly at her, his uneven white teeth to the fore. "It hasn't taken you much time to follow, has it?"

It hadn't. Cate's success had been nothing short of meteoric since she'd bought her little shop in Ferrara. At first, she'd sold only to locals, but they began recommending her label, Zabor, to small shops in other Italian towns. Within a year, Cate's reputation had spread exponentially and she found herself supplying larger retailers in the cities. Success demanded staff and Madeleine Zobbio had helped her find suitable employees, plus the occasional charitable case. Cate always happily obliged and before she knew it, she had a small but industrious team.

Shortly after had come her spark of luck. A British fashion chain called Suba Q had shown interest in her collections and had asked her to produce a few lines for them. They had just broken into the US market, opening several shops. They were an overnight success and of course, Cate's designs went with them. Her success riding on theirs, she was faced with a dilemma. She could supply the American retail stores that expressed interest in her label or she could choose a vertically integrated business model and open her own stores. The latter was riskier, but she decided the only way to find out if she could succeed was to open a small store in a location where women spent freely on their wardrobes. She chose Miami.

Her subsequent success had more to do with Zobbio than with her modest advertising budget. Her mentor phoned every socialite for whom she'd ever designed a gown and herded them to the store. Within a year, Cate's designs were appearing on the social pages and she was being invited to the parties that really mattered. Several Palm Beach heavyweights invited her to stage a fashion show at a charity event, and Cate hadn't caught her breath since.

Now, only eighteen months after her Miami launch, she was planning her second store, her showpiece, here in Manhattan. She'd traveled over from Italy to finalize the location and store concept, and to press the flesh with her investors. It was difficult to believe the progress she'd made even working at breakneck speed, operating day and night to cope with her rapid growth. She was exhausted but thrilled. Just thirty-three years of age, and she owned a successful fashion house and would soon boast two brand-name retail stores.

Only now did she feel ready to strike at Seraphim. Her plan was quite simple. She would take market share from Seraphim. She would make her brand more sought after, then offer unbeatable discounts to stores willing to drop Seraphim lines in favor of Zabor. She would pay various nitwit celebrities to promote her label and when stores ordered items they saw in the media, she would decline to supply those who stocked Seraphim equivalents.

She wouldn't be the first designer to insist upon a certain degree of exclusivity among stockists of her brand. If she defended her turf aggressively, shutting Seraphim out wherever she could, she could squeeze hard enough to make her father think twice about propping up the company any longer. It was a shame they weren't publicly listed. That would have made things easier. Cate could simply have purchased shares as values declined, eventually becoming the major stockholder. However, her plan would see the business flounder and Ms. Beauty with Brains would be no more. Her father would discover the mistake he had made in writing Cate off.

"Well, what do you think?" Jeremy asked. At Cate's blank stare, he swept a hand around. "This, darling. My little function."

"Little function?" Cate surveyed the lavish surroundings, and the abundance of food and drink. "This must be costing you big time."

"Aye, but you have to keep the punters happy. Besides, I have that *enfant terrible* reputation to keep up. It's tough at this age…with all those so-called new generation designers snapping at one's ankles."

Jeremy paused as a gorgeously dandified boy tapped him on the shoulder and whispered something in his ear.

He turned back. "Caty, darling, I've got to go mingle…strut my stuff. I'll catch up with you later. By the way, I love the new concepts. Let's talk about broadening the color range."

Cate spent the next half hour talking to other guests and making some useful contacts, until hunger won out and she headed for the food.

"I can recommend the chunks of lobster, and the mango sauce is to die for."

Cate turned her attention away from the appetizer trays, seeking the source of the clipped British diction. She found herself staring directly into a pair of luminescent green eyes.

"You don't remember me, do you?"

Cate didn't.

"I'm Zoë Parker. We met several years ago—briefly—when you first showed Jeremy your designs. I was at that meeting…graphic design." She offered a hand.

"I'm sorry, I don't remember." Cate thought she spied a flash of disappointment and it drove her to continue the handshake for longer than necessary and to soften her answer. "I was so focused on making sure Suba Q got what they wanted that day, and we signed the contract, I wasn't paying attention to much else."

"There was never any doubt. That's why they flew you over to England in the first place. Jeremy loved your stuff."

"Right." Cate had thought the passing conversation over but Zoë seemed to have an agenda.

"I saw you at Silverlakes that night. I really wanted to come over and say hello…buy you a drink…" She laughed self-depreciatingly. "But I was a tad shy. By the time I'd garnered my courage you were dancing with some other woman."

Cate couldn't imagine that Zoë had ever suffered from a lack of confidence. She'd spent only three days in Dudley, where Suba Q was based, but she'd managed to find Silverlakes, a popular lesbian bar in the Midlands. None of the women she'd met there seemed reticent.

"I thought I wouldn't make the same mistake again," Zoë trilled.

"Sorry?"

"Wait too long and let someone else whisk you away."

It suddenly dawned on Cate that she was being chatted up—and by a very pretty woman. Zoë was taller than her and slender to the point of being delicate looking. She carried herself with an attractive touch of arrogance many Brits seemed to have, full frontal confidence toned with a splash of diplomacy. It was as if the country's old Empire days still resonated within each of them.

She leaned forward past Cate, and hooked a green olive which she deftly placed in her mouth. The light caught her straight long brown hair, producing a shine that suggested vitality and health. Leaning back, she looked at Cate expectantly. When she didn't get a response, she said, "There's a really good club not too far from here. I'd love to take you there. It would give me that chance to finally buy you a drink."

Cate felt a surge of discomfort rush through her. Her modus operandi was all about control. She was always the one who led in these matters, the one who approached a potential date, who made the moves when summing up the possibilities of a one-night stand. And casual encounters were all she was ever interested in. Simple. Uncomplicated. No ties. She had no time to invest in a real relationship, the kind that required energy and commitment. Perhaps one day…

She returned her focus to the woman in front of her, surprised that she felt awkward and gauche. She wasn't used to this reversal of protocol—someone asking her out. That was probably why she had so few dates; she knew her demeanor didn't encourage flirtation. People only hit on her occasionally, both men and women, and Cate was an expert at delivering a subtle brush-off that wouldn't offend potential clients.

She had the perfect excuse at her fingertips, this time, she realized with relief. "It's a nice idea but I have an early flight out of Newark, so I'm planning to catch a few hours' sleep before I go."

Cate was surprised to see disappointment in the eyes that stared back. She felt a heel, like she'd punched a hole in Zoë's self-confidence. Not so British after all, then? It hadn't been her intention to wound, yet she could see Zoë felt she simply wasn't interested in her. Not quite true. Another place, another time…under Cate's conditions. She hastily sought some way to communicate this. "I hope I see you again, Zoë."

"That doesn't seem terribly likely." A bright smile followed. "Have a safe flight. And a nice life."

Cate watched in silence as Zoë walked away. She knew that after a drink or two, they would have ended up in bed together and would most likely both have had great sex. So what was her problem? The small, frankly unimportant incident had actually disturbed her. Zoë had seen something in her that she desired, and Cate also felt a pleasant flicker of interest. So she'd have missed out on a night's sleep, but the flight back to Italy would resolve that. She wasn't sure why she'd turned Zoë away, or why it was so important to her that everything was on her terms. Why was she the one who always had to be in charge?

Cate couldn't remember desiring control when she was a child. No, this element of her nature had appeared in her late teens when her father had started boxing her in. He had controlled every aspect of her life, her friends, where she went at weekends, what she did socially. And Cate had rebelled, wanting her independence. Her father had never given in, and once free of his shackles, she had sworn she would never let anyone control her life again.

Lately, however, she'd been questioning the constraints she imposed on her social life. Maybe it was because now, in her thirties, she was beginning to wish she felt closer to people. She felt she was missing out on something. In her work, she was succeeding beyond her hopes, yet the satisfaction she felt was tempered by another emotion. Dismay gripped her as she identified the feeling. Loneliness.

Cate set her lobster down untouched. Glancing at her watch, she realized it was one o'clock in the morning. She'd intended to bid Jeremy farewell, but she could talk to him later. For now she needed to get some sleep before the journey home to Ferrara.

CHAPTER FIVE

The coastal town of Amalfi was usually a busy Italian tourist resort for both countrymen and foreigners, its natural beauty and close proximity to Sorrento, Positano, and Capri, the lures. But now, the holiday season barely over, the resonance of the place turned to a calmer, more tranquil refuge, leaving just the natives and a few indulgent travelers like herself. There was a plaque in the center of the town that declared:

> FOR THOSE NATIVES OF AMALFI WHO ARE CALLED TO PARADISE,
> JUDGMENT DAY WILL BE JUST ANOTHER DAY.

Whoever had written those words, Dita understood the sentiment the author tried to convey, for there was something that moved this place beyond beauty, and toward an indefinable conveyance of complete happiness. Yes, many might call it paradise. And in her comfortable state of mind, she allowed herself to contemplate how she might go hiking tomorrow, to spoil herself with more of this country's spectacular beauty.

From her chair in the hotel courtyard, she could see out over the cliff top to the sea. The sun would soon go down. Streaks of shimmering light spilled across the ocean, and as a gentle, almost caressing breeze warmed her, she pondered that this place would lift her spirits and give her back some of the energy she seemed to have lost of late. Perhaps she might even have the opportunity to indulge in one of those brief holiday romances novelists so loved to write about. *Unlikely.*

At a polite cough over her shoulder, she turned to see a hotel waiter balancing a tray of coffee. His face lit up in a bright, radiant smile. She fought not to smile in return as she recognized the attraction she'd sparked in the handsome young man.

"*Signorina*, your coffee."

She indicated the table next to her.

The waiter was not conversant in English, but tried to make his mark with her anyway, offering an observation about the romantic view and the weather. His words were disjointed, and his over-enthusiasm wonderfully obvious. This was nothing new. Everywhere Dita went, she incurred the same response from the male population. Her elegant blond looks were a magnet for the opposite sex.

She thanked him for the coffee, offering a tip which he fervently refused. *Definitely smitten!* He slowly backed away from her, maintaining eye contact for as long as possible. Once he'd gone, she allowed herself a smile. The little scenario had lifted her sagging spirits. If nothing else, she could still "pull," even if those drawn to her weren't often her type.

Closing her eyes, she threw her head back and relaxed into the chair, allowing the fading heat of the evening sun to warm her face. Hopefully a few days here would replace its pallor with some color.

❖

Madeleine Zobbio regarded Cate angrily. "No, no, no. I don't care that you are busy and have so much to do. No one can take the candle and burn it at both ends like you and not suffer the consequences."

Cate's reprimand in her mentor's office was reminiscent of being in front of the school principal, something she remembered too well. "I've just got off an international flight," she started to explain.

"Bah! You look dreadful. You've lost weight and you have bags under your eyes."

"Oh thanks, I feel much better now."

"Do not reduce this to humor, Cate. This will not do." Madeleine wagged a finger at her. "If you don't slow down, you're going to make yourself ill." The elderly woman was clearly exasperated. "Is it not enough that you now have such success? What more do you seek, child?"

Cate had not expected this sort of welcome, and she was shocked at the extent of Madeleine's concern. "You're right," she said, trying to mollify her. "I'll take things easy for the next couple of days."

This rare concession fell on deaf ears. "You. Must. Stop," came the retort from Madeleine before she softened. "Won't you even admit to me that you are tired?"

How could Cate lie to her? This was the one person she really cared for, the only one she could ever be open with. Surrendering, Cate exhaled noisily as she moved to a chair and sat down. "Okay, fine. I am tired. Point made. Things have been a bit busy these last few months, that's all. But if it'll please you, I'll take a few days off and go nest in my apartment with a good book."

"You will not. I know you. You'll be looking at business charts and spreadsheets…your precious financial predictions." Madeleine threw her arms up in disgust. "You need a good holiday, somewhere with plenty of good fresh air and peace."

"I can't take a holiday now. I just signed a lease. Renovations on the Manhattan building begin next week."

"You've signed the legal papers, so what else are you needed for? You are not an engineer."

"Something could go wrong."

Madeleine shrugged. "Then you will receive a phone call. You can handle such a conversation anywhere in the world."

"No, I need to be close enough to make contingency plans…to see people here if I have to." Cate fell silent, realizing she'd just accepted defeat and they were now discussing the terms of her exile.

"I know just the place," Madeleine said with satisfaction.

"All right. But I can't be away for more than a week."

"Two weeks," Madeleine said sternly. "I'll make the reservation."

Cate acquiesced with a weak nod. She would take work with her, of course. But she wasn't going to tell Madeleine that. "Let's go out for dinner tonight," she suggested. "I owe you a fine meal. Without those Palm Beach clients of yours I'd still be waiting for the Miami store to turn a profit. And Manhattan would just be a dream."

Madeleine gave a small snort. "You forget, I know you. Those dreams…*you* make them happen. Nothing stands in your way. And no one…"

❖

Amalfi was a gentle place, Dita thought as she took an early evening stroll along the harbor before dinner. Or maybe it was just because she'd arrived at the closing end of the tourist season. No matter. She felt sure this place would prove an inspiration to the designs she was working on.

She watched the crews of fishing boats and private yachts pulling down their rigging, making fast and secure for the night. At the far end of the harbor road she found a small nest of shops, all geared toward seafaring maintenance. There were the general ship fitters, the rope and riggers, the woodworkers, and the sheet metal stores. Despite the late hour, most were still open and no one seemed in a rush to finish. Several workers smiled and waved at her as she passed.

Turning back toward the hotel, she thought of William. It was a shame he'd never married again, and a waste. Someone out there was being deprived of a wonderful husband, a genuinely decent human being. But she guessed William had found his one mate in life, and when he lost her that was it for him. She was sure he'd kept Seraphim going as a memorial to Helena. While it still existed, in some small part so did she.

Dita had been naturally inquisitive in her early days at Seraphim, wanting to know more about the man willing to risk hiring an unfledged twenty-six-year-old to run a fashion house. She'd also been curious about his reasons for keeping the struggling brand afloat when most businessmen would have cut their losses. There was a painting on a wall at Seraphim of its founder, Helena Canton. She was an extremely elegant and attractive woman with beautiful deep blue eyes.

She'd remarked carefully on the picture to William one day and in the briefest of answers, he'd merely agreed that his wife was a lovely woman. Dita had asked him about children, and he had answered with a monosyllabic, "Two," and then walked away.

Dita had heard something in his tone. Pain.

Intrigued, she'd tried to find out more about the two children over the subsequent weeks, but not many of the original staff still worked at Seraphim. Marcus Abner would never be drawn into any conversation regarding the Canton family. The topic seemed to make him uncomfortable. She guessed it was loyalty, for he had worked for them since the beginning of Seraphim, originally hired by Helena.

All Dita had managed to find out from one of the clerical staff was that William had a daughter who was killed in a car accident. There was another girl, too, but she'd been a problem and had left home quite young. No one knew what had happened to her and they'd never dared to ask their boss.

Dita never pushed the point with him herself, accepting that William was a deeply private man who did not talk of his family beyond his wife's connection with the business. She respected his wishes, knowing too well how the past could hurt. She had only to think of her own mother, who had discarded her. The memory still generated raw emotion, and she had no desire to open old wounds by discussing the past.

Thoughts of William, of his great love for Helena, stirred something in Dita and she paused near the hotel, turning to look out to sea. Normally she enjoyed her own company. She was self-sufficient and so preoccupied with work she never had time to dwell on the sense of isolation that sometimes enveloped her, or the fact that, at almost thirty years of age, she still hadn't found her mate in life. She was beginning to wonder if she ever would.

Of course, she hadn't been a nun. She'd known early in her teens that she was gay but didn't have her first real relationship until college, where she'd met an older woman, Alba Dolley. They'd lived together for three years, but when college finished, so did the relationship. It had run its course. Dita had dated several women since, but it seemed she couldn't meet that special someone. She was beginning to think she was broken goods.

Dita chastised herself inwardly for her self-pitying thoughts. She had so much going for her now, with the rising success of Seraphim. It was foolish to feel inadequate over her unspectacular track record in romance. She had plenty of time to succeed in that sphere as well. Still, it would be nice to find love—true love.

Maybe one day, she thought.

❖

The elevator seemed to take forever as it shuddered and cranked its way up the levels of the hotel in Amalfi. The Hotel De Prati had been in the family for generations and Cate didn't doubt the elevator had been, too. She lurched forward as everything came to an abrupt halt, then waited for what seemed an eternity until the doors finally parted—slowly—to reveal that she had made it to her floor. She couldn't imagine what on earth had possessed her to set out on this holiday, let alone allow Madeleine Zobbio to choose the hotel. But the elderly director knew how to get her way, and she'd used every emotional blackmail technique in the book. She'd insisted that Cate would find no place prettier on the seafront, and that the hotel was full of rustic charm and only a short distance from the *Piazza del Duomo*, the main square that housed Amalfi's famous tenth-century cathedral.

And here she was.

"Hmm," Cate muttered as she turned the large antiquated key to her room. "We will see."

She entered a small but welcoming room. The floors were tiled in mosaic patterns of white and blue with small pieces of rug at appropriate places. The bed was large by Italian standards and the white sheets looked crisp and inviting. Cate was shattered. She'd been traveling all day—an early taxi to Ferrara airport, the linking flight to Milan and then here. Though it was early in the evening, the setting sun was still powerful and Cate was glad the wooden shutters were closed, sheltering the room from its intensity.

She efficiently unpacked her luggage, hanging clothing up, placing stuff in drawers, laying toiletries out in the bathroom. She hadn't brought much for she didn't intend to stay more than a few days, even though Madeleine had booked the room for much longer. Cate had far too much to do, and being stuck in a coastal resort, no matter how lovely, was not going to help. Even now she had pressing phone calls to make. She picked up the phone and dialed Saul de Charlier, the manager of her U.S. operation. The phone was answered immediately. She liked that. Saul was efficient. He dealt with work in an effortless manner, making it look easy when it wasn't.

Though Cate had not been keen to employ someone, initially, she had grudgingly acknowledged that Madeleine was right. She couldn't be in two places at once, and she needed someone to share the day-to-day responsibilities. Almost from the moment she'd met Saul, she knew she had her front man. He was handsome, cultivated, and full of charm, the ideal public face of Zabor.

Cate had never been much good in that role herself. She'd already built a reputation for being somewhat shy and aloof. Her desire for privacy only seemed to provoke the fashion press. She knew she should take advantage of their infatuation with her while it lasted, but she preferred to have someone else handle the photo opportunities and interviews. No matter how carefully she orchestrated her contact with the media, they were always intrusive, asking awkward questions and claiming they needed a lot of background material so they could write the "personal angle." When her creations started appearing at various fashion shows, she was never seen. Whilst the Italians unwillingly accepted this, Americans did not. They had the public to satisfy and demanded someone to deal with.

Saul was perfect in the role. Though he was raised in America, his father was French, so he had dual nationality. He also spoke the language like a native, and it suited them both that he appeared to all as a Frenchman, emphasizing the genteel accent of his European roots, something which charmed the fashion world. It was a mild deception, but a money spinner as far as Cate was concerned.

His business credentials were equally impressive and Cate had wondered, at first, why such a qualified man would want to be second best behind her. But Saul was one of Madeleine Zobbio's charitable cases, a man from the school of hard knocks. Cate had chosen not to ask him about his past, and he never volunteered any detail. It was enough that Madeleine trusted him implicitly, and though early days, it seemed her trust was not misplaced. Cate was establishing a strong working relationship with him, for they were both like-minded in matters of business.

"Has that taffeta arrived yet?" she asked him. A shipment from India was late.

"Bit of a problem," he replied in his straightforward manner. "It's here but it's the wrong color. Needless to say, the pattern cutters are annoyed because they're already working to tight schedules and this delay won't help."

Cate didn't flinch; these problems happened all the time and she had learned to take them in stride. Besides, the tight schedules were the ones she'd imposed to cover all eventualities…like this one.

"Pull the Suba Q project forward," she calmly directed, "and let them work on that."

"Already done it," he said.

"Then get back to the suppliers and tell them we have no intention of paying for their error. If they want their fabric back, they'll have to pay for the shipping. Meantime, we need that color."

"I had that conversation with them. We can keep the problem fabric, their compliments."

A slight smile touched Cate's lips. Saul was not only efficient, but effective, too. "Good. I'll touch base again tomorrow. If anything changes, please contact me."

"Understood."

Conversation over, Cate kicked off her shoes and collapsed back on the bed, letting her head sink into the generous pillows. She really was exhausted. However, she was certain just a few days would recharge her batteries. She closed her eyes, and her mind wandered. It felt good that her hard work had paid off, that she was now in a position to put her plans in action. She'd been delaying the inevitable, reluctant to move back to the U.S. until she had no choice. With the Manhattan store taking shape and the rapid growth of her ready-to-wear lines, the day had come. Thinking about Seraphim once more, Cate smiled. She was ready.

Too tired to sleep, she got up and threw open the wooden shutters to her balcony. Perhaps after dinner tonight, she could sit out here at the small table and relax with a good bottle of wine. She glanced down into the courtyard below as a tall blond woman entered from the street and dropped her bag down next to a chair. A young male waiter rushed up instantly, attentively smarming over her. They exchanged a few words. Cate caught the general gist. Tourist talk about sights to see. Their conversation became a little louder and more animated when the woman said something about hiking in the surrounding hills.

"No, *Signorina.* That path is...*pericoloso*...no good." The waiter was obviously struggling for words. "Many ladies...they go to Pontone...la Valle dei Mulini. It's beautiful...*una bella escursione.*"

Cate didn't catch the reply. As the young man moved away to speak to a couple who had settled at another table, the woman lifted long, slender arms with graceful hands, smoothing back her hair. Her every move had the liquid elegance of a woman who knew she was beautiful but made little effort to play on her looks.

Feeling she was invading another's privacy, Cate was about to reenter her room when the lovely blonde glanced up as though sensing she was being watched. Cate took in a fragile face with long pale features. Frowning, she automatically stepped back into the shadows of the balcony, hidden but still able to see the tourist.

The woman sank down into a chair and, after a few minutes, accepted a glass of wine from the waiter. Cate watched her for a little longer, then went back into her room and picked up her organizer. She extracted the picture she'd torn from that aggravating article the previous week and studied it for a long time. When she looked toward the balcony once more, her heart was racing. Was it possible?

Cate shook her head. No, she was exhausted. She would probably run into the stranger tomorrow and discover that she looked nothing like Dita Newton. Just to be certain, she made sure the blonde was still in the courtyard then picked up the phone and called the front desk.

"Please put me through to one of the other guests. Dita Newton?"

There was no hesitation. "Certainly. A moment please."

Cate's mouth went dry. As soon as she heard the first ring, she ended the call, setting the receiver slowly back in its cradle. Her enemy was right here. Cate didn't know if that was a blessing or a curse.

CHAPTER SIX

*F*ind a penny, pick it up...
Wasn't it funny the things that went through one's head at the most perilous times? Dita had found a one cent coin lying on the concrete sidewalk as she'd left her hotel to catch the early morning ferry. It had brought her to the bay where many went hill walking.

All the day you will have luck.

Like that worked, she thought as she hung onto the small rocky hillsides for dear life. Locals had warned her that this particular trek was treacherous, and that only experienced hikers and those who knew the area well should take it. She should have listened but instead she'd decided the physical challenge would do her good. Now she was not quite hanging vertically, but at enough of an angle that if she moved, gravity would take hold and she'd slip down the crumbling embankment and plunge straight over the edge to certain death. Her fingers ached as they tired of their strenuous hold. She felt herself panicking. How much longer could she hang on?

She'd been stuck there for over ten minutes, well away from the beaten track that so many hill walkers took. At first, she'd tried calling out for help, but the movement of her body as she inhaled had caused her to slip further down the rough ground she lay on. There was nothing stopping her further descent other than her poor fingers and what was left of her nails, for her feet were already hanging over the edge. Dita felt like crying, but couldn't because one breathless sob would start the perilous downward motion again—and this time, she knew she wouldn't stop.

Her long dead grandmother's voice taunted her, too, reminding. It reminded her to pick her feet up, that she was a natural klutz and that if she didn't pay more attention, there was going to be some horrible accident. *Guess what, Gran, this is the day. Keep an eye open, I'm about to join you!* Forcing her body to almost merge with the rough terrain, she tasted the dusty soil as her mouth kissed the earth.

Every breath felt perilous, yet she couldn't calm the rise and fall of her chest while in the middle of an anxiety attack. She found herself methodically analyzing every single movement she could make that might get her out of this dismal situation. Not a single fingernail was left out of her calculations. The result was a depressing recognition that she could do absolutely nothing but stay very still and hope someone from the hotel eventually came looking for their missing guest. Perhaps the handsome waiter would remember their brief conversation about hiking trails the previous evening. He was one of those who'd warned her to avoid this route.

Suddenly, more dust and stones tumbled down from above, the grit invading her eyes. Horrified that the sliding fragments might take her with them, she prayed with earnestness that she wouldn't be caught up in the momentum. In the midst of her spiritual ramblings, she became aware that she wasn't alone. Someone was moving on the path above her. A calm female voice cut through her fear.

"Keep hanging on, I'm going to grab you. I just have to get a foothold."

Unable to move or look at her would-be rescuer, Dita placed all her trust in the unruffled command. She heard the woman trying to get lower, cursing when she slipped. Seconds later, she felt a strong grip around her wrist, followed by a tug which lifted her away from the rocks she'd been clinging to. She was being pulled back up the steep slope.

"Dig your feet in, get a hold," husky tones instructed.

Now able to look up, Dita briefly got a glimpse of her rescuer, an auburn-haired woman who was squinting against the power of the midday sun. Dita obeyed her without question, picking up on the confidence she exuded. Another powerful tug and she was on the safer side of the embankment. Dita quickly scrambled back onto the treacherous pathway she'd slipped off only a short while ago. On her hands and knees, and panting from anxiety and exertion, she couldn't look up immediately. When she'd regained her senses she finally faced the woman who had, without question, put her own life in jeopardy to rescue her. The stranger stood, with her hands casually on her hips as if saving a life was an everyday occurrence.

"Thank you. I don't know what I'd have done if you hadn't turned up." Dita hardly recognized her own voice, thinned by adrenaline.

"Give yourself a moment," her knight errant said.

"I'm okay," Dita wheezed. "Just need to…get my breath."

Unemotional, the stranger trained her gaze on the beautiful panoramic view which had enticed Dita up here in the first place. She was surprisingly short and wiry for one with such strength, and her clothing was not exactly the classic attire of a seasoned hill walker. She wore tailored white linen slacks and a pink cotton shirt with long sleeves turned up to the elbow. Dust from the rescue bid streaked her pants and white sneakers. *Definitely not a seasoned hill walker.* Something resonated in the back of Dita's mind. She always remembered faces, and this one seemed familiar.

Still shaking, she got to her feet and inefficiently tried to dust herself down. Nothing came easily. Her legs wobbled. Her long hair blew in her eyes and she could hardly swallow, her throat was so sore from yelling for help. She pushed her hair back and tried to cram it into the ponytail that had loosened as she'd slalomed down the hillside. Her actions were fast. Breathless. Nervous.

The woman, who looked around the same age as her, said, "You should've been paying more attention. These tracks are dangerous."

"Yes, I was warned," Dita admitted in embarrassment. "It's going to be a long time before I do something stupid like this again."

"Let's hope so."

Dita was mildly taken back by the abrupt tone but offered her hand, feeling introductions were needed. "I'm Dita…Dita Newton. I'm here, sort of on a business holiday."

The stranger didn't attempt to return the handshake, but moved her compact body to a small bush to pick up the backpack she'd obviously discarded hastily before the rescue. Dita chose to ignore the standoffish behavior, for after all, this passerby had done her the favor of a lifetime.

For a moment, it seemed she wasn't even going to reply, let alone introduce herself. Dita arched her brows slightly, waiting for some response. Rather slowly, it came.

"I'm Cate."

As Dita waited for Cate to say more, she moved her hand over her chin, only now aware from its stinging that she'd grazed it in the fall. She inspected her fingers and the sight of blood immediately seemed to magnify the shock of her ordeal. A cascade of bottled-up emotions choked her unexpectedly, and unable to stop herself, she lurched forward and grabbed Cate in a bear hug, hanging on for dear life. "I thought I was going to die," she whispered desperately in her ear, barely able to talk and hugging her even tighter. "Cate...I owe you my life."

When she became aware of the stiffness of the body in her arms, Dita was mortified and let the stunned woman go. Cate staggered back a few paces, clearly shocked by what had just happened. Dita's eyes watered. She immediately regretted her impulsive behavior. It made her look like some overly emotional type, which she wasn't—and it had clearly embarrassed Cate.

Passing a trembling hand across her mouth, Dita said, "I'm sorry. I was so scared. I was slipping and I couldn't have held on for much longer." She laughed nervously. "I don't usually get this emotional but..." She couldn't finish.

The passing traveler, having steadied herself, cast Dita a shadow of a smile, as if her facial muscles weren't used to the expression. "I can understand that," she said rather mechanically. Looking uncomfortable, she wiped her dusty hands down the sides of her trousers. "Maybe we ought to be getting back. You've had a shock."

Caught in the moment, and feeling as though she'd lost direction, Dita let the word "shock" sink in. Yes, she did feel as if she was in a haze of shock. Maybe that's why her body was trembling and she was acting like a pathetic idiot, grabbing onto a total stranger on a mountainside. But then, she did have a reason. It wasn't every day she nearly slid off a rock face and got herself killed.

"Yes, I feel pretty shaken up," Dita admitted. "Let me buy us both a drink. My hotel isn't far away. The Hotel de Prati. Do you know it?"

Her heart still hammering in her chest, she gave Cate a look that conveyed she really was sorry for her emotional outburst. All she received was a cautious nod, as if Cate was forcing herself to be polite in the presence of a complete lunatic.

They began their slow descent in awkward silence, and as they fell into step beside each other, Dita linked her bare arm through Cate's, seeking support, for she was still shaking and her trembling legs felt like blobs of Jell-O. The last thing she wanted to do was lose her footing again. She sensed tension in her escort's wiry arm and Cate gave her a strange sideways glance, but she did not withhold her support, and shortly after, she actually reached over and placed her hand on top of Dita's. It was a small, insignificant gesture but it brought Dita comfort, especially coming from such a reticent woman. Sometimes, the smallest actions surpassed the essence of words.

Dita found herself lost for a reply. She'd never been an overly verbal type, but compared with her companion, she was an absolute rent-a-mouth. The woman at her side definitely fell into the strong, silent type, making no attempt whatsoever to talk. It suddenly occurred to Dita where she'd seen Cate before. It was at her hotel. She'd observed her jogging in the grounds early that morning before breakfast.

Dita felt overjoyed. Part of her hoped she'd just made a friend, or at least someone she could share a little time with over the next few days. Although, looking at her unresponsive companion, she didn't feel the sentiment was returned.

When they reached the base of the hill, they took the bus that went back to the fishing village and boarded the ferry, sitting next to each other, the sun warm on their backs. Despite not wanting to appear rude, though conversation was probably never going to be excessive, Dita dozed most of the way home, the earlier surge of adrenaline having depleted her energy levels. She remained mildly aware of the buffering of the waves on the sides of the boat, its gentle up and down motion, and of Cate, occasionally stirring beside her. It seemed her newfound buddy couldn't get comfortable on the hard seats.

When she opened her eyes after a while, the ferry was only a short distance from its destination. The pretty inlet of Amalfi grew larger, the town nestled cozily at the foot of the steep hills that surrounded it. Dita glanced at Cate, whose eyes were closed, her head tipped back, asleep. Choosing the moment to study her, she couldn't help but be appreciative of what she saw. Cate was good looking, with auburn hair that fell slightly below chin level. She had a strong, attractive face with clear unblemished skin and a good tan. A minute amount of freckles smattered her nose, and Dita noticed that her lips rested in a natural smile, something that disappeared when she was conscious. She swept a quick glance down the body, noting small breasts, a flat stomach, and trim, well-shaped legs—a runner's legs. Cate's hands rested in her lap and Dita thought how beautiful they were, slim and elegant, the nails not excessively long, and neatly filed.

It was then, as her eyes moved further down Cate's outstretched body, she noticed fresh blood on the bottom of one of her trouser legs. There was a growing patch of red highlighted vividly against the white of the material. The source of the stain seemed to be a few inches above Cate's ankle bone, but the blood had made its way onto the top of her shoe and had trickled down to the heel.

"You've hurt yourself!" Dita proclaimed, unable to hold back.

Cate jerked awake. Confusion lodged on her face.

Cate was dismissively indifferent. "It's only a scratch."

"I don't think so." Dita's response was quick as she moved forward, eyeing the injury. "There's blood on your shoe and your slacks."

Cate bolted into an upright position and quickly moved her leg to the side, away from Dita's fussing. "I said it's nothing, now leave it alone!" The warning was implicit, the words glacial. Sharp, intense eyes bored into Dita's, causing her to sit back quickly, shocked. Seeing the effect she'd had, Cate adjusted her tone. "It's only a graze. They always look worse than they are."

A graze it was not, but it was obvious that Cate didn't want drama. Without further discussion, Dita extracted a wad of tissues from her backpack. "Here," she said, handing them over. "At least wrap these around the wound until you get back to the hotel."

Cate accepted them awkwardly and bent down, lifting the trouser leg enough for Dita to see a nasty-looking gash. Quickly and without ceremony, she stuffed some tissues over the wound and pulled up her bloody sock to hold the temporary dressing. When she sat upright again, she mumbled, "Thank you."

Silent once more, they both jerked in their seats as the ferry bounced against the harbor wall. The engines throbbed at a lower pitch as the boat maneuvered alongside, and an agile youth jumped onto the quay and began securing the vessel. Then everyone was suddenly standing and surging forward to disembark. Dita quickly became separated from Cate in the swarm of tired travelers eager to get back to their lodgings, probably for a hot soak in a tub, a change of clothing, and then off out into Amalfi for some fine local cuisine.

She looked around as the crowd thinned out, but didn't see Cate again. Disappointed that her rescuer had been so keen to escape, Dita walked the short distance back to the hotel. She wished she'd asked Cate's last name. The least she could do was send her some flowers and a card.

❖

Cate limped into her hotel room, her leg the last thing on her mind. She threaded her fingers through her hair in astonishment.

Unbelievable.

If she'd had any doubts yesterday that the blonde from the courtyard was who she thought she was, that was all in the past. Even having her call transferred by the hotel desk hadn't completely convinced her. But hearing Dita Newton introduce herself was like walking into Bloomingdale's and being told she was the millionth visitor and the winner of an amazing prize. Cate couldn't believe it. What were the odds of bumping into her nemesis, at the same place, the same time, the same hotel? The coincidence, if that's what it was, seemed too fortuitous to be possible.

Cate tried to arrive at a more logical explanation. The name she'd been using for almost fifteen years—Cate Morgan—had no obvious connection to Seraphim, but perhaps Dita had become aware of Zabor's presence in the U.S. and had come to Italy for a closer look at her competitor. Could Saul or Madeleine have said something to a contact who'd then circulated the information that Cate was in Amalfi? Given the timing it seemed unlikely. Cate had only agreed to the holiday on the spur of the moment, and Madeleine had chosen the hotel. Besides, Dita was already here when she'd arrived; she must have planned her travel well before Cate let herself be talked into this vacation. Puzzled, and still reeling from the events of the day, she moved across to the window and pushed open the wooden louver shutters. Leaning against the frame, she slowly exhaled and unresponsively surveyed the magnificent vista before her. The blazing sunset cast a flaming orange-red hue over an iridescent sea, and vibrant flecks of gold mantled the hills as the light slowly surrendered to an approaching dusk. The location was everything Madeleine Zobbio had promised, a panacea for low spirits. Yet the uplifting panorama was wasted on Cate, who saw nothing, her attention consumed with her new dilemma.

What was she going to do about Dita Newton? Nasty thoughts started to run through her mind. She could learn a lot by getting to know her. It seemed obvious that Dita had no idea who she was, and that she felt beholden after their experience on the mountainside. Her guard was down, and if Cate allowed her to buy that drink they could enter one of those short-lived holiday camaraderies. Cate could show an interest in Dita's work and maybe she would get to see her upcoming designs. She would encourage Dita to talk about her business plans. Cate sucked in breath—how dishonest that would be. But then she reminded herself of her goals. This was the woman her father had praised in that damned article, the one who had turned her mother's business around, and who now posed a real threat to Cate's ambitions.

An ailing Seraphim would be easy pickings for her. She could bide her time and wait until the company was near collapse. But Seraphim's rebirth as a viable fashion house changed everything. She couldn't allow Dita to build on the momentum she'd created. If Cate wanted to regain what should always have been hers, she had to act quickly to reverse Seraphim's fortunes.

Uneasily, Cate considered that it was one thing planning to undermine Seraphim by means of a remote, impersonal operation executed in the shadows of anonymity; up-front contact was another matter. Not what she'd had in mind at all. But fate had delivered an opportunity, the chance to learn more of the Beauty with Brains, and get a real sense of what she was up against.

Playing this card would be dishonest and unethical. This was not who she was. And yet, wasn't her plan to shut Seraphim out equally underhanded? This was merely a different means to the same end, and she would have to look her enemy in the face rather than simply sneaking around behind her back.

Never turn down an opportunity, her dark side whispered. This was not the time to become weak. This was war, and war was not for the squeamish. If she wanted her mother's business, she had to be ruthless. She had been preparing herself for this moment since she was nineteen. In all she'd done, facing every obstacle she'd overcome, she had one end in sight—Seraphim. Dita Newton was now playing right into her hands, and Cate owed it to herself to take full advantage of the situation. She took one final look at the view, still failing to see its beauty. A change of plan, then. Dita wanted to be friends with her. Cate could play that game, and she would set the rules.

Smiling, she picked up the phone. This time, when she asked to be put through to Dita's room, she knew her call would be answered.

❖

I just know I'm going to regret this. Dita cringed as she stood outside the hotel room on the second floor. She was relieved that Cate had phoned, and that she seemed genuinely sorry they'd lost each other back at the wharf. She said she'd waited for a moment, then hurried back to her room wanting to clean the deep graze quickly. She'd planned to dress the injury, then, having learned they were at the same hotel, phone Dita to make a time to meet for that much-needed drink. But once she examined the abrasion, she realized she needed help to pick out all the tiny stones before bandaging it. She was going to call housekeeping.

Dita had interrupted her then, and swiftly offered her first-aid skills, thankful for the chance to repay the debt of conscience she owed. Now that she'd reached Cate's room, however, she felt unaccountably nervous, recalling her emotional behavior after the rescue. She was probably the last person Cate really wanted to see. No doubt she'd only made contact because she realized their paths would inevitably cross. It was one thing to rebuff someone you didn't expect to see again, but another to have to avoid a guest in the same small hotel. It would be absurd to see each other at breakfast and have to act like strangers.

Dita had the impression that courtesy was important to Cate. She had obviously decided their life-changing adventure warranted a pleasant conclusion. Dita was in full agreement. They would share that drink, have a casual conversation, and part on good terms. She had no intention of pressing Cate into a holiday friendship she clearly didn't want. Dita was surprised by her desire to get to know the woman who'd saved her. Socializing with strangers had never interested her, and she'd arrived in Amalfi looking forward to solitude and tranquility. She suspected she and Cate had that goal in common.

Resolving to reassure Cate on that score if necessary, she knocked on the door. It swung open almost immediately and for a few seconds, she and Cate stared at each other. Though Dita had a height advantage, it didn't stop her discomfort as Cate surveyed her up and down without a flicker of emotion. She wanted to bolt under that hard, cool gaze, but held her ground and offered a friendly smile.

"I'm so glad you phoned me, Cate."

"I didn't want you to think I'd blown you off." Cate stepped back. "Please. Come in." The words "fight or flight" unhelpfully crawled their way across Dita's thoughts and choosing the former, she feigned a charm offensive. "I happen to have a really good first-aid kit with me, something I always travel with. I brought it along."

Cate lowered her eyes to inspect her leg. She was dressed in simple khaki shorts and Dita noted an amateurish attempt to cover the gash with a flimsy piece of tissue, held together with two ridiculously small pieces of band aid. The surrounding flesh was already red and angry, the skin swollen and pulled tight. Looking at the inflammation, Dita didn't doubt for one minute that it was painful.

"I was going to visit the pharmacist, but by the time I'd started cleaning it, everything was closed." She made eye contact again with Dita. "I'll go first thing tomorrow if it's no better."

Another of those awkward silences stretched.

"Does it hurt?" Dita asked, then rebuked herself inwardly over the lame question.

"Yes." One word said enough.

Dita edged forward. "Well, this won't take long. I have some good tweezers in the kit. Once we get all the gravel out, we can apply some antiseptic cream and bandage it properly."

Feeling more assertive, she instructed Cate to sit on the edge of the bed and raise her injured leg. Pulling up a chair, Dita sat down then removed the unsatisfactory dressing and examined the wound. As she started to rummage in the first-aid kit, she could see she was being viewed warily.

"Don't worry. I'm quite good at this. I've had a lot of practice."

For the next few minutes neither spoke as Dita concentrated on cleansing the wound and picking out the tiny stones that could cause irritation. Methodically and with care, she applied an antiseptic salve.

Flinching, Cate asked, "So, how often *do* you do this? You said you'd had a lot of practice."

"You may not believe this, but I'm a bit accident prone."

"I believe you."

The dry humor in Cate's tone made Dita look up, and she found herself staring straight into eyes the color of dark cornflowers. She momentarily considered how nature could produce such contrasting shades, her own irises so light and translucent, Cate's heavy and deep. Caught off guard, her contemplation made her frown.

"Is something wrong?" Cate asked. "Do you think it needs stitches?"

Dita shook her head as she reached for a surgical dressing. She continued her earlier conversation. "No, I think this will do the trick. I'll leave you with some extra dressings so you can change them whenever you need to. I always travel with plenty. The last thing you want if you're hurt is to have to hunt this stuff down."

"Thank you. I guess this would have been a real mess tomorrow if I'd left it."

"Yes, and an infection could have ruined your holiday. How long are you here for?" Dita watched the question play across Cate's face.

Like someone trying to avoid an incriminating answer in a court of law, she gave an evasive answer. "Until I feel like leaving. I've no other plans at the moment."

Interesting response. "That's nice, having that luxury. What do you do?"

Cate hesitated. "I'm self-employed. I play the stock market. Investing, selling, speculating." She continued in a cavalier fashion, as if it were nothing. "I buy when prices are low, sell when they're high, that sort of thing. As long as I can access the Internet, I can work anywhere."

Dita was impressed. Stocks and shares, and everything to do with trading them had always mystified her. She'd heard the usual horror stories about people who speculated unwisely and ended up buried in debt. "You must be good if you can make a living from it. I guess my mind isn't wired that way."

Nonchalantly glancing around the room, Cate looked as if the whole conversation bored her. "Day-trading isn't for most people, but I do okay. So, what's your mind wired for?" Her head swiveled back.

Reminded of a bird of prey, Dita smiled. The deflection to another topic didn't bother her; rather she found Cate's behavior interesting. Even now, though she'd asked a question, she communicated no real desire to know the answer. Dita gave it anyway.

"I'm a fashion designer, not a particularly successful one yet, but I'm trying."

"Fashion. That must be…creative."

Cate's face was hard to read but she didn't seem impressed. To someone engaged in the equivalent of legal gambling for a living, Dita imagined designing garments probably sounded as exciting as watching paint dry. Oddly disappointed by her lack of interest, Dita leaned back and surveyed her work.

"There, finished. How does it feel?"

Standing just a little too quickly, like she wanted all the fuss over, Cate gingerly pressed her leg to the floor. She tested it a few steps and then thanked Dita politely. "I think I should be the one buying the drinks," she said without enthusiasm. "You saved me a visit to the doctor."

"If you're not in the mood tonight, we could take a rain check." Dita packed up her first-aid kit. "I'll probably turn in early. I feel quite drained."

Relief flickered across Cate's face, yet she missed the opportunity to extricate herself completely. "Maybe we could have breakfast tomorrow morning."

Surprised by the suggestion, Dita said, "Only if you want to get up at the crack of dawn. I'm leaving early on a day trip to Herculaneum."

Cate didn't respond immediately. The hands at her side closed then slowly opened again as though she was consciously releasing tension. "That's the town buried in the Vesuvius eruption, isn't it?"

"Yes, just like Pompeii, but smaller. A lot of the buildings are supposedly in better condition, and there's the Villa of the Papyri." Dita allowed her excitement to show. "I've always wanted to see it. There was once a great library there and when archeologists started digging they found about a thousand scrolls."

Something in Cate's expression changed. Her eyes sparkled and she searched Dita's face as if intrigued. When she spoke, her voice held a warmth Dita hadn't heard before. "That sounds fascinating."

Unsure if Cate was really interested or just making conversation, Dita said, "You could join me if you wish. It's an organized tour, but they'll probably have room for a last-minute extra. If your leg's okay," she added.

"I'll see how I feel."

"If you decide to come, just show up in the lobby around seven thirty a.m." Dita didn't doubt for one minute that the leg would be fine, but she'd given Cate an excuse if she wanted one. Not pushing the invitation, she thanked her again for her timely rescue and wished her a good night. She doubted she'd see her tomorrow.

CHAPTER SEVEN

Y ou're here!" Dita emerged from an early breakfast to find Cate waiting for her on the sidewalk outside the hotel.

"An offer I couldn't refuse." Cate squinted hard against the brightness of the early morning sun, tilting her head to the side as she regarded Dita. "See an old ancient ruin full of fossilized people or read a boring novel while I sunbathe? I'll take the ruins any day. And before you ask, the leg's doing fine."

Genuinely pleased, Dita touched Cate's arm. "That's great. I really didn't think you'd show, and when you weren't at breakfast—"

"I'm not a breakfast eater. I prefer to run." Without making a show of it, Cate extricated herself from the contact at the earliest opportunity.

Dita remembered how Cate had recoiled from her hug on the mountainside yesterday. *Not a woman comfortable with emotion? Doesn't like to be touched?*

"They say it's the most important meal of the day. Might make you run faster," Dita jested lightly, a warm smile on her lips.

"Perhaps. Anyway, I don't always skip breakfast, I sometimes have a few cups of coffee."

"Nutritious!" Dita mocked.

Cate waved a finger. "Never ignore the humble cup of coffee. Once I've had a few of those I feel ready to take on the world."

"Or at least rescue stupid tourists off mountainsides." She wasn't sure why, but Dita thought Cate didn't want to be reminded of her feat. Maybe she was one of those shy, reluctant hero types. "Anyway, I'm really glad you're coming on the trip. Now I'll have someone to talk to."

Cate glanced around at the chattering tourists. "They look like a friendly bunch."

"I have no doubt." Dita lowered her voice so only Cate could hear. "The only trouble with being a single traveler is that people either think you're a social inadequate and steer well clear of you, or they try and adopt you. You then end up getting stuck with people you really don't want to spend the day with."

Cate nodded. "But you can't break away from them for fear of being rude and ungrateful."

They both laughed.

"I think our tour guide wants us on the bus." Dita watched an older gentleman speak to bus driver, who immediately started waving everyone on board.

Cate glanced up at her, a slight smile resting sensuously on her lips. "Maybe two social inadequates should sit together?"

Dita let herself stare into those deep blue eyes for a few seconds longer than a new acquaintance should. "I'd love that."

❖

The tour was everything Dita expected. At Herculaneum, their guide had been a retired history professor who, besides having a remarkable knowledge of the site and an engaging sense of humor, had also impressed on the party a feel for the personal lives of those who had once lived—and died—in the buried town. Never in a rush to push the tourists through the place, he hovered at each notable building, allowing everyone to see as much as they desired. A lover of all things historical, Dita was fascinated by the ancient designs, the shapes and lines. She took a myriad of photos, trying to capture the rustic colors and vivid images that whispered of the past. Her imagination set free, she could feel her creative juices soaking up the energy and ambiance of the place, and the essence of a people who had tragically died all those centuries ago, suffocated by the gases and lava of the volcano. Such beauty amidst the horror. If only she could capture something of the former, and return it to life via her designs.

Throughout all of this, the enigmatic Cate quietly remained at her side, accompanying her as she retraced steps, and never once complaining. Dita had suggested that she might like to go on to the museum or the small coffee shop, but Cate had stayed, insisting that she was enjoying herself.

Dita wasn't sure if this was true. It was difficult to read the woman who kept her emotions so much to herself. As Cate patiently followed her around, often holding her backpack as she searched for the best angles and light for her photos, Dita found herself wondering whether, beneath the frosty indifference, there might be a warmer Cate, one less reserved. Occasionally, as she studied some dusty relic, she would glance up to catch Cate watching her, a strange, indecipherable look on her face. Dita would smile at her, and slowly Cate would smile back.

Cate—she didn't even know her surname—intrigued her, and strange though it was, especially given the woman's testy behavior, Dita felt drawn to her. Maybe it was the quiet strength Cate exuded or something more basic: chemistry. Dita acknowledged that her acceptance of Cate was unusual. Though she appeared easygoing and friendly, this wasn't entirely true. Dita found relationships, any real relationships beyond that of acquaintance, difficult. This was probably because for the first six years of her life, she'd been raised by her mother, who'd never shown her a shred of love.

Dita's young life had been one of physical neglect and emotional starvation, but her salvation had come when she was sent to live with her grandmother. Despite her subsequent happiness, Dita knew she still carried the scars of her earlier parental rejection. They had left her marked in so many ways, it had taken her a long time to be able to handle intimate relationships, to learn to place her trust in any person other than her grandmother. She'd never really had any close friends, and from an early age when she'd recognized her attraction to her own sex, she'd felt alone in learning to deal with it.

College had helped in her emotional development. So had her relationship with Alba Dolley. A flamboyant and emotionally demonstrative lover, Alba had taken her time, building trust and encouraging Dita to talk about her disturbed childhood when she was ready. Dita had tried to come to terms with the deep hatred she felt for her mother but even now, she found it difficult to think about her and she seldom spoke of her past.

"This is incredible," Cate said as they entered the House of Neptune and Amphitrite.

Slowly they approached the vividly hued wall mosaic, awaiting their turn for a photograph. There were probably better images for sale at the museum, but Dita was just as interested in the architecture as she was in the famous mosaic. After she'd photographed the walls, she angled her digital camera and took several shots of the villa before training her lens on Cate, who was studying the cobalt blue pattern above an archway.

As she zoomed in on her face in profile, Dita felt the familiar stirrings of recognition once more. She took another picture and zoomed in closer, wondering where she could have seen Cate before this week. They hadn't met or she would remember. Maybe they'd passed on a street somewhere and she'd experienced a fleeting instant of enchantment. Like the one that held her captive now, as her finger clicked down.

Cate turned her way sharply. "Did you take my picture?"

Dita lowered the camera. "I was photographing the arches." She attempted to sound nonchalant, with little success, so she reverted to ponderous ruminations. "There's an austerity to so many of the houses from the exterior. Yet when you stand inside, it's so easy to imagine people in these rooms. Laughing. Eating. Kissing their children… It's truly poignant."

As she chattered, Cate's eyes never strayed from hers. They darkened to a shade of deep gentian when Dita licked her dry lips. Her stomach hollowed and she became aware of the noise of her own breathing and the sandy echo of footsteps nearby. The air seemed warmer than it was just moments ago. The collar of her thin cotton shirt clung to the back of her neck. She took a step back as Cate started toward her. That sensual smile became almost teasing. Cate stretched out a hand. Automatically, Dita started to lift her own, then let it fall when Cate reached for the camera.

"Let me see that."

Flustered, Dita tried to press "delete" on the display without making her intentions obvious. She was too late. Cate plucked the camera from her hands and inspected the latest images.

Dita winced. "I have a few better ones of you outside the Deer House."

"Oh, that's a relief." Cate laughed. Lifting the camera, she instructed, "Look at me."

"You're standing too close for a photo."

"Smile," Cate invited softly.

Dita gulped.

The picture was taken. She was afraid to look at it until they were on their way back to the bus. She locked herself in a stall in the restroom and scrolled back. A shiver twitched between her shoulder blades as a face filled the small screen. The eyes were over-bright and the mouth was slightly parted. She looked like she'd just been kissed.

❖

Dita and Cate sat silently at the front of the coach as it traveled back from Herculaneum to Amalfi along the amazing coastal drive of hairpin bends, with azure sea vistas to one side, and majestic granite mountains the other. One of the more gregarious Italian holidaymakers in their group chose a particularly nerve-racking moment to get out of his seat and lurch along the aisle, passing out candies.

After almost falling into their laps, he flashed an array of uneven teeth at them and announced, "I always give these to the pretty ladies." Dita reached politely into the little white paper bag and took a Galatine, a milk candy that seemed commonplace everywhere she went in Italy. Cate followed suit, and thanked the man for his generosity. As he staggered away, she stole a sideways glance at Dita, and with unusual spontaneity, started to laugh.

She should smile more often, Dita thought as she tried to tear open the idiot-proof white wrapper. Unexpectedly, a well-manicured hand reached out, took the sweet off her, and in one swift movement, the Galatine all but leapt out of its wrapping. As Dita reached for it, Cate caught her hand.

"Your fingers, what did you do to them?"

They weren't pretty. Nearly all of the tips had been grazed in her fall the day before, and on two fingers, the nails had broken, leaving an ugly, jagged mess she hadn't been able to file neatly. The contrast between her rough fingers and Cate's elegant ones couldn't have been more vivid. Dita felt embarrassed, as if the poorly presented fingers indicated a lack of basic hygiene on her part.

"I did it yesterday, when I was trying to hang on to the rocks," she explained. "They don't hurt. They just don't look nice. Maybe I should have just let go. They could have buried me with a decent manicure."

"Don't!" Cate said sharply. She dropped Dita's hand like it was on fire.

"I was trying to see the funny side, that's all." Dita wished she understood what made this woman tick. Cate had been such good company today, and yet now Dita felt as if she'd aggravated and displeased her.

"There is no funny side," Cate whispered, half to herself.

She stared out at the passing scenery, confused by the strength of her emotions. Dita's words had provoked an image she couldn't get out of her mind, and with it came a guilty knowledge that for one horrifying instant on that path, she'd almost allowed the fall to happen. She'd been frozen, watching Dita slide toward death and knowing she had to act, but her legs had refused to move.

Afterward, on the ferry, she couldn't stop thinking about that perilous inertia. It wasn't unusual, she'd told herself; people witnessed accidents and were paralyzed. Later, if a life had been lost, they agonized, wondering if they could have saved the day by reacting more quickly. Cate was desperately thankful that she didn't have to carry a burden like that. She'd saved Dita's life. And yet, she was haunted by the suspicion that her hesitation was prompted not by shock, but by a darker instinct. After all, with Dita out of the picture all Cate's desires would have become reality.

Whatever it was that unconsciously churned around the deepest layers of her mind, it made her feel dirty, and she pressed her hands together between her knees. They felt clammy. Was it possible that she'd unconsciously chosen inaction, that a part of her wanted Dita to go over the edge? Worse still, had Dita sensed that malevolence? Was she trying to minimize her brush with death by joking about it? Cate realized she should have laughed, too, but the comment had pushed her buttons and she'd reacted like she had a guilty conscience.

With good reason.

She'd followed Dita that day. At a distance. Plotting, thinking about her ruination. *Be careful what you wish for.* Cate absently rubbed the place where she'd grazed her leg. Dita had tended to her wound with such gentle and genuine ministering, Cate felt ashamed of her scheming. When was the last time anyone other than Madeleine Zobbio had bothered about her well-being?

She glanced uneasily at Dita's damaged fingers. They must have been hurting dreadfully when Dita cleaned and bandaged Cate's leg. How could she have missed that? Was she so blinkered by revenge?

"I would never have let you slide off that cliff," she said, needing to hear herself speak the words. Whatever fleeting impulse may have gripped her, she was still a good person. She had done the right thing and she didn't regret it.

Dita's eyes registered surprise and Cate realized she'd sounded more vehement than she'd intended. With a warm smile, Dita said, "I know. My joke was in poor taste. What do they call it…gallows humor?"

"Something like that."

"For a few minutes I really thought I was going to die," Dita said. "When I heard your voice, it was like a guardian angel was talking to me. I *knew* I was going to be all right."

Cate let her eyes wander over Dita, who wore very little makeup, which only served to show how much of a natural beauty she was with her well-defined cheekbones, striking eyes, and generous lips. Dressed simply in faded blue jeans, a light-colored sweater, and an old suede jacket, she was an understatement of loveliness with her willowy form and her blond hair tied back loosely in a ponytail.

Guardian angel? The touching comment sat badly as Cate knew she was anything but. Had Dita Newton been any other tourist, Cate's wary heart might have enjoyed the companionship of someone so visibly appealing, but more, apparently rather wonderful on the inside. She stared up at the high walls of rock lining the one side of the road, anything to avoid looking at the woman who was starting to play with her moral compass. Dita Newton didn't have an ounce of harm in her. Yet in order to win control of her mother's business she would have to bring down this lovely, decent human being.

"You've gone quiet." Dita leaned closer, her breath caressing Cate's cheek.

"I was only thinking what a wonderful day it's been."

"It has, hasn't it," Dita said with enthusiasm. "You have no idea of how much I've enjoyed your company, today. Thank you, Cate."

Cool blue eyes bored into Cate, who could only smile back mindlessly. Though she didn't want to admit it, the thanks should have been all hers for she was strangely grateful to be sitting here, sharing Dita's life for just this short time, even if under false pretenses.

Immediately uncomfortable, she sought escape and tapped one of Dita's hands, drawing attention again to the badly mauled nails.

"You know, I think if you soak those tonight in really hot, soapy water, you might be able to get scissors low enough to cut off those nasty ragged bits."

"Do you think so?"

"I do."

Dita webbed her fingers out before her, studying them before grasping Cate's hand in hers. She said something, but Cate didn't hear a word. All she knew was the shocking contact of Dita's hand. The warm sensation bothered her.

"I said you have beautifully manicured nails," Dita repeated. "You really are miles away, aren't you?" Soft laughter rose.

"Ocean air," Cate quipped politely as she retracted her hand.

"Well, I hope you're not too tired. I want to lure you out this evening for dinner…I promised you that, and I really want to express my thanks for your rescuing me."

Cate's conscience swung like a pendulum. Dinner would be another opportunity to learn what she could of her opponent, but more deceit would be necessary. Her stomach twisted at the innocent expectation on Dita's face. "That's very kind of you, but there's no need. It's been a long day for both of us. I…"

Cate's throat closed as she watched the liveliness drain from Dita's eyes.

"Of course." Dita's voice sounded even huskier than usual. "Whatever you prefer."

Her disappointment seemed genuine, and although Cate hated to admit it, she wanted to make that spark return. "How about tomorrow?" she asked hastily. Did she really just say that?

"I'd be delighted." Dita immediately began enthusing about the various cafés near the hotel.

Cate nodded and, against her better judgment, agreed with whatever she said. Her mind was a cacophony of opposing inner voices. Her conscience noisily protested her underhand tactics and her common sense warned her to walk away before she did something she would regret. She already knew that the urge to spend time with Dita was no longer about her industrial espionage agenda. The anger she'd harbored for so long, her desire for revenge, were rapidly being overtaken by an attraction to the woman she was supposed to detest. Cate had a choice to make, and only a few days ago she would not have been in any doubt about her next move.

But everything had changed the moment she reached for Dita's hand. Suddenly she seemed no longer completely in control of her destiny. Cate hadn't experienced that feeling since those suffocating years when her father dictated her life, and she didn't like it. Taking short, shallow breaths, she stared down at the choppy sea through the windows of the bus and made herself a promise. She would carve out the future she'd promised herself, the future her mother would have wanted for her. She would not allow anything, or anyone, to stand in her way. Whatever this confusion was about, it would pass, along with this fleeting holiday attraction. All she had to do was stay on track.

❖

Cate closed the hotel door behind her and turned slowly to face the wall. With both hands against the cool surface, she proceeded to gently hit her head against it several times. *Fool. Fool. Fool. You were supposed to keep your distance, be the unseen observer, but no, you had to change the rules.*

"Know thine opponent" didn't mean pulling them off mountainsides, letting them paw bits of her broken body, and becoming their traveling companion. Damn it!

Before she did irreparable damage to either her head or hotel property, she crossed the tile floor and sat on the edge of her bed, staring at an unexciting wall painting that the hotel management considered art. Things were not going the way she wanted. Her thoughts turned uncomfortably to her father. She wondered what on earth could have possessed William Canton to hire someone like Dita to head the family business. Certainly, Cate had not expected her to be so vibrant, or as young. She'd assumed a woman with years of experience, primarily because of the way she'd managed to turn Seraphim around and so quickly. Dita really was pushing the business in a new and vital direction. Yet, this clever woman was also able to mock herself. Cate found this refreshing *and* endearing, and couldn't help but feel a grudging respect for her rival.

She pondered whether her father had been duped by Dita's sexual appeal. Cate doubted it. He was the ultimate business shark and would have hired Dita purely for her talent, something she obviously had in abundance. Cate had been following Seraphim's collections via the Internet and had seen the last one at Fashion Week when it was presented in one of the Atelier shows. Dita's designs were refreshingly different. One in particular had stood out. A plum-colored suit so simple, yet elegant. The box jacket fitted easily on the hips, with three little buttons down the front and with small inlet pockets. The skirt was straight just to middle knee, but wonderfully cut.

God, she'd thought when she saw it modeled, *this woman has it.* The Coco Chanel inspiration was obvious but Dita Newton's designs built on the great couturier's legacy without losing their contemporary freshness. None presented as overtly sexual or brash, but her fabrics softened lines and emphasized curves, and the alluring look she created brought a lump to Cate's throat. She herself had always strived for elegant simplicity within a modernist style, and Dita had captured that sensibility perfectly. Seraphim wasn't out of trouble yet, but if Dita continued to make a name for herself, the company couldn't fail.

Cate lay down, listlessly consulting the ceiling. When had she ever felt ashamed of herself? She couldn't recall a time, not even during the dark days of her youth when the school had levied insulting accusations against her. But she felt it now as she compared herself to Dita. Glorious brilliance versus seditious darkness. It was all very well to study someone from a distance, but to deal with them face-to-face, to have to lie to maintain anonymity… Cate didn't like this duplicity. But did she have any option, given what she wanted?

She contemplated backing out of the dinner date but knew what it meant if she chose to retreat now, having come this far. Despite her growing ambivalence about her tactics, she needed to secure Dita's trust and stick with her plan. A creeping awareness moved over her like clouds that hinted of thunder. Far from being the victim of her life, some actor in a sorry dramatic production still being played out and awaiting the last act where revenge is reaped as the final curtain falls, she could see herself morphing into someone repellent. Someone her mother would never have been proud of.

Was this how she wanted justice—at any price?

CHAPTER EIGHT

I suppose I'm a bit like you really," Dita mused over dinner. "You simply need the Internet for your job, I simply need a sketch pad and pencil."

You're nothing like me. The words tripped through Cate's head and she wasn't sure what they meant. Was it that she was the smart adversary gaining the data she needed to destroy Seraphim, or that they were poles apart; one decent, the other dishonorable?

Trying to relax, she swept a quick look around the café. It was a pleasant place some streets away from the main square and, at this time of the season, less busy than usual. Everything about it was quaint with its checkered red and white tablecloths, and little fresh central flower arrangements. There was a relaxed feel to the place and the staff seemed in no rush to move diners on.

"Did you get your designs finished?" she asked in a casual tone, referring to some work Dita had mentioned when Cate called her room earlier to confirm their dinner date.

Dita's wolf-like eyes focused on her as though assessing her to see if trust might be well placed. After a long hesitation, she indicated a large folio propped against the wall several feet away. "Almost. I brought them with me."

"To show *me?*" Cate asked.

"Only if you promise to be flattering," Dita said with good humor. "I have an ego to take care of."

"I'm honored." Smiling, Cate lifted the portfolio and set it down on the table. A pulse of excitement beat through her. She was about to see Dita's latest designs and she realized how privileged this made her. No designer ever showed their work to anyone they didn't trust. Certainly, Cate always guarded her own like a state secret. So Dita trusted her? This was a major breakthrough.

She took her time, scanning each design. Now even more she saw the correlation between Dita's style and Chanel's, simple classic lines but modernity thrust to the forefront. Strong colors, flattering cuts. Perhaps not quite so stunning, for the French designer had innovated, often startling both critics and admirers. But Dita was a chip off the old block, drawing inspiration without slavishly copying. Cate wondered why it had taken the industry and media so long to recognize her talent.

"Who do you sell these to?" Cate asked, hoping she sounded politely curious rather than overly inquisitive.

"Most of these designs are for Nordstrom. Getting that order was quite a coup, but…"

Cate prompted, "But?"

"Sometimes, it's almost as if we're a fated business. Seraphim was in such a mess when I took over. It has the same few lovely people working there that have been there for years. They're very loyal and dedicated, but they aren't business or fashion people. They need leadership and I don't think there's been any real artistic direction since my boss's wife died. He's been propping the business up financially for years. I think he does it because it's all he's got left of his family, memories he doesn't want to lose." Dita stretched a tanned arm out. Resting a hand on Cate's shoulder, she said, "I'm sorry. You don't want to hear this."

Cate forced a smile. "Please…I'd like you to continue. Besides, never turn away a willing ear. Unless…you're worried about talking business with a stranger."

The manipulation worked beautifully, and the hand on Cate's shoulder kneaded the area. "You're no stranger, Cate. Not to me. You're a friend I'm still getting to know."

Cate hated that response. "So this Nordstrom order is pretty important."

"It's a make or break deal for us," Dita said candidly. "I have a phone call arranged for late this week, just to make sure we're still on the same page."

"From what I've seen here, you can't lose." Cate meant it. If these designs went in to Nordstrom they would do the deal. She was certain of that. Which was why she had to get them to Saul.

He'd been very industrious on her behalf, making certain Zabor was a step ahead of Seraphim at every opportunity, pushing for more brand exposure, squeezing buyers, and dropping hints about their rival's imminent collapse. If he had these designs before the Nordstrom buyer signed off on them, he could present something very similar but at a more competitive price.

"I don't know." The light went out of Dita's eyes and worry lit her face. "We've come within a hair's breadth of closing several big contracts over the past year, only to have the retailer pull out at the last minute to chase 'a more lucrative deal.'" She mimicked the last few words, obviously something she'd heard too often.

Cate let her eyes wander over Dita's lean body and those ample breasts. Dita, in her pencil slim red jersey skirt and a lace black blouse with a dipping neckline, looked completely stunning. Cate had been trying all evening to avert her eyes from the abundant soft skin that was revealed. Fighting the distraction, she was thankful for the smokescreen of eating and conversation.

"I guess that's business," she said with her head lowered. "You can never count on anything."

"We're offering these retailers a good deal," Dita snapped. "Any deeper discounts and we'd be giving our range away."

Cate managed to nod sympathetically.

"If I didn't know better," Dita continued, "I'd say someone was deliberately out to get us, poaching our best customers." She laughed weakly. "But that would be paranoid, wouldn't it?"

Cate didn't answer the rhetorical question. She closed the folio and leaned it against the wall. There was only one way she was going to be able to "borrow" the designs. She had to find a way to slip them out of the folder over the next few days without Dita noticing. That would mean gaining access to her room. Cate sipped some water as she considered the options. There was no reason for her to drop by the room unless they were meeting for an outing, and she would never be able to take several large drawings without Dita noticing.

Short of breaking in while the room was empty, there was only one way to get the opportunity she needed. Sometime before the end of the week, she would have to spend a night with Dita.

❖

"This was a good idea," Dita said, stretching her long body out on a sun-lounger by the hotel pool.

"It was the most energetic thing I could manage," Cate said.

The unpredictable Mediterranean weather this time of year had turned hot again. The air was still and dry, and the best way to stay cool was to take an occasional dip, then dry off in the shade of one of several big blue and white umbrellas on the patio. She cast an eye over Dita, admiring the long, nimble body with the ample breasts yet slim waist resting on curvaceous hips.

"You have a beautiful figure." The words were out before she could stop them. Cate could have kicked herself. Damn, clumsy compliments weren't going to get her into Dita's room, and the week was slipping away. Besides, she hadn't intended to flirt, she'd simply been honest.

Dita pushed up on her elbows, apparently taking the unguarded observation as a compliment. "Thank you."

There was something intimate in that voice and Cate thought Dita's look rested on her too long. She felt awkward and glanced away quickly, rubbing her tired eyes. Nightly guilt trips were messing with her sleep pattern. Over the past three days, since the outing to Herculaneum, she and Dita had spent much of their time together. They'd explored the neighboring towns during the day, shopping and sightseeing, and had fallen into a comfortable evening routine, watching the sun set as they drank wine and coffee in the courtyard. An odd combination, but they shared the same enthusiasm for it, another of many preferences they seemed to have in common.

Cate never forgot why she was there, and was gradually finding out about her companion's business goals, but she wasn't even close to sneaking the designs out of Dita's folder. Her efforts had been half-hearted to say the least, and the more she got to know Dita, the worse her nights became, consumed by strange dreams that left her feeling exhausted the following day. No sleep for the wicked.

Feeling irritable, she messed with the height of her lounger's back rest and rearranged the neckline of her bathing suit. Her discomfort didn't go unnoticed.

"You seem out of sorts today," Dita noted with a gentle smile. "Have you had some losses?" At Cate's frown of confusion, she added, "On the stock market."

"Oh. No, everything's fine," Cate said hastily.

"I was doing some reading about your line of work. It's hard to understand. Are you more of a swing trader or do you close out your positions right away?"

"It depends," Cate said vaguely.

"I suppose if you're short-selling a stock, things can get pretty dicey."

Cate hoped her eyes didn't look glazed. She slid her sunglasses back on. "Hell, you really have been reading."

"I've had time on my hands." Dita laughed. Turning on her side to face Cate, she propped herself up on an elbow, her head resting in her hand. "I never thought I'd admit it but I needed this break so badly."

"It's been rough, huh?" Cate slid down her lounger and turned correspondingly, inviting openness.

"I was desperate for this job and don't get me wrong, it's wonderful and I wouldn't change it for the world. But sometimes, it all gets too crazy."

"You can't delegate more?"

"Not really. It's a small operation."

"But the company's growing, isn't it? Why don't you hire an extra pair of hands?" Cate frowned, as though deep in thought. "I guess it's not your decision. What's he like...your boss?"

Dita lay back down and resumed her original sunbathing position. "I told you. He's great."

Cate couldn't take her eyes off Dita's full lips. *You told me, but not enough detail.* "Yes, I remember you talking about him, but there was a bottle of wine being consumed at the time, which always strips me of any retentive capacity," she joked, her tone languid. She remembered *everything* she'd been told.

"I'm very lucky." Dita spoke with sincerity. "Obviously, he wants to know exactly what I'm doing. We meet weekly, but beyond that, he's given me full autonomy and never interferes with my artistic direction."

"And is that the right direction?"

"I hope so." Dita sighed and as she did, her well-hidden exhaustion grew more evident.

"You don't seem convinced," Cate pushed, wanting more.

"We've worked very hard to give the business the face-lift it needed, *all* of us, and we've had some notable success. I've had to release a few of the smaller, less profitable stockists—the ones that only cherry-pick the range and then expect preferential supply of the few items that make it onto the pages of *People* magazine."

"Sounds like common sense. Any business has to serve the customers whose sales are worth the most."

"Yes…I want to prove that Seraphim can be successful. That William's faith in it *and me* isn't wasted. He deserves that." Dita stopped talking and her searching stare made Cate feel naked, as though she'd somehow given herself away.

"You seem to have quite a close relationship with your boss," Cate said tightly.

"William's a gentleman. I'm so lucky working for him. Sometimes I—" Dita broke off with an embarrassed shrug.

"Tell me," Cate coaxed, reassuring herself that Dita didn't know who she really was or they would not be having this conversation.

"One of my colleagues says William treats me like a daughter." She turned quiet and subdued. "I'm not so sure, but I'd like it if he did."

Something painful caught in Cate's throat and she wanted the ground to open up and swallow her. She could barely force a half smile. "You don't have a father?"

In a spontaneous response, Dita's whole body went rigid. "No. Nor any mother worth remembering."

An underbelly, Cate thought, but far from pleased to know she'd found fragility in Dita, she felt a thread of compassion…a connection with someone else who'd had a rough ride in life. She fought to subdue it. She could not be weak.

Dita's abruptness subsided and when she next spoke it was with softness. "This will sound really stupid, but I sometimes feel her presence…William's wife. When I'm at Seraphim late at night, it's as if she's there watching over me, willing me to make something of her business. I know it sounds crazy but I think she likes my designs. Both

Marcus and William have commented that some of my work is like hers." Dita looked a thousand miles away. "It would be nice, wouldn't it, to be haunted by the woman who once had so many dreams for the business she started but never finished." Glancing back at Cate, she asked, "Cate, are you okay? You look so pale…"

It took a while before she could answer. "I'm fine, really. I think I jogged a bit too far, too quickly this morning…then this heat…the humidity…" She poured out her excuses in quick answers to try and deflect Dita's obvious concern.

Cate knew she must look awful because she felt *terrible*. How was she supposed to cope with all of this? She had to get away from Dita and from this place. She needed to breathe. "Let's go indoors." Dita sat up and reached for her robe.

"No, I really am okay," Cate said, this time more insistent. "If I just get out of the sun and into the shade, maybe lie down in the cool… I'll be fine." She stood and rapidly gathered her things together.

Dita wasn't convinced. "Let me walk you to your room."

Deliberately pausing, and faking semi-revitalization, Cate lightly touched Dita's elbow. "You'll only make me feel worse if I interrupt your sunbathing."

"I don't care about sunbathing. You're my friend."

The statement rocked Cate. There was nothing but genuine sincerity from Dita. She cared and wasn't afraid to show it. Cate knew she should exploit the opportunity, maybe hint that she could use Dita's company or ask for her help, but she really was going to be sick if she didn't get away from her now, and fast.

With what little control she had left, she became an Oscar-worthy actress. "The minute I get to my room, I'll stick my head out of the window and wave so you know all's well. Okay?"

A side window in her room overlooked the pool area. She prayed her ploy would satisfy Dita, but it took a few seconds.

Dita scrutinized her like a lab rat, until hesitantly agreeing. seemingly taken in by Cate's performance. "You'll phone me if you need anything or if you feel ill?" she demanded.

Cate nodded. "Of course."

"Dinner tonight, then?" Dita asked.

Cate nodded again, reminding herself that it was tonight or never and she couldn't leave Amalfi empty-handed. "Definitely. And this time I'll expect to see those designs."

Dita laughed. "Oh, the pressure."

"You're the one who keeps telling me they're almost done." Cate forced a nonchalant shrug. "I'll believe it when I see it."

As she walked away, Dita called after her, "You win. I have to be satisfied with them sometime."

Cate waved brightly. "See you later."

When she got to her room, she replayed their conversation, unable to stop tormenting herself. She had a father who probably thought of her as dead and seemed to view a complete stranger as his surrogate daughter. And her mother's ghost was "haunting" this substitute who was running a business that should have been Cate's. Cate felt like someone had stuck a knife in her and was twisting it around. Tears streamed down her face.

Seraphim is all my father thinks he has left!

❖

After dinner that evening, Cate invited Dita back to her room for coffee and drinks, and Dita was quick to accept—bringing the portfolio. In the balmy evening air, they sat on the balcony talking as Cate liberally poured Frangelico liqueurs from a bottle she'd purchased on one of their shopping trips.

"I don't usually drink so much," Dita gushed. "So it only takes a glass and I'm giddy."

"Nor me, but it seems a lovely way to finish such a splendid evening, doesn't it?" Cate cast a slow grin and was surprised to see her dinner companion blush. She speculated that it was the alcohol, and that Dita was telling the truth about her tolerance levels. Cate had noticed how little wine she consumed during their meals together.

"Don't you find this view romantic?" Dita purred dreamily, indicating the ocean vista lit up by a full moon.

"Yes, I suppose it is. I hadn't really thought about it."

Dita laughed. "You intrigue me. How can you not be stirred by something as beautiful as this? Doesn't it make you feel anything?"

Cate theatrically pursed her lips and tilted her head at first toward the view, then back at Dita. "Okay, it's a romantic, beautiful view. Are you happy now?"

"I've been happy all evening, Cate. You're very good company, you know."

Dita stood and stretched her arms above her head. Cate worried that her guest was about to make a departure whilst correspondingly noting how a back wall light revealed the form beneath Dita's blouse.

"You're not leaving?" Cate could hear the edge of concern in her own voice. She made sure not to glance at the portfolio, standing against the wall, its contents beckoning. Dita would take it with her when she left. *If* she left.

Dita, who now leaned against the balcony railings studying the view, glanced back. "Not if you don't want me to."

Cate caught something in the voice, something inviting, and for the first time realized that Dita had misread her anxiety. Her pulse jumped. She topped their glasses up.

"I'm not sure more Frangelico is a good idea." Dita's eyes held Cate's with homing missile precision. "I might say things I shouldn't if I drink too much."

Cate's heart skittered past a beat, but her head ruled. *Let's test the theory.* She already knew that Dita was gay; she'd suspected from the moment they first met, but she hadn't raised the topic and neither had Dita. They had settled, instead, on an unspoken awareness. Those subtle intimate signals, whether intentional or not, were only ever reserved for the gender one was attracted to, and Dita's cues were unmistakable. The only thing Cate wasn't sure about was whether to take them personally. Dita was, she suspected, one of those women whose sensuality communicated itself to others, inviting wishful thinking and a lowered guard. But Cate had no time for frivolous conjecture or tempting fantasies, she had a mission to procure that portfolio… and there were other questions she wanted answers to, if Dita was in a careless frame of mind.

"Seraphim," she mused aloud, yet again drawn by the wonderful transparency of Dita's blouse. "No family standing in the wings waiting to take over the business?"

Dita turned to face her, the blouse twisting to reveal a good expanse of flesh. "No, none that I know of."

She caught Cate looking at her breasts and smiled seductively.

Cate averted her eyes, caught between self-consciousness and opportunism. She could see how this was going. Dita was flirting with her. All she had to do was relax and allow one thing to lead to another. Wasn't this what she wanted? Unable to answer that question with any certainly, she reached for her drink, buying time.

Dita sighed, leaning against the railings, her head tilted back a little, exposing her throat. She seemed let down by Cate's disinterested response. "William's children were in a tragic car accident." She frowned as the once light conversation now turned heavier. "I think one daughter survived."

The change of tone had also affected Cate. No longer able to smile, she asked, "So there is someone?"

"There are rumors." Dita spoke to fill the silence but immediately regretted doing so. It didn't seem right to speak of such personal things. She felt disloyal to William. Damn the drink.

"Rumors?"

"Oh, nothing really, and I'm boring you." Dita wanted to retract and kill this particular thread of conversation. But it was too late, Cate wanted to know more. Her eyes gleamed with military attentiveness.

"You're not boring me, and I promise this goes no further." Cate leaned forward, reaching out to fleetingly touch Dita's arm. "Of course, if it's too personal…"

Dita hesitated. She wanted to be discreet, but she also wanted Cate to feel she was trusted. Their building friendship meant a lot to Dita, even if that was all it was destined to become. She had never met a woman she felt so at ease with, yet Cate also stirred her on a much deeper level. Tonight, when Cate invited her to her room, Dita had allowed herself to hope the feeling was mutual. But every time she thought she detected a quickening in the fine thread of tension between them, Cate severed the connection. "Things slip out," Dita said. "It seems the surviving daughter was a bit of a bad seed, messed with drugs, got expelled from school and gave William nothing but trouble. I think she was the cause of the accident, but I'm not sure. Anyway, she left home a long time ago and no one has heard of her since. Everyone acts as though she's dead, or as good as."

A red-hot needle lanced through Cate. "Even her father?"

"No." Dita shook her head. "William never talks about any of this, and I'd never ask him. We've become close, good friends over the last few years, but there are things that remain wholly private. Whatever happened back then, you can see it in his face…he's haunted." Questioning, she looked at Cate. "You would be, wouldn't you? Children aren't supposed to die before their parents, and he didn't just lose one daughter. Somehow he lost them both."

Dita glanced up at Cate and stopped talking, realizing that something she'd said had touched a nerve. The face that stared back at her was wooden, but the eyes were anguished. It was as if something dark had reached inside Cate, tearing her apart to reveal a raw sorrow she couldn't hide.

"I'm sorry," Dita said awkwardly. "I've ruined the *joie de vivre*, haven't I?"

Cate shook her head before slowly answering, "No…it's just sad…tragic."

Dita shivered and pushed off the railings, wrapping her arms around her. "Lousy conversationalist that I am, I think I ought to go. I'm getting cold." She walked into the room, dismayed that she'd been insensitive. Somehow she had stumbled onto a topic that upset Cate, perhaps reminding her of unpleasantness in her own past. Dita should have guessed. Whenever she probed a little about Cate's childhood or her personal life, she ran into a wall.

"No, wait." Cate bolted up and followed her inside. "I'll make us a hot drink and…I have something you can wear." She rifled through a drawer and produced a soft pink button-up sweater. "Here."

She wrapped the cardigan around Dita's shoulders and pulled it together at the front, all but holding her captive. It was then that time stopped. They made eye contact and, for once, Cate didn't look away. Taking a chance on what she saw in the dark depths of her eyes, Dita leaned in and planted the lightest of kisses on her lips.

Cate simply froze. Dita withdrew enough to smile, run a hand down Cate's soft cheek, and move in again for another kiss, but Cate stepped back abruptly, letting go of the sweater.

"Stop," Cate said, struggling for control.

She watched confusion flow slowly, like treacle and molasses, into Dita's eyes. She tried to say something but no explanation made any sense. She wanted Dita. Her lips felt swollen from her very faintest touch. Her breasts felt heavy and her body ached. But she couldn't bear to reduce this moment to nothing but the means to an end. She couldn't depersonalize what was happening. Wanting to start again, this time with the truth, she tried to find words, but it seemed her face betrayed her turmoil, for Dita stepped back, too, and was apologizing, blaming the drink and excusing herself.

Within seconds, the door had closed and Dita was gone.

But she had left the portfolio.

❖

Cate's withdrawal dominated Dita's thoughts as she drifted toward sleep. Only a fool would have missed the desire in her eyes, but Dita knew she was missing a crucial piece to the puzzle, a reservation that drove Cate back just at the very moment Dita had sensed her reaching out. Unknowingly, she had touched a raw nerve in the woman she was beginning to care for more and more deeply with each day that passed. At first she hadn't noticed Cate's deep vulnerability. She was so strong and confident, so decisive in her interactions with others, it was easy to look no further than the smooth surface she showed the world. But there was so much more and Dita was only now learning how to read her.

She racked her brain as to the cause of Cate's discomfort and realized the hopelessness of her task, given she knew so little about her. That would have to change. Dita had always been concerned for how others felt. She could never accept causing anyone pain or suffering, but with Cate her feelings were more personal and stronger. She knew her fascination for Cate lay in an increasing attraction toward her. It was becoming important to learn more about the mysterious Cate, for she *was* mysterious. She was a bundle of conflicting signals, at times distant and aloof, possessing an almost granite disposition of someone unfeeling, uncaring. Yet at other times, Dita sensed behind the unemotional façade someone far different and kind-hearted, but unseen because of the barriers she'd erected. *So many questions, so many things I don't understand about her.*

Dita wondered if Cate knew the profound effect she had on her. While the alcohol had affected her judgment, it didn't create feelings in a vacuum. The intensity of her desire shocked Dita, for when had she ever been this powerfully attracted to another, and so quickly? Not even in college. Did it have something to do with the fact that she'd placed her life in Cate's hands on that mountainside? Had that level of trust created a shortcut to Dita's heart?

Somewhere between grappling to understand the complex woman whose emotions turned on a hangnail and trying to identify her own feelings, Dita had allowed Cate to worm her way into her affections, and deeply. It was strange what attracted one person to another, and how often there were no signs to suggest an attraction would even be likely. The essence of the heart was such a well-kept secret, but then that was the mystery of life itself, why people fell for those who, analytically on paper, they normally wouldn't touch with a pole. And Dita *was* falling.

Forcing her thoughts back to Cate's polite rejection, she realized the only significant clue she had was that of context. She'd steered the conversation to family, love, and loss. Was that the key to Cate's discomfort? The traumas and unresolved problems of one's youth could linger in adulthood. Dita's mind conjured up a plethora of disturbing scenarios. Perhaps Cate was adopted or fostered. Perhaps she'd suffered a tragedy in her youth. The possibilities were endless.

Whatever the reason, Dita mentally kicked herself. Like wearing symbolic Doc Martens, she'd trodden all over Cate's vulnerable psyche. It was the last thing she'd wanted to do. Cate was beginning to matter to her...a lot.

CHAPTER NINE

I don't know much about you," Dita said as she and Cate walked along the harbor wall the next morning. When she received no answer, she continued, "I mean, I don't even know your last name. I don't know if you're married, single, divorced, bereaved, gay, straight, children...whether you have any family at all." She wanted to ask if there was anyone important in her life, a *significant* other, but refrained. From the outset of their walk, it had been obvious that Cate had not slept well and was irritable.

This time, there was an answer but Cate's voice was tetchy. "And that's important to you, is it, to know everything about someone?"

"No," Dita immediately defended herself, gently tugging on Cate's arm. "No," she repeated softly. "It's just you never talk about yourself, almost to the point of being evasive. You always hold back, as if you've something to hide or that you don't want people to get to know you."

"Guilty as charged," Cate said dryly. "Some of us like our privacy."

"There's no middle ground for you?"

"Not if it involves treating every social situation like a talk show, telling the whole world my life story." Cate's eyes were fixed on her with flinty defensiveness.

Determined to get her point across, Dita said, "You left the pool yesterday saying you didn't feel well, but I think the real reason you left is because I said something, and I hurt you." As she recklessly plunged on, she felt Cate grow more prickly. "I don't know what it was I said, but I do know I inadvertently caused you pain, and I loathe having done that, Cate. But it made me realize that it happened because

I know so little about you. Maybe if I'd known more, I'd have avoided sticking my big foot in...something. That's why I ask, and that's *why* it's important to me."

But far from her appeal having any positive affect, Cate only seemed more moody...and *angry*. Dita wondered where this anger came from and why? At her own peril, she ignored the warning signs and pursued her quest to unravel the mystery that was Cate. "It's like you don't trust people, like you don't want to share yourself—"

"Maybe I'm not a nice person to know and I want to keep that hidden."

Dita flinched at the cold response. Cate's reaction pushed their tenuous friendship back to the early days of its fragility. This was not what Dita had wanted. "I'm not asking for your complete ancestral history, Cate. But give me something, *anything*." She attempted to lighten the moment. "Right now, I'd even settle for your shoe size." Her humor fell flat. "Oh, Cate. I just want to know you better."

The plea rattled Cate. Why couldn't Dita Newton have been someone else, someone less likeable and less disarmingly honest? The comparison between them couldn't have been more obvious and it only fueled Cate's anger. She was still stinging from what had been said yesterday, and she simply had no energy to be nice this morning. Dita should have left her alone, let her lick her wounds until *she* felt ready to face her again. Cate found herself wondering why she'd bothered to stay on at Amalfi. She didn't know the answer to that one...perhaps she was so upset she simply wasn't thinking straight. All she'd wanted to do today was stay in her room, in her bed, and pull the covers over her head.

"You think I should be more like you?" she asked Dita sharply. "Up front and friendly, someone who tells a complete stranger everything, a stranger who could use that information against her?"

Dita straightened a little, taken aback by her abruptness, but her eyes sparkled and she responded with gentle humor. "Unless I've missed a news item, we're not living in a communist state where people report on each other."

"That's not what I'm talking about." Cate couldn't hide her frustration. "You've told me everything about *you*, without knowing *me*, and who I am. I could be an adversary and you'd never know it." She wasn't sure why she said that. Was she making a point about Dita's stupidity in trusting her of all people? Or was there another reason? Was she trying to caution Dita...to give her fair warning?

"An adversary? Why would you be an adversary? This is silly." Dita's warm eyes focused on her. "Okay, maybe I am too trusting—with the right people—but isn't that better than suspecting the worst? I feel sorry for anyone who goes through life not believing there are right people out there." She paused, a small frown forming. "It actually took me a long time to learn to believe in people. I had to be taught. But it's a lesson I'm glad I learnt because, for the most part, I haven't been disappointed."

"Whoever taught you that was an idiot!" Cate bit back. "Have you ever considered that your infantile trust in people is probably what's standing in your way of having a successful business? No wonder you're struggling."

Cate's words hit Dita like a slap in the face. She'd never bared her soul to anyone about her business worries, and now she was being criticized for sharing her concerns? "I'm sorry? Are you saying I shouldn't be honest and open with a friend?"

"I'm saying you've only known me for a few days."

"Sometimes a few days are all a person needs," Dita said quietly.

It could only have been seconds but it felt longer as Cate stared back at her. "Really? A few minutes ago you didn't seem to feel that way. You wanted me to tell you more about myself. But now you're saying you know enough to trust me?"

Sensing Cate's withdrawal, Dita tried to close the gap between them. "It worries you that I trust you so much, doesn't it? But I do. Is that so difficult to understand, so difficult for you to live with?" She reached for Cate's hand, but was shunned. *I'm losing control of this.* "Cate. I happen to like you, even if I think you don't always seem to like yourself."

"Who do you think you are?" Cate blazed, backing away like a cornered animal. "What gives you the right to think you know who I really am? You have no idea."

Stunned, Dita said, "Cate, what's wrong? I don't understand any of this."

Then, like a flash of lightning, she started to realize that she'd probably made the biggest mistake in seeking Cate's friendship... and if she was honest, perhaps something more. It seemed there was nothing to seek, and worse, the person before her might actually resent her somehow. The way Cate was looking at her now, Dita certainly thought so.

"You think we're friends?" Cate whispered caustically. "You're a fool."

Dita could find no answer as Cate turned and started back toward the hotel. Only now, watching her walk away, did she realize the truth. They weren't friends. They never had been—and she *was* a fool to have thought otherwise.

Two days later, Dita sat on the top deck of a ferry bound for the island of Capri. She'd wanted to go home immediately after the incident with Cate, but was trapped by a business appointment, something that had fallen out of the Milan seminar she'd attended. At the time, she'd considered the unexpected contact a blessing, now she wasn't too sure. The only thing she did know was that as soon as the meeting was over, she was going home. She was miserable and didn't want to be here anymore.

Unable to relax, she stood and walked over to the bow of the ferry and leaned against the railings, fiddling with an old Polaroid camera her grandmother had bought her years ago. Despite its age, it still worked, and given its sentimental value, Dita would never part with it. Just holding it, she felt the reassurance of the love her grandmother had always given her without reservation, and right now, she needed that memory. She ran her fingers over the body of the instrument as her thoughts stayed with her grandmother. It was she who had taught her to be more trusting of people. *You got that wrong, Gran.* How stupid and naïve she'd been, allowing herself to fantasize over some tourist. Dita couldn't stop thinking about her error of judgment. Stupidly, she'd believed they were becoming friends. She still didn't understand Cate's irrational behavior that day and she abhorred how Cate had made her feel. If their paths ever crossed again, she'd certainly let her know what she thought of her.

It was chilly on the top deck, and wanting to forget how wretched she felt, she decided to go below deck and buy a hot drink. Carefully negotiating the metal stair ladder, she descended into the refreshment area. The ferry was crowded below, with tourists occupying most of the tables. As she waited in line, Dita scanned the area for an empty seat and blinked in disbelief when she spotted a familiar form. Cate was sitting at a table reading a newspaper. *Oh, for heaven's sake.*

Dita instantly backtracked, hoping Cate hadn't seen her. Damn it, she'd really wanted that coffee. Retracing her steps to the upper deck, she mercilessly kicked herself for being so spineless and running away. *If I ever see Cate again...* Her previous thoughts taunted her. Like she was really ready to confront her! She hadn't seen Cate since that day and had been sure she must have checked out of the hotel. To find her now, on the same ferry trip? Fate had a peculiar sense of humor.

Flustered, she moved down to the far end of the ferry, and looked out over the railings. *Please don't let her come up here,* she prayed and found herself thanking the gods when the wind picked up a little, discouraging even the braver tourists from remaining on the cold upper deck. When the few final stragglers gave up and went below Dita sighed with relief. Far too slowly, her mind and pounding heart calmed down as she drew up an emergency plan to stay back and exit the ferry last. That would give plenty of time to make sure she didn't bump into Cate...

"Hello."

Ice shards crystallized down Dita's spine as she recognized the composed voice. She turned to find herself face-to-face with Cate. "Hello. What a surprise."

"I thought I might find you here." Cate's gaze was cautious. She gave a nervous smile.

Every single memory of their last encounter surged back, and taking a deep breath, Dita drew herself up from her hunched position at the railings and frostily replied, "If you don't mind, you can leave me alone." She moved away from Cate, toward another part of the deck, aware that her heart was hammering out of rhythm.

Cate silently whistled as she watched Dita walk away. When they'd last been together, she was so angry she'd said things she shouldn't have, that she didn't mean. After that anger had abated she'd realized with winter cold clarity that none of what had happened was Dita's fault. It certainly wasn't her fault that Cate's father had hired her. That she was talented, bright, and capable of turning Seraphim around. Or that others saw in her work a similarity to Helena Canton's. It certainly wasn't Dita's fault that even the ghost of Cate's mother might spring late-night visitations on her. And so what if her father liked Dita? Cate liked her too—a lot, though she didn't care to admit it.

And now she owed her an apology. *How crazy is that? I'm about to apologize to the woman who runs the business I'm trying to smash.* But it wasn't Dita Cate's revenge was targeted at, and she felt bad that she'd let everything get so personal the other day. Feeling apprehensive and uncomfortably sheepish, she walked over to the solitary figure on the other side of the ferry.

"Dita, I wanted to say I'm very sorry for my unacceptable behavior."

Without looking at her, Dita said, "Well, now you've delivered the apology, you can leave me alone, or do I have to call the staff and tell them I'm being harassed?"

"I was hoping you might accept my apology," Cate said humbly. Whether from the gusting wind or the frosty reception, Cate shivered and crossed her arms, placing her hands under her armpits. Squinting against the direct sunlight, she stared at Dita's face, hoping for a response. She got nothing except an unsympathetic and stony stare-down. Taking an exaggerated deep breath, she let her hands fall to her sides and very calmly started to talk in bullet points. "Single. Never married. Never divorced." She paused to smile a little before continuing. "No children…and no family to speak of." Still there was no flicker of any emotion, nor any answer from Dita. "My surname is Morgan," she said, quickly excising a twinge of guilt. She'd used her mother's maiden name ever since her arrival in Italy. Only now was she considering reverting once more to Canton, for her business dealings in the U.S. "And, oh yes, I'm a shoe size seven, although I prefer a size eight for running."

Annoyance flashed in Dita's eyes. "Are you done?"

"Not quite." Acknowledging the stone wall of contempt, Cate pushed on regardless, determined to hand Dita the information she'd once seemed keen to possess. "Do I have friends? Not too many, probably because of my definite lack in the 'cute and cuddly' department." Cate remained somber beneath Dita's unforgiving gaze as she confessed the next part. "And probably because I have an inability to trust people, *even the really special ones.*"

She hoped her last words might evoke something from Dita, but those icy blue eyes were devoid of emotion. Struggling to think of what else to say, Cate waited for a moment, then reluctantly turned to leave. As she reached the stairwell, she stopped to glance back at Dita, speaking with a depth of genuine affection which surprised her. "It's cold up here. You really should come below, you'll catch a chill."

"You're amazing," Dita hurled at her. There was undeniable pain in her voice, which contrasted with the fury on her face. "You think you can call me a fool, accuse me of having infantile trust, criticize my business ethics, and throw my friendship back in my face, and then offer some lame apology. That's supposed to make it better?"

Cate ran a hand through her windblown hair. "I acted badly, I was out of order and I'm truly sorry." And she honestly was. It was disconcerting the way her conscience had decided to make a comeback. "I don't know what else I can say, Dita. I think I answered all the questions you asked me, but if there's something else you need to know, just ask and you've got it. Only, can we do it below, where it's warmer and there's coffee?"

Dita stiffened. Just a few days ago, she would have been thrilled to receive any sign of Cate's friendship, to know more about her, but not now. She hadn't heard anything that excused Cate's hurtful remarks, and she wasn't going to wait around for new insults the next time Cate had a bad day. "Don't freeze on my account," she said. "I don't have any other questions. I've seen all I need to see."

Groaning a little, Cate placed her cold hands back under her armpits, and edged toward her. "Dita, I've spent the worst forty-eight hours kicking myself and wondering how to put things right, and I realize I'm not doing a very good job of this." She emitted a hollow laugh as she truthfully stated, "My only excuse is that I don't do the 'apology' thing very often, which probably tells you the sort of person I am. But the fact I'm trying—"

The ferry suddenly lurched upward as it hit a rogue wave, and Dita grabbed the rail to steady herself, but her treasured camera slid from her fingers and careened along the wooden boarding, out toward the ocean. Grasping for it, Dita leaned perilously out over the railing's edge. Just as her fingers closed on the small cord that dangled from it, she felt gravity shift and her feet left the deck. The weight of her body swung over the wrong side of the railings and she flailed, on the brink of falling overboard.

As she felt herself slipping downward, two strong hands grabbed her shoulders and clumsily yanked her back up and over the railings until she was safe. Out of harm's way, and with her feet firmly on the deck again, Dita let herself lean back into the body shielding hers.

Cate's hands slipped around her waist and linked together tightly across her stomach. Her voice trembled in Dita's ear. "You are, without doubt, the most accident prone person I have *ever* come across."

Ignoring the sensations that danced through her body, ones she didn't want to feel, Dita heard the tightness in her own words. "You can let go now."

"No—I can't," Cate whispered. "Not just yet."

Dita shrugged away and stepped back a little. Only then did she see that Cate was visibly shaken. Clutching the camera, Dita said, "I think we should go below."

Unable to make eye contact, Cate muttered, "I hate heights…and I absolutely hate water."

"Then what in God's name were you doing up the mountainside that day?" Dita questioned crossly.

"I like challenges," Cate whispered limply, still fighting to regain her composure. A kind of lie but not really. That morning, when she'd realized that Dita was going hill climbing up some of the most treacherous passes imaginable, she'd balked and nearly aborted her reconnaissance mission. It had been truly challenging to follow her.

Confused, Dita was at a loss what to say. "You could have been pulled overboard with me." Spoken with impatience and almost accusatory, the comment forced a laugh from Cate.

Looking at Dita as though she'd just spoken the blindingly obvious, she said, "No kidding. And then where would we both have been? Two blobs bobbing up and down in the water as shark bait."

"I don't think there are sharks around here," Dita replied with a slight thaw in her tone.

Picking up on the infinitesimal improvement, Cate smiled cautiously at her, and was heartened to see the smallest incline of her lips. A seagull flew overhead screeching. They both looked up and then Dita spoke in the first really civilized manner since Cate made her apology.

"I suppose this means you've saved my life—again."

Did Cate detect humor? She responded with warmth. "No, not

this time. They'd have fished you out. Embarrassing, but you'd have lived."

"I guess." Dita watched Cate draw deep breaths as she kept glancing over the side of the boat. Rather unkindly, she remarked, "Long way down, and plenty of water."

Cate shuddered visibly. "Thanks. I hadn't noticed."

Dita couldn't help but smile, her tension and resentment easing. She never had been one to hang on to anger—only where her mother was concerned. "So, what now?" she quizzed Cate.

The gentle gauntlet thrown, Cate responded with a tight little shrug. "I suppose that you, with your wonderfully trusting nature—which I wouldn't ever want to change—grant me a chance to redeem myself." She felt vulnerable as she stood in front of Dita, trying to apologize. "Let me please try to salvage this friendship I don't want to lose, and to try and show you I'm worthy of it."

Something was happening to Cate and she knew it. She genuinely wanted Dita's friendship, even though that opened up a family-sized can of worms she had no idea how she was going to deal with. But one step at a time. She wanted to put right the wrong of the other day and somehow take back the things she'd said. She cared enough to want to make Dita feel better, even if Dita chose not to let her or now shunned her. At least she would try. *I care! When have I ever felt like this before?*

Seeing the indecision on Dita's face, she offered a low-stress option. "We could start by going below for a cup of coffee. Then maybe…if it's okay, you'd let me accompany you today. You have my word of honor I'll be nice and well behaved." She had never been so humble.

Dita hesitated. She might have calmed down but she hardly felt like resuming a friendship. Cate might be an interesting woman but she was too dangerous, too volatile, and even though she was trying to make amends, Dita wasn't ready to return to the easy footing of the past week. Cate had hurt her, and could easily do so again. But she'd also saved her life and Dita couldn't simply crush her attempts at making amends. Despite her better judgment, she agreed to the coffee and they smiled nervously at each other, a moment of connection moving them forward to a better place.

As Dita led the way down and onto the lower deck, she caught a glimpse of Cate's reflection in one of the glass panes. Cate was about to touch her shoulder, as if in affection, but the hand hesitated and withdrew. Cate's expression was hollow but its emptiness spoke volumes. It was the look of someone who thought she'd lost something…maybe even still felt she had. It almost made Dita stop and turn, to try to wipe that dreadful look away, but then she remembered how badly she'd been treated by Cate only a few days earlier and continued on.

They ended up spending the day together, allowing Dita to witness the Cate she'd glimpsed often enough over the past week that she'd yearned to know her better—the woman who was mellow and gentle, light and peaceful, and who seemed grateful for her company. Cate went out of her way at every opportunity to try and please her. Though the absence of her usual edge was welcome, Dita found it unsettling that Cate seemed so desperate to try and win back her favor. There was something sad about it all…that mystery Dita had sensed, always in the background.

The last thing they did before their return trip was to ride up to the highest point on Capri, a route traveled on a rickety chairlift. The view from the highest part of the island was stunning with its cliffs and surrounding panorama.

Gazing out at the view, Dita stepped back from Cate, drawing her camera to her eye.

Cate put her hands to her face and turned to one side. "I don't like having my photo taken."

Mildly aggravated, Dita said. "For heaven's sake, Cate, I'm taking a photo, not capturing your spirit god! I'm sorry if you don't like this, but it's for creative purposes." Looking confused, Cate dropped her guard and Dita took advantage and clicked. Pleased with herself, she smiled broadly. "Relax, this is why I lug this old Polaroid around."

Seconds later, a photo emerged from the camera and Dita watched the image on it slowly develop, then rifled round in her bag for something to draw with. Placing the camera in Cate's hands, she positioned the photo on the top of a wall and started to draw over it.

"And there I was thinking you wanted a photo of me," Cate said wryly.

Dita stopped drawing for a second and scrutinized her deflated companion with mild humor before returning to her task. Finally, she picked the finished product up and showed it to Cate. "Look at this.

Imagine a mid calf length dress in something sleek like parachute silk. Give it an A-line here, and do this on the hips…" She spoke rapidly. "It should be a very fluid dress, with a draping shape. Very flattering." She looked up to see what Cate thought. "So?"

Before Cate could say anything, Dita was off again. "Maybe the material should be silver, gold, or even scarlet. This is a dress that screams 'I'm making an entrance'…right?" She stopped to catch her breath. "Say something, Cate. You have my permission to talk."

Welcoming the playfulness, Cate could only stare at the birth of the design before her. It was amazing. Everything was sketched over a picture of her in a pair of khakis and a long sleeved T-shirt. The rough design was flattering, sophisticated, and though only a draft, it already suggested lightness and something that would dazzle.

"It looks impressive, but I don't know much about fashion," she lied, and again her conscience stabbed at her.

"Maybe not, but you've inspired me."

Eyes dancing, Dita reached out to retrieve her camera, and for one second, Cate thought she was reaching out to touch her. Something flashed through her, a deep craving for Dita's touch. When she realized it was the camera Dita sought, not her, she was so disappointed she forgot to draw her next breath. Struggling to understand what she was feeling, she failed to notice when Dita snapped another photo of her.

This one's all for me. Dita grinned.

As they left the scenic overlook to return to the ancient chairlifts, Cate cautiously touched Dita's arm. "Would you have dinner with me tonight?"

Dita wasn't sure. Even though Cate had earned back a few gold stars today, her recent behavior still sat raw. "I don't know, Cate…"

"Please," Cate begged. "I'm desperate."

A shaft of light fell upon the angel and it stirred.

Though it still could not move, slowly the grime that lay heavy on its wings began to dry, and as it did, so the weight became lighter until the dirt crumbled and fell like dust.

CHAPTER TEN

The Marina Grande, once a simple beachside café, had transformed over its eighty-year history to become a white tablecloth establishment. During the day, tourists rented loungers on the beach below and waiters would serve them pizza and wine from the restaurant. In the evenings diners sat on the sprawling terrace just above the breaking waves, or indoors in more intimate, elegant surroundings. Cate had reserved a window table overlooking the beach, and after ordering antipasti, she and Dita sipped Amarone and watched the sun paint the ocean in brilliant cerise and gold. Soft jazz music played in the background and Dita found herself mesmerized as Cate reminisced about other parts of Italy she knew well.

It was difficult not to be bowled over by her. Tonight she wore loose-fitting black linen slacks and a charcoal gray shirt that made her eyes seem even more blue and her hair almost Titian in its fiery brilliance. Cate was an enigma, quiet and self-assured, yet often moody. When she was relaxed she exuded an inner strength Dita was drawn to. Right now, smiling as she recounted a tale about getting lost in the winding cobblestone streets of Siena, she was so warm and charming, it was easy to forget her harsh words a few days earlier. The reward of friendship didn't come easily, she reflected, but it crossed her mind yet again that she might like more than friendship from Cate.

"What?" Cate had stopped talking. Perhaps sensing that Dita was not entirely focused on her travel anecdotes, she asked, "What are you thinking about?"

"Oh, nothing." Dita quickly averted her eyes, embarrassed to have been caught gazing at her like a moonstruck adolescent. She reached for her wineglass. It was empty.

"Allow me." Cate filled it with more of the ruby liquid that had already gone to Dita's head.

Promising herself to slow down, Dita said replied lightly. "I was just thinking how much I'm enjoying this evening. With you…the real Cate, the one I'm attracted to."

Cate's eyes lingered on Dita's mouth. "Have I allayed all your fears now?" she whispered.

"Not fears, Cate. Never fears." Dita grew bold and returned the intense gaze, but after a few seconds she weakened, worried she was being too forward and giving away too much of what she felt. A wayward thought crossed her mind, and she gave voice to it almost before she realized she'd let the words slip out. "Peter Parker…"

"What?"

"Spider-Man."

"Spider-Man?" Cate raised an eyebrow.

"Peter Parker is Spider-Man." Dita laughed at the bewilderment on Cate's face. "Don't tell me you've never heard of Spider-Man, the comic superhero. He has special powers, which he uses for the usual things…combating villainy and rescuing damsels in distress?"

"What are you talking about?"

Incredulous at her companion's ignorance, Dita waved her arms flamboyantly in front of her. "How can you not know this? Have you lived in a vacuum all your life? Didn't you read comics as a kid? Haven't you seen any of the hugely successful movies? Peter Parker is Spider-Man, the superhero who climbs walls and buildings like a spider, who can eject webs from his hands and scale great heights, moving rapidly over the city tops, rescuing those in trouble."

"I hate heights." Cate was being deliberately obtuse.

"You're missing the point," Dita frowned playfully. "Parker hides his secret powers and real identity from everyone."

"I guess you would too if you covered cities in cobwebs," Cate parried.

"Nobody knows who he really is."

"Your point?"

Dita's eyes narrowed as she leaned across the table and whispered.

"*You* are mysterious, Cate. Like Peter Parker, you go to great lengths to hide the real you." Her manner grew more serious. "I think you wear a mask too, and I find myself wondering who you really are, and what you're taking such pains to hide."

If Cate thought this was an accusation at first, she only had to look at Dita to see that she was reaching out. A desire for intimacy had driven her comment, and acknowledging the same urge in herself came too close for comfort, Cate needed to divert the conversation. "How many glasses of wine have you had?"

Cate's grin had returned. Dita liked it. She pushed forward even closer, seductive, her voice seductive. "Ah, there you go, Parker, deflecting any serious enquiry. Always hiding behind the mask."

Cate rested her chin in the palm of her hand and studied her dinner companion. As Dita's predatory eyes bored playfully into her, Cate felt the unwelcome resurrection of guilt. She wasn't sure if it unsettled or warmed her that Dita could read her like a book…she just didn't know the subject matter of the story.

With a suggestive lilt that purred out words from across the table, Dita asked, "So, are you a superhero?"

Somehow she made the ridiculous question sound like a come-on. Watching the rise and fall of the breasts demurely revealed by a low-cut dress, Cate said, "Not quite."

"But you have secrets," Dita pursued.

"Maybe I do," Cate answered candidly, realizing she'd become less playful.

Though subtle, Dita caught the hint of sadness in the response. "Would you ever share them with me…your secrets?"

Cate found herself thinking seriously about the question. Would she ever share the truth with Dita? Could she? Only a few weeks ago, she would have adamantly declined, but now she wasn't sure. Something about Dita made her question herself, made her question *everything* about herself, and that was unnerving. Cautiously, she answered, "I might consider it…one day." Then she turned wistful, almost challenging Dita, wanting to test a possibility. "But would you like what I had to tell you?"

"I can only answer that when I know your secrets," Dita replied affectionately.

"Yes, of course," Cate said solemnly, a rawness in her throat.

Somewhere in the playfulness over a superhero, the conversation had moved to an underlying subtext, and something undefined, but important, was being discussed. Dita seemed to recognize it, too. She let a few seconds pass before asking, "Are you happy, Cate?"

The question jolted Cate and she realized she was holding her wineglass so tightly the stem would probably snap at any moment. Willing her fingers to open, she said, "I was just thinking what a lovely evening this is." Evasion or not, she recognized she meant every word.

"I don't mean *now*. I mean, in general." Dita leaned on an elbow and ran her hand through her pale, shimmering hair. The movement caused her perfume to waft over to Cate who found it so intoxicating, she could barely breathe.

She struggled to remain focused. "Am I happy, *in general*?"

"Hmm." Full red lips pursed.

Cate stared absent-mindedly into the glass of wine she now held loosely. "Rather a strange question."

"But not entirely without context," Dita said with a hint of challenge. "You must admit, you're not always in the moment."

"Granted." Cate smiled benevolently at Dita. How perceptive she could be.

"I sometimes wonder where you go at those times. Memory… fantasy?"

"Usually work," Cate said.

Dita recognized deflection. "So, are you?"

"Am I what?"

"Happy?"

Cate realized that the question wasn't going away until she gave an answer. "Happiness is a state of mind. It's entirely relative."

"And you're very good at not answering questions." Wolf-blue eyes danced below Dita's arched brows.

She didn't know if it was the wine, but Cate was beginning to find Dita irresistible. Something to do with the seductive smiles that kept coming her way, the red lips against a light complexion, and the enticing view of beautiful breasts. She could feel herself being pulled toward this woman, and she had less and less resistance. "Whether I'm happy or not, I try to rise above it. We all have to, don't we…and simply get on with our lives?"

"Mystery woman," Dita muttered, and Cate laughed, unable to break eye contact.

Dita warmed to the sound of that laugh, with its gravel-like resonance and unusual husky quality. She sipped her Amarone and brazenly studied Cate. She could see how she was being admired—she liked it. "You should laugh more often."

An almost tangible intimacy pulsed between them.

"You think so?" Cate's voice dropped lower and her smile faded.

Dita felt a chill of excitement rush through her. "I do. You can capture hearts with that smile."

Her words drifted into silence as she met Cate's eyes and felt warmth flood her body. She sensed a change in Cate, an opening up. She knew she was being invited in, but hesitated at the threshold, half expecting Cate to retreat once more behind her barriers. The reasons she avoided being vulnerable were anyone's guess, but Dita could see in her a great capacity for compassion, an instinctive nurturing. Why Cate chose to repress those gifts was a mystery Dita was drawn to solve.

She touched Cate's hand and felt her flinch at the slight collision of their flesh. Dita felt equally sensitized to the current that coursed between them. "Let's go," she said.

Cate swallowed half a glass of wine in a single gulp and waved for the check. She couldn't speak. It was all she could do to breathe.

❖

The stroll back to the hotel seemed to take forever. It was a sultry evening, the weather warm and caressingly humid, the sky a myriad of diamante stars set against the blackest of backdrops. At the furthest point of one of the town's two piers, a group of young teenagers were harmlessly skylarking. The boys were trying to impress the girls, who were trying to impress the boys. The circle of life never stopped.

"A penny for them," Cate said, seeing the faraway look in Dita's eyes.

"Only that it's been a long time since I've felt this relaxed, this happy."

The gaze that came back to settle on Cate's face held an unspoken message, but Cate sensed its significance. She coughed uncomfortably, wondering how things had progressed so rapidly and in this direction, without her intention. She felt the embers of guilt stir again inside her and could only offer a trite reply. "I'm glad."

"And your thoughts?" Dita asked.

"I was wondering what they put in the drinks." Cate heard herself trying to dull the exquisite tension between them with humor, and wondered why she felt the need. She wanted Dita, there was no pretending otherwise. And the feelings were mutual. Why not give in and accept all she was being offered? Cate wanted to imbibe and soak herself into oblivion tonight, even as her heart and mind clashed in pursuit of her soul.

Dita's arm slid through hers and she leaned into her. "I think I've had far too much to drink. I feel dangerous."

And I haven't had enough. Dear God, she felt out of control, no longer the one holding the winning cards. Worse still, she wasn't sure she even cared anymore. Did she really have to dictate every moment of the game?

"I love this place, and I'm going to hate leaving," Dita said.

"You're leaving?" Cate couldn't hide her disappointment.

"In a few days." Dita heard the genuine regret in Cate's tone and it pleased her beyond reason. "I need to get back to work…things to be done."

"Of course." Cate's emotions were on a seesaw. The designs. Dita would be submitting them to Nordstrom. She would be devastated when they walked away from the deal.

Dita tugged gently on her arm, bringing them both to a halt. "You know, there is one question I wanted to ask you, but didn't, and I guess I'm just drunk and brave enough to ask it now."

Cate faced her, her nervousness and tension rising. "Oh, and what's that?"

Dita had wanted to ask Cate if there was anyone special in her life, but as she looked at her, her words faded before they even found sound. Instead, impulsively, she leaned in and kissed Cate, who didn't pull back. Growing braver, Dita pushed her tongue past the receptive lips to gain access to the warmth and taste beyond. She moved gently up against Cate and slipped her arms about her.

It felt so good to be held, Cate arched her back, bringing their bodies into full tantalizing contact. The warm lips her eyes had been drawn to all evening settled more firmly on hers and Cate invited deeper exploration. Closing her eyes, she responded to every delicate caress of lips and tongue. Dita's fingers dug softly into her back and her kiss became more urgent. Cate slid a hand up to cradle Dita's head, working her fingers up through the satin heaviness of her hair.

Dita shivered. With a soft moan, she moved her lips from Cate's and kissed a slow path across her cheek to her ear. "I want to spend the night with you. Cate, I—"

The hoarse murmur was roughly severed by the sound of running teenagers screaming and laughing. The moment broken, Cate drew back and they just looked at each other silently, waiting for the rowdy youngsters to pass. When they had gone, Dita tried to connect with Cate again, reaching a hand out to touch an elbow, but Cate stepped away, shock sprawled across her face.

"This can't work." The words seemed to be wrenched from her.

"It can't?" Confused, Dita said, "Why not?"

"Because it just can't. I'm sorry. It's that...this isn't right." Floundering uncomfortably, Cate could barely look at Dita, aware that her snub was blunt and unkind. A battle raged inside her. Part of her wanted to kiss Dita again and stop resisting the inevitable, but another part knew this could not happen for both their sakes.

"What are you saying?" People talk about time standing still at important moments. Only now did Dita understand their meaning, for apart from being aware that she was still breathing, it felt as if her entire world had imploded. She felt cold from the inside out. "Is there a significant other?"

Sometimes, it really was acceptable to tell small white lies, if it was a way to gentle the pain delivered to another. And right now, Cate didn't want to hurt Dita, not anymore. "Something like that...yes."

"My loss then." Dita's look of rejection was almost immediately eclipsed by a calm so fragile Cate was reminded of a fresco at the Herculaneum.

And like a simultaneous crack of thunder accompanied by a blinding flash of lightning, she realized she was in love with Dita.

❖

How strange it was that she had joked to herself only a short while ago that she longed to have a summer affair, an engagement of the heart. Now it had happened, she wished it hadn't. Three o'clock in the morning and Dita, unable to sleep, leaned over the bathroom wash basin, gazing at her reflection in the mirror. From an early age, people had told her she was a natural beauty and though she hoped she avoided being vain or egotistical, she had the wisdom to accept the gift that life had bestowed on her. She had a body with all the right proportions including generous bountiful curves that accentuated her femininity, blond hair that fell in Hollywood waves, sensuously caressing her face and resting slightly below her shoulders, and a creamy paleness of skin set vividly against the pale intensity of her eyes. Add to that the final brushwork of a master, the redness of luscious full lips… Life had been good to her. It had made her beautiful, and doors opened for beautiful women.

But that meant nothing at this moment. For how could it be that both men and women were forever falling over themselves to be with her, wanting to seduce her, to love her, but the one person *she* desired seemed unable or unwilling to return the affection? Dita raised her hands to wipe tears that had appeared from nowhere, and realized her eyes were swollen and red. *Not so attractive now.* Real love, that breed of affection that knows no boundaries, had never come easily to her. That it should come now, and find rejection, turned her heart into an aching mess. Miserable and full of self-pity, a rare characteristic that only served to make her feel worse, she pondered if this was to always be the way of things. Thirty years old and, apart from her grandmother, she'd never known true, deep love, the love that offered permanency.

Knowing she wouldn't sleep tonight, Dita reached for her sketch pad, hoping her work might bring her solace. When she awoke hours later, chilled and achy after having dozed off over her sketches, she realized that it was midmorning and she could hear the maid outside, pushing the service trolley down the corridor. She poked her head out through the doorway and, in broken Italian, told the woman not to bother cleaning her room, trying to explain that she had slept badly and wanted to catch up on the missing sleep.

The maid seemed more than happy with the arrangement—one room less to clean.

❖

One kiss. One single, most beautiful, intoxicating kiss, and Cate's whole life, like a house of cards, had come tumbling down. What was it about the experience of such intimacy that a single kiss could evoke? Was it the subtle, innate precondition that the act itself implied, a trust and willingness to open up one's heart, and body, to be loved by another? Did she love Dita? Did she desire her? Did she care for her beyond herself—the real definition of love? The answers to all three questions shocked her. *Yes. Yes. Yes.*

Yet in that moment of sharing, of spontaneous and naked truth, Cate had panicked. Why? Her love and desire for Dita were real, yet she couldn't grant herself what she longed for. Everything she felt seemed tainted by deceit. What she was doing was wrong—pretending to be something…someone she wasn't. Only now did she truly understand to what depths she had sunk.

Like a bucket of ice cold water thrown over her, her new awareness scared her. Cate found herself torn between the goals that had driven her for so long—possession and reclamation of what she perceived as rightly hers—and, now, something greater, something far beyond materialistic value. She had a chance to love and be loved. In a passage of so little time, Dita had reached some place deep inside her, a dark wretched last sanctuary where once a betrayed, fragile young heart had gone into hiding. Dita had tenaciously pursued her heart and torn down the walls of its asylum, nurturing the damaged vessel back to health with care and love.

In the distance, Cate heard church bells ringing out the time. Was this her moment of reckoning? The realization of what she'd become and how far she had traveled—away—from that younger, vibrant Cate of fifteen years ago who'd been brimming with passion and integrity. Was it not a crime what life could sometimes do to the heart?

As the last bell rang out ten o'clock in the morning, its tone echoing into the distance, Cate wondered if she'd been given a choice: continue on her current pathway and most likely succeed in achieving what she'd ruthlessly worked toward for so long, or abandon her dreams and alter her course, drastically. Which road would she take?

Lying there, gazing up at the whitewashed ceiling, Cate stopped breathing for several seconds when her mind and heart came together. The occurrence was so rare, she waited for the moment to pass in case it was mere fabrication, the last resort of a person trying to justify a decision that flew in the face of common sense. But when her certainty only deepened, Cate knew she had just experienced an irrevocable change. Her reality had altered and the path she had to take was suddenly as clear and bright as the sunlight streaming through her shutters.

Filled with purpose, she picked up the phone and dialed the international number for Saul. When he didn't pick up, she left a brief message on his answering machine, telling him to hold off on taking the competing designs to Nordstrom until she returned home. Cate no longer had any intention of pursuing this course of action, leaving the field open for Seraphim. Her reasons for this change of plan were too complex to explain over the phone, and she wasn't sure how she was going to account for her decision.

But as she replaced the receiver, she felt a weight fall from her shoulders. Finally, she felt she'd done something honorable, something her mother would be proud of. She didn't know what this meant with regard to her future and if she had any with Dita, for she *would* have to share the truth with her, and soon. That might change things between them, but for the moment Cate was free to pursue the direction of her heart, not her head.

Glancing at her watch, she realized she was running late for the coach trip to Ravello, something the two of them had agreed to yesterday when they'd returned from Capri. Her heart racing with the anticipation of seeing Dita soon, she hurriedly grabbed her jacket and ran out of the room.

CHAPTER ELEVEN

D ita reclined in a chair on her balcony, gently dozing in the sun. The hotel overlooked a quiet, winding side street lined with pale villas. Beyond the rooftops a myriad of small fishing boats could be seen nestled in a tight corner of the harbor. Dita loved the view but she was too exhausted from lack of sleep to enjoy it as she usually did, content to watch passersby chatting in the street. Lulled into slumber by the gentle, distinctive metal rattling of the rigging on the boats nearby, she drifted in and out of sleep and dreamt uneasy dreams. Somewhere in the tangle of her mind and her senses, she became increasingly aware of familiar laughter, of whispers on a breeze, of something tangibly welcome. The distant sensations became closer and more physical as something landed in her hair, waking her as it rolled down and into her lap. Opening her eyes she examined the offending article, a Galatine. Still caught in the remnants of sleep, she was wondering where it had come from when another one hit her squarely on the nose.

Sitting up and peering over the side of her balcony, she saw Cate wearing the biggest grin, about to fire off another of the milk candies. Her tanned face beamed with affection and her infectious laughter was reminiscent of childhood, when nothing was held back. Its sound brought joy to Dita, like ice cream on a hot, humid summer's day.

"Hey, sleepyhead, what happened to you this morning? We were supposed to go to Ravello, remember?"

This time Dita caught the Galatine. She smiled back apologetically. "I'm sorry, I didn't sleep well last night...and I forgot. You're back early."

"Never went." Cate couldn't hide her joy at seeing Dita. "When you didn't turn up, I came to your room and saw the 'Do not disturb' sign. The maid said you wanted a sleep-in, so I thought I'd leave you alone for a while. But now I'm bored."

Again, the familiar grin reappeared, only serving to remind Dita that she had fallen hard for the unobtainable. "I should have called you this morning and let you know. I'm sorry…I've ruined your day."

Cate saw the change register on Dita's face, saw the lines of tension appear that had not been there a second ago. "You are okay, aren't you? Can I come up?"

Dita attempted to conjure up some excuse, but Cate had already disappeared and even as she leaned further out to try and see her, there was a gentle tapping on her door.

"Did you fly up here?" Dita asked as she opened it.

Standing there, out of breath, Cate wiggled her fingers in the air. "Spider-Man, remember?"

She immediately sensed Dita's discomfort. Usually happy and vivacious, she seemed unable to make even the simplest conversation. In the limited time Cate had known her, she'd never been short on words. Her concern grew. "Are you sure you're okay?"

Dita waved a hand, dismissing the question. "Yes, really. Just woken up, that's all."

Cate didn't believe a single word and knew Dita's awkwardness had everything to do with what had happened last night. Hoping to ease the tension, she moved across the room to pick up a sketch, one of several scattered over on the desk. "Are these new?" She studied the design closely. "This is beautiful," she said, impressed. "I adore your colors."

"This is my next collection, what I've been working on while here." Now distracted by her work, Dita relaxed a little. How easy conversation turned when it hinged on the professional, not personal, context. She wrapped her toweling bathrobe more tightly around her and moved toward Cate, who was deeply absorbed as she studied the other sketches. All were different drawings for various articles of clothing, but based on a similar theme. Dita thought it amusing that Cate was so taken with the designs, almost to the point of being oblivious to her presence.

Dita glanced at the one Cate was studying. It was a cocktail dress cut on the cross and in a stunning midnight blue, classically simple but very effective. "I think that's my favorite. It's not finished yet, needs a lot more thought."

"I recognize that one." Cate pointed to a basic outline of a dress that had started its creative life as a rough sketch over her photo in Capri.

Dita went to pick it up and as she did, her fingers touched Cate's. She moved her hand away as if it had been burned, then tried to cover up her odd behavior. "I've made changes to it, remember?"

"Yes, I do." Cate gave her a quick sideways glance, warmth in her eyes and a tender measure of understanding on her face.

Dita blushed, then moved away on a paltry excuse of looking for a sketch on the other side of the room. "I'm very pleased with what I've done so far, but the collection's not quite there yet, and I can't seem to get these right." She pointed vaguely to several other outfits, aware that she was talking too quickly. "I know the material I want to use and the colors, but the pattern and cut has to be right and I can't quite marry them all together, but it'll come."

"You're very talented." Cate didn't hide her admiration and awe. "I really mean it. You deserve to succeed with designs like these."

For the first time since she'd entered the room, Dita actually looked at her directly, nervously biting her bottom lip and growing more uncomfortable by the minute.

Unable to bear it any longer, Cate put the sketch down. "I'm concerned that I upset you last night."

"No," Dita interjected quickly, glad that the source of her discomfort was out in the open. "No, *I'm* sorry, Cate." She closed her eyes wishing the whole embarrassing situation would disappear. It wasn't right that Cate was apologizing to her. Dita was the one who'd made the first move.

But Cate didn't see it that way. "Why would you be sorry? I was the one who pulled back."

"You probably think I make a habit of coming on to strangers. I don't. My behavior last night...I'd like to say it was the effects of what turned into a wonderful day yesterday, then complemented by a good meal, excellent company, and large amounts of fine wine." Dita sighed. "But I'm afraid it was me, stupidly overreacting and misreading signs, believing I was seeing something that wasn't there." She thought again of how Cate had looked at her all through dinner, her expression intimate and inviting. "But the wine's worn off and I'm now very sober, and I can see you were just being polite and that I...embarrassed you." She rattled on nervously. "Hell, I've embarrassed me."

Dita tried to laugh, to make light of it all but failed miserably, and worse, she could feel her eyes stinging. Her heart was thumping so noisily, maybe that was why she didn't see or hear Cate move and was suddenly surprised when she felt a single finger rest on her lips.

"Stop." Cate stood a hair's breadth in front of her, her voice caught in that gravelly tone Dita loved so much.

Refusing to stop before she could finish what she wanted to say, what she *had* to say, she brushed Cate's hand away and continued, "Like an idiot, I thought you might feel the same way I feel about you."

There, she'd said it. The words out in the open, time came to a standstill. Did anything else move or exist in the universe, but them? Had it not been for a boat's horn lamenting in the distance, she could almost have believed they were the only two living, breathing occupants in the world. Reality returned only when Cate, very slowly, very deliberately, placed a feather-like kiss on her lips.

"But I *do* feel the same way, and you weren't coming on to a stranger," Cate whispered, caressing the lips she'd just kissed and tasting the salt from Dita's falling tears.

"You do?" As Dita spoke, she saw how Cate's eyes searched hers, lit with warmth and compassion...and love. Soft hands rose and cupped her face tenderly, fingers touching her ears and sending tingling sensations down her body. Cate looked as if she was holding the most valuable thing in her life.

"I shouldn't feel like this," Cate said softly. "This shouldn't be happening."

"The significant other?" Dita didn't want to know but she had to.

Cate didn't answer the question. "Maybe your Peter Parker was right." Her hands still on Dita's face, she wiped a tear away with a thumb. "People shouldn't get too close to him because he's dangerous. People might get sucked into the bad things that happen to him."

Unable to believe what was happening, Dita took one of Cate's hands in hers and, turning the palm upward, kissed its center. "Sometimes risk is a part of love."

"But what if the risk is too great?" Soft words, but Cate's voice seemed to cry *Caution!*

But Dita no longer wanted words, her body cried out for a deeper depth of communication. She needed to satiate herself in the arms of this woman, to let herself give passionately to this strange human being before her whose vulnerability and fragility cried out for attention. Was Cate so unobtainable? Probably. Could Dita settle for so little, and then see even that disappear? A fleeting encounter wasn't what she wanted, but with Cate she would take whatever she could. She leaned in and kissed Cate, this time not holding back the passion that burned inside her like a furnace.

The moment their tongues entwined, Cate felt her heart explode, and the corresponding and overpowering desire for Dita consumed her. Out of control, her hands raked over the Dita's lithe body as she pushed the robe off her shoulders and tasted her flesh, from the succulent lips, to the delicate throat, down to the valley that formed between supple, taut breasts. Dita did not resist as Cate backed her against the wall for support. She thrust her hips against Cate and clawed her light clothing away, quickly discarding it. Nothing was said as the force of nature moved into control.

Barely aware of what she was doing, Cate urgently pulled Dita toward the unmade bed and pushed her down onto the pillows. There was only one moment of hesitancy, as Cate gathered up several sketches lying on the covers and gently placed them on the desk. Then, tugging at the Velcro on her sandals and discarding them carelessly, she sank down onto the bed, her lips eagerly seeking those she had thought about all morning.

In the buildup of heat and sweat, as desire reigned, there seemed no time for teasing. Cate's leg instantly lodged itself between Dita's. A firm thigh pushed itself up against an already wet sex as they lay naked, breast against breast, their kissing intensifying, tongues dancing, Dita thrusting herself down on the rocking movement of a muscular limb.

Sheets and blankets were vigorously pushed to the floor with naked feet as bodies writhed and twisted rhythmically to some unheard musical beat, accompanied by panting and breathless sounds, the occasional moan. Dita's hands slipped down Cate's torso, exquisitely discovering a firm, strong, and lean body beneath her fingers, but as those fingers neared their objective, Cate resisted and promptly turned Dita on to her back. Pinned by Cate's weight, Dita felt her sensitive, aroused nipples taken one at a time. Cate's slim fingers teased as they penciled a snake-like dance, moving sensuously down Dita's stomach, causing her to tremble and shake in anticipation of what was to come. Her groans urged speed.

When the fingers stopped their travel south and found time to play seductively with her hardened clitoris, she cried out, unable to contain the tidal wave of feelings that flooded her. When Cate's fingers found her opening, wet beyond belief, she slid in easily then rested for a moment as if to taunt her.

"Please!" was all Dita could whisper, and Cate began to push into her and set a gentle rhythm and depth that slowly built until Dita felt herself rise and fall over some unseen chasm. A burst of energy exploded inside her as she wrapped her legs around Cate's body. As it hit, she stopped moving and clung to Cate so tightly she could feel the sweat between them, blending, saturating into their bodies as if they were one. The orgasm hit her like shock waves, one after the other, until the breathtaking sensations slowly faded and she lay satiated and exhausted in the protection of Cate's arms.

Abruptly motionless with Cate's resting fingers still inside her, a thumb placed on her clitoris, Dita looked down on her lover, who lay with her head resting below Dita's breasts, her shoulders rising and falling quickly as her breathing returned to normal. Dita wondered if there was ever any time, place or moment more wonderful and humbling than this. To share such intimacy, such intense and natural communication with another at such a level, could anything really surpass this?

After a short while, she ran her nails down Cate's soft back, evoking a dull moan from her. Then she moved them sensuously over the exposed rib cage, the sign of a fit runner who stored little excess flesh. She reached for Cate's breasts, wanting to return Cate's gift with equal passion. But instead of reacting to the promise of what was to unfold, Cate rose up on her elbows and shifted up the bed to kiss Dita again.

"Your turn," Dita whispered, but Cate only shook her head.

"No." Though spoken softly in the breath of love, it was an adamant response.

Frowning, Dita moved so she could see Cate's face, and she found sadness waiting there. It frightened her that perhaps she hadn't been enough, or done enough, and had somehow lost Cate.

But Cate saw her doubt and raised a hand, pushing it into Dita's hair. "I want you to love me, Dita. I want you so badly, but..."

Dita sensed that something...or *someone* lay between them. "You must love this person very much." It was meant to be a simple statement of what seemed so obvious, this *other* coming between them, but she hadn't expected to see such loss in Cate's eyes. Was this what it was all about? Was there another lover out there? Someone who possessed Cate's heart, a past lover, or worse...someone in the present?

"No questions, please?" Cate implored softly. "Not now..."

Dita allowed herself a smile as she pushed the hair from the face that watched her so intently. She said nothing, but nodded and then changed the subject, needing Cate to smile again. "I like your eyes. Sometimes they're so blue. But when you're angry, do you know they turn gray, like slate?"

"My father used to say that all the time." Cate's eyes were blue now and full of passion.

"Is he still alive?" Dita probed, but when Cate was silent, she placed a kiss on her forehead. "You don't want to talk about that either. I'm sorry."

"Don't be," Cate said. Wrapping her arms back around Dita, she pulled her close. Together like that, they fell asleep.

Later when they awoke, they remained entwined in each other's arms, watching strange shadows creep across the ceiling and listening contentedly to the street sounds and the clanking of boat rigging in the distance.

"Why won't you let me make love to you? I want to, you know." Dita leaned over Cate to kiss her forehead.

Cate closed her eyes and welcomed the love that Dita so unreservedly gave her. She answered slowly, not yet ready to return to her world of reality. "I know. It's not right. Just...not yet."

"Not yet? You mean there might be a time?" Hope burned in Dita's heart. She waited for an answer, but none came. "Don't disappear from me, Cate…don't go mysterious again." She kissed Cate's neck below an ear. "Is it the other person?"

Cate took one of Dita's hands in hers, kissing the fingers delicately one by one. "Maybe Spider-*Woman* wants to come out from behind her mask, but can't yet. Maybe she wants to know if a certain person she's grown *so very fond of…*" She checked to make sure Dita was in no doubt who she was talking about. "Maybe that person might give her a little time to sort things out?"

She was full of riddles. Dita found herself clinically observing Cate as she spoke, looking for clues, anything, that might give her a greater insight, but this passionate lover still gave so little of herself away. "I think she would wait forever," Dita whispered hoarsely.

Cate hadn't expected to hear that and couldn't hide her shock. "Forever is a long time."

Dita only smiled and then moved a hand to run fingers over the old scar above Cate's left eyebrow. "How did you get this?"

"I don't remember." Cate didn't want to remember, and the incident seemed a lifetime away. "Probably some tree I fell out of as a kid." She could see she wasn't believed, but wanting to push the bad memories far away, she playfully nudged Dita in the ribs. "We should get up, go out and eat. I'm starving."

Dita laughed. "Me too, but I don't want to move from here. I want to stay here, cocooned here with you." *Forever.* "Why don't I order room service?"

"Appealing…" Cate bent down and kissed one of Dita's breasts, feeling her instantly respond beneath her. To make love to her again was very tempting but no, food was paramount now. She finished her sentence breathlessly. "Very, very attractive woman spends all day in hotel room. Orders large meal for two. They'll gossip in the kitchen."

"I'm sure they're used to it." A dreamy answer. "Anyway, I don't care."

You should. Reputation is everything. It's who you are. Cate's past fleetingly returned to haunt her, a sore that seemed never to heal, never allowing her to forget who, until now, she'd been. Before Italy. Before Dita. *But that's all changed now. I've changed.*

❖

When Cate returned to her room later that evening, after she and Dita went out for pizza, she kicked her shoes off and allowed herself a smile as she fell onto the bed. Slowly the smile became a gentle laugh, and she couldn't stop. Cate laughed because she was happy, a feeling she seldom experienced, and yet one she could remember from her youth.

How had her life turned so fast from dark to light?

She knew only that she wouldn't sleep tonight, for all she wanted to do was remember everything about Dita, the way she'd felt under her hands, the smell of her soap and perfume on her skin, the scent of her hair, the smell of her sex. Feeling inexplicably light of heart, all because this wonderful woman was so willing to love her, Cate found herself praying. It was another of those things she hadn't done for so many years, but tonight she did. She prayed and asked God to give her a second chance at joy, a life that offered more meaningful rewards than success in her field and admiration from her peers. If granted, Cate asked also to be able to share that life with Dita. She no longer wanted to be the ruthless woman who'd arrived in Amalfi only a short time ago. She wanted to be new, reborn again…to have a chance to be someone else for whom the opportunities seemed limitless. *A second chance at love, please.*

Earlier, lying next to Dita, Cate had wanted to tell her everything but she'd held back, not because she was afraid, though she was—she was apprehensive of what Dita might think once she knew all of the truth. She could see how happy Dita was, and she hadn't wanted to ruin the moment. She had hurt Dita's feelings too many times, and a few more hours of secrecy wouldn't hurt before she delivered the awful truth. And if she was honest, Cate had wanted that moment of happiness too.

She would let Dita have a decent night's sleep before she told her everything. Tomorrow, after breakfast, they would go for a long walk and she would tell her the truth…tell her who she really was and beg her understanding and forgiveness.

Resolute and determined to confess everything, Cate got up and headed toward the bathroom to take a shower. As she finished brushing her teeth, she heard her cell phone beep. She didn't want to think about work, but she had been waiting all day to hear from Saul. His text message drained the strength from her legs and she stumbled onto the bed, clammy with shock and dismay.

Nordstrom on board. All signed. Water tight. Stop worrying.
See you soon. S.

❖

Dita held off ordering breakfast for nearly an hour, but when Cate didn't show, she made her way to the hotel reception and asked them to phone Cate Morgan's room. A new member of staff she'd never seen before looked confused and asked her for the name again. Irritated, she gave him Cate's room number. The man's face lit up in recognition and he politely informed her that the lady had ordered a taxi very early that morning and had checked out.

"Are you sure?" There had to be a mistake.

"Quite sure, signorina. The lady said urgent business had arisen, and she had to go home."

Despite what the desk clerk had told her, Dita went straight to Cate's room where she found the door open and a maid already cleaning it. She asked if the guest had switched to another room, but the maid spoke no English and seemed confused by Dita's Italian. Thinking that Cate must have left her a phone message, Dita returned to her room but there was none. She decided Cate was being considerate and had not wanted to wake her at such an early hour. But it was now past nine o'clock. Dita called reception to see if any messages had been left for her. Nothing.

For the rest of the morning, she waited in her room, convinced that there was a reason for Cate's silence. She was probably on a plane or dealing with the business emergency that had called her away. Watching the rain pour down and the electrical storm rage above Amalfi, Dita tried to concentrate on her sketches but she couldn't settle. Pacing her room, constantly checking her phone for messages, watching the clock, she waited for a call that never came.

❖

An impressive bolt of lightning cut across the sky, along with a loud bang, and for a moment, the lights flickered inside the airport terminal. With every flight delayed due to the atrocious weather conditions, life in the departure lounge was getting more noisy and unpleasant by the minute. Frustrated, Cate stared out of the large glass plated windows at the tumultuous dark gray sky and the driving rain. Quite why, she didn't know, but she found herself thinking of her mother and was suddenly overwhelmed with feelings of loss. She found herself yearning for that closeness that had existed between them. She remembered how the two of them would sit together at home on the back terrace, watching electrical storms dance overhead. Cate had been frightened of thunder and lightning as a young child, but her mother used to hold her hand and explain that it was only angels running around upstairs above the clouds, playing with flashlights.

Cate's eyes brimmed with tears and she wondered why she was suddenly missing her mother more than ever. Even before the question had played itself out in her mind, she knew the answer. The loss of her mother had been unbearable, and the thought of losing Dita had brought those old sorrows rushing back. Cate wanted to get away from the feelings. She wanted to flee Italy, but she could only sit here alone with her emotions and the inescapable knowledge that she had fallen in love with Dita even as she was plotting to ruin her.

Try as she might, she couldn't place Dita in some mental file labeled Business Venture: The Means to an End. Her dishonest ruse had turned into something far more personal. She had found herself opening up to Dita, and not because of her beauty—Cate was not that shallow. In the fashion industry, she was used to being surrounded by stunning models. Her attraction to Dita was much more than that. Dita was one of those rare people who possessed an unpretentious beauty of spirit, an inherent kindness that drew others to them. She was someone the world had not tarnished. Although, maybe that would change now. Maybe Cate's impact would be just as destructive as she'd once hoped.

If she'd had any guts, she would have stayed and admitted everything. Even now she could phone Dita and try to limit the damage. But Dita would despise her once she knew who she really was, and what she'd done. And Cate couldn't stand the rejection that would bring. The guilt she'd felt ever since receiving Saul's text was awful. She was scared like a child, knowing that something horrible had happened and she was no longer safe. Out of her fear had come sheer panic and like a child, she had run. There was no going back. Her inability to stop the Nordstrom contract going through had ruined everything. It would be impossible for Dita to believe that even as Cate was stealing her designs, she was changing. Even as her plan bore fruit, she was falling in love with the woman she resented so bitterly. Dita would never forgive her.

Oh God, what have I done?

Chapter Twelve

I have to take a phone call," William said, showing Dita into the living room instead of their usual meeting place, his study. "I'll be with you as soon as I can. Make yourself at home."

Dita thanked him and crossed an expansive room formally decorated in rich, dark colors. Every muscle in her body was tense as she settled into a dark brown leather sofa and prepared herself for the difficult meeting to come. Since learning of the collapse of the Nordstrom contract, she and Marcus had worked all hours to try and source other retailers to replace the loss. She'd lost count of the phone calls she'd made, the e-mails she'd sent, and the fashion stores Marcus had physically visited. Even as she'd left the office, he was next door on the phone setting up more appointments.

It was depressing. All this hard work and so far the results were not promising. It was the worst time of the year to be seeking major new contracts. The only good thing that had happened to Seraphim was the arrival of a young designer, Leona Jarvis, who had recently finished an advanced fashion program and who wanted nothing more than to work for Dita. Fortunately she was willing to work for a pittance as long as she could understudy Dita, a process she described as "becoming the magician's apprentice." When Dita had queried the word *magician*, Leona explained that some of her designs were "simply out of this world, magical." If Dita hadn't been so tired, she'd have let her ego run rampant.

Although she knew Seraphim would be plunged back into debt if she didn't increase their orders soon, Dita had hired Leona anyway, and quickly recognized her potential. Along with a willingness to work all hours, she produced excellent results. If—*if*—Dita could keep the business afloat and not get sacked in the meantime, she and her young apprentice might have a good working future together, bouncing around creative ideas.

Dita cast her gaze around the room, taking in antique oriental carpets, a Georgian style fireplace, and a unique, heavy coffee table with an inlaid wood design. It was one of several statement pieces she would never have thought of placing together, yet the eclectic combination worked. Dita wondered if it was the late Helena Canton's hand she was seeing in the careful choice of furniture and the mix of styles, or if William had employed an interior designer. She hadn't seen much of his home, other then the study, where they always met, and the kitchen where they sometimes snacked after a long discussion, but she appreciated the atmosphere of family and security. She missed that feeling. Coming home to a dull, empty apartment was not the same as stepping into a warm room and seeing the face of someone she loved. For the hundredth time that week her thoughts strayed to Cate Morgan.

She'd tried to find her contact details, using the Internet, but she knew nothing about her. There was no centralized list of day traders she could search, and with thousands of Morgans all over the world, Dita had concentrated her search on major U.S. cities, since Cate was American. She had worked her way fruitlessly through phone books for a month after returning from Amalfi, all the while ignoring the obvious—Cate knew how to find *her*, but had chosen not to make contact.

Dita had reached the painful conclusion that Cate had fled because of the other person in her life. That was where her loyalties lay and Dita had to respect her decision. Still, she couldn't stop analyzing and re-analyzing the situation, wondering if she could have done something differently to make Cate stay. She wasn't a home-wrecker, but everything seemed to have come together for them in Italy, or so she had thought, and Cate didn't behave like a woman in a happy relationship with someone else.

Dita's chest constricted as she thought about their lovemaking. There had been such tenderness and warmth, such a depth of connection. She knew that whatever she had felt for Cate, it had been returned for she had seen it in Cate's eyes. Such powerful feelings were not easily hidden, yet Cate had not allowed Dita to reciprocate and make love to her, and she'd initially resisted Dita's overtures. In the light of subsequent events her reluctance made more sense. On bad days, Dita concluded that she'd pressured Cate into something that was little more than a summer affair she had immediately regretted. A momentary frolic in the sun could be dismissed as meaningless. Such encounters posed no challenge to the status quo unless discovered, and Cate was so secretive Dita could easily imagine her partner, if she had one, knowing nothing about the way Cate spent her time. Perhaps they were having a bad patch. People made uncharacteristic choices when their relationships were in trouble. Perhaps Cate had come to her senses and rushed back to the other person, filled with remorse.

Dita set her satchel aside and got to her feet, restless and depressed. She couldn't accept the idea that their connection was one-sided when every instinct told her that something profound had happened between them. But could she trust her feelings? Turning philosophical, she wondered if it was really possible to fall in love with someone so deeply in such a short time, or whether the scientists were right and these emotions were merely hormonal overdrive. The world was littered with people like her, who read too much into brief affairs that blossomed in the absence of reality, only to die in the harsh light of everyday life.

She moved aimlessly around the room, pausing at the windows to gaze out at the lamplit gardens. The trees had dropped most of their leaves and the flower beds had been readied for the coming winter. Dita couldn't help but compare the bleakness of the outlook before her with the warmth and brilliant hues of Amalfi. She drew the heavy drapes together, closing out the gloom, and her gaze shifted to the antique mahogany sideboard on the same wall. An array of photographs stood around a Chinese vase, and curious to know more of William, a man who hinted so little of his private life, Dita wandered over to look at them more closely.

They appeared to be family photos, some formal, some less so. She spotted one of a much younger William, darker haired and thinner, standing happily next to a tanned, relaxed woman whom Dita recognized from the painting at Seraphim as his late wife, Helena. Though the fashion and styles suggested the photo was probably taken several decades ago, Dita found herself drawn to the woman, for there was something familiar about her. She studied the image closely. The smile, the shape and color of the eyes, and slowly it dawned on her that although the face was more angular, the woman bore a striking resemblance to Cate Morgan.

Dita set the photo down and scanned the others rapidly. The same woman appeared in a photo with William and two young girls, both barely teenagers. The older, taller one was leaning casually into her, and the younger stood behind a seated William, her arms playfully wrapped around his neck. In what appeared to be the setting for a formal photo, the photographer had gone ahead and captured a moment of fun, for all four in the picture were laughing, seemingly unaware of the camera. In the split second of a shutter frame, the camera had caught a scene of undoubted family love and closeness.

But Dita wasn't interested in that. What held her attention was the face of the young girl behind William. With a paralyzing fear, she knew she was looking at Cate Morgan. Whatever the name she used, she was William's daughter, the "bad seed" who had made her father's life hell, if Seraphim gossip were to be believed. Hardly able to breathe, Dita somehow managed to hide her shock as William entered the room. Internally, she waged a war, arguing that she had to be wrong, that this was all some huge mistake and an amazing coincidence. There were doubles for everyone, wasn't that a well-known fact? She stared at the photograph and again and knew in her heart that there was only one explanation for the resemblance, Cate wasn't a look-alike, she was the real thing.

"My wife and daughters," William said, confirming her conclusions. He smiled as if reliving happy memories, and on a rare personal note, added, "I miss them all."

Dita wanted to blurt out that she'd found his deceitful, delinquent offspring, but she couldn't. She could only guess at the pain Cate had brought him. The last thing she wanted to do was hurt him and reopen old wounds.

Somehow, she managed to get through the evening, informing him of how business was proceeding. Even as she did, unpleasant seeds began to germinate, ones she was almost too frightened to face. Her mind was conjuring up a story she didn't want to recognize, a story that gave life to a suspicion she'd harbored for some time. All the failed business deals and broken contracts suddenly seemed less random. The pattern that took shape was one of a quiet but sustained undermining of Seraphim. Dita couldn't put her finger on a common thread but, if there was one, she now suspected it would lead back to just one person. Cate.

Was she trying to ruin her father? Dita felt physically sick as she contemplated the subtleties of that scenario. Obviously Cate's presence in Amalfi was no coincidence, and her hasty departure was almost certainly prompted by a fear of discovery. A bitter taste flooded Dita's mouth. The affair she had agonized over ever since she'd stared into Cate's empty hotel room finally made horrible sense. A scheming daughter with a desire to hurt her father had pumped her for information and seduced her into lowering her guard. Cate's hurtful words echoed. *I could be an adversary and you'd never know it... You think we're friends? You're a fool.*

"I just opened a decent pinot noir," William said pleasantly. "Would you care for a glass?"

Dita contemplated asking for a stiff drink of whiskey instead, but said, "Yes. Thank you," and followed him to the sofa and chairs in the center of the room.

Her legs all but buckled beneath her as she sat down. Dazed, she pulled her notes for the meeting from her satchel. William returned with the wine and she did her best not to gulp down the entire contents of her glass.

"Rough week?" He settled into the armchair opposite her.

Dita nodded wordlessly. A tear slid down her cheek and she wiped it away, hoping her emotionality hadn't been observed.

William's gentle tone suggested otherwise. "Do you think it's time to close the doors?"

"No." Dita shook her head vehemently. She now knew the truth about her Amalfi distraction. She had been used, but she refused to go down without a fight. Now that she knew their enemy was not mere marketplace competition, but likely sabotage, she could maneuver accordingly. "I think we can ride this season through. But we'll have to adopt a new strategy moving forward."

"You have something in mind?"

"Marcus and I are working on it," she said with more confidence than she felt. "We'll have our plans ready to present to you in a couple of weeks."

"You still feel we can do this?"

Anger lit a flame inside her, making her brief answer an emphatic "Yes."

"Then that's good enough for me." William raised his glass. "To success next year."

Dita joined the toast. The hand holding her glass shook, but even as she sipped the wine, a steely calm came over her, invading body and soul. She didn't know whether she was simply numb, or if this was how love was forged into hate. Whatever the feeling, she drew strength from it. This fight was far from over and, by the time she'd finished, she intended to teach Cate Morgan—Canton—the lesson of her life.

❖

Cate took her gym bag from the passenger seat and locked her car. Her late-evening trips to the sports center were a lifeline that helped her to relax, and right now, she needed all the help she could get. Though her work schedule was no less hectic, living in Manhattan took more of a toll than she'd anticipated.

She had envisioned dividing her time equally between Ferrara and New York, but her U.S. operations were expanding so rapidly she could already see the impracticality of her plan. Even after the building of her flagship store was complete, she knew she would have to be here to build the relationships that would make Zabor prosper. Saul was already talking about a third store, in Las Vegas.

But Zabor wasn't the only factor in her decision to remain in Manhattan after her frantic trip here the day she left Amalfi. Her mind taunted her with continuous self-reproach and remorse over Dita. She'd arrived too late to undo the damage with the Nordstrom contract, but had then set about trying to put right some of the mess she'd created over the past two years. Her first move had involved one of her best young designers, Leona Jarvis, whom she'd sent to "apply" for a position with Seraphim under explicit instructions not to reveal her previous employer. Through Leona, Cate planned to drip-feed new contacts that could help keep Dita's business solvent. So far, the subterfuge seemed to be working, even if Cate's conscience knew no peace.

She swiped her membership card in the door and entered the gym. The skeleton late-night staff already knew her and one of the trainers waved and said he would set up the weight circuit for her as soon as she'd finished on the treadmill. Cate preferred to run outdoors, but there was a lot to be said for a running machine. She found the rhythmic pace therapeutic, and it allowed her to zone out, a welcome respite for her troubled soul…but not tonight.

Tonight, things were different. For the last few days her mind had been playing tricks on her. Yesterday, on a drab and sunless afternoon, on the way back from a business meeting, she'd crossed a street and collided with a woman on the sidewalk. The stranger had not been paying attention and had run slap-bang into her. She'd apologized profusely, smiling with embarrassment before continuing on her way. Though entirely different in stature and shape, she had worn Dita's smile. Then today, on the phone, the client Cate was speaking with had laughed, but it was Dita's laugh Cate heard.

Irritated, she adjusted the treadmill controls, increasing the incline. As beads of perspiration collected on her brow, she began to wonder if she was losing her mind, for in everything she did, every place she went, all she heard or saw was Dita. It was as if her subconscious was obsessively searching for her. She couldn't go on like this and deep down, she knew the only way she would find any true peace was to seek out Dita and tell her the truth. Was it too late? Maybe, if she really did bare her soul…just maybe, Dita might forgive her. Wiping the sweat that trickled into her eyes, Cate felt a slight lifting of her spirits as she made the important decision to find Dita this week and tell her everything.

She made her plans as she completed her run and weights. She would fly to Boston, then phone Dita and ask if they could have dinner. If Dita refused, Cate would go to Seraphim and insist on a meeting. She was ready to deal with anger, even complete rejection, she was so desperate to see Dita again. She hoped the feeling was mutual. Cate longed to hear her voice and gentle laughter. Perhaps, before she confessed, the two of them might hug, and Cate would catch the scent of Dita once more. She hated the thought that it could be the last time Dita would allow her to touch her, but whatever the outcome, she had to take the risk. It didn't matter to her that Dita might not believe the story of her past and accept her reasons for deception. It *did* matter that Dita would believe she was sorry, and that she was in love with her… that the love between them had never been a sham.

Cate thanked the trainer and headed for the showers. She was the only client in the women's change area, which, since the wall clock announced one thirty a.m., wasn't surprising. She'd already discovered, however, that the Manhattan working day knew no bounds. Stepping beneath the hot water, Cate tilted her face into the refreshing spray and directed her thoughts to more mundane matters like whether she had enough food in the apartment. She disliked cooking and usually ordered in or ate at one of the countless restaurants within walking distance of her apartment, but she kept her refrigerator stocked with fruit, salads, and various antipasti.

Cate allowed the excess water to run off her body before wrapping the towel around her and stepping around the corner into the small locker room. Her snack planning came to an abrupt halt at the sight of the tall blonde standing there. Shocked and speechless, Cate stared into Dita's granite eyes and hardened face. This time her imagination wasn't playing tricks, and she didn't need a clairvoyant to tell her Dita wasn't waiting here for pleasantries, or a coincidental late night workout. The smartly dressed woman before her was angry.

What had Dita found out? Whatever it was, it appeared to be enough to bring her all the way from Boston to Manhattan, and at this late time of night. How had she even gained after-hours access to the gym or known where to find her? Was she following her?

"Not who you expected to see, am I, *Miss Morgan*?" Dita's voice rang out coldly. "Or should I address you as Miss Canton?"

Cate could only tighten the towel around her as a million thoughts raced through her mind and her anxiety levels hit the red zone. She'd dreamt of reclaiming Dita's love, but there was no look of smoldering lust on Dita's beautiful face, no emotional embers still burning there that hinted of the love they had shared. Cate saw only revulsion.

"Dita…" she mumbled, not knowing how to start. It was irrelevant anyway since Dita had no intention of letting her continue.

"Oh, you're clever. So cold, so calculating, and I, like a fool, fell for it all." Dita barely seemed to breathe as she stood there, still and controlled, but dangerously threatening.

Cate wisely remained motionless. She was briefly thankful when another late-night client entered from the gym. The woman took in the unfolding drama with a quick, nervous glance, getting more increased heart activity than she'd bargained for.

"Well?" Dita demanded, glaring at Cate.

The red-faced newcomer mopped her face with a towel and grabbed her sports bag. "I can see I'm interrupting something, so I'll leave you right to it."

After she all but ran out, leaving them alone again, Dita said, "I kept wondering why Seraphim was losing customers. Imagine my surprise when I saw the promotions for the range Nordstrom selected instead of ours. If I didn't know better I could have sworn I'd designed it myself. Oh wait, I did." She cast a long, scrutinizing scan over Cate, her eyes moving down the toweled woman and then back up again in a dismissive, trivializing manner. "And here's the really good bit." Sarcasm oozed. "Cate Morgan, the woman I thought I'd fallen in love with, was the only other person who'd seen them. No wonder you felt the need to comment on my...*infantile trust*?"

The woman I thought I had fallen in love with. The words resonated in Cate's head. "Dita, please, let me explain."

"What could you possibly explain? Are you denying that you stole my designs?" Dita didn't wait for a response. "I doubted it myself at first. I thought no one would sink that low. No one would do something so morally reprehensible as to deceive another in that way. How could that special person I met and fell in love with possibly be the same dishonorable spoilt brat who messed with drugs and ripped the heart out of her father? Who could be such a cold and calculating piece of vermin?"

Dita could have punched Cate in the face and done less damage. To hear the wrongful accusations of her youth return to haunt her, and to hear them from the woman she loved? Pain sliced through her like a cleaver. She had thought she couldn't be hurt anymore, not after all these years, but that was something else she'd miscalculated.

"You're wrong, Dita, it wasn't like that," Cate whispered.

Dita raised a hand. "Please, don't insult me with more lies. I know all I need to know about you and your sordid past. I hired an investigator after I found out who you really were. Silly me, I didn't want to misjudge you, so I obtained proof."

"Dita, I—"

"Even now, you still think you can manipulate me." Dita shook her head incredulously. "And you still think the world owes you. I can't believe the lengths you've gone to, to harm your father's company. How very resourceful that you would bother to seek *me* out. But best of all, using sex." She laughed mockingly. "I certainly fell for that, didn't I? You must have laughed your head off at how easy I was to lay."

As Dita's cynicism rose, Cate's heart plummeted. In the mirrors lining the change rooms, she could see the blood draining from her face.

Dita stepped closer and hovered over her, making their height difference very obvious. "Can't even defend yourself, Cate?"

"I know this looks bad, but I—"

"*Looks* bad? All those lies about being in stocks and shares...but then nothing should surprise me about your actions. And it's fascinating that so many of your staff appear to be reformed drug addicts and prostitutes. Hell, even your sales manager has done time."

He has? After Madeleine Zobbio's recommendation to hire him, Cate had never probed into Saul's past, something which he'd always hinted regret at and the need to move forward. If it was true, she felt no animosity for him, only sympathy.

Dita, on a vitriolic roll, moved toward the ridiculous. "Maybe you do a little drug business on the side, some trafficking? I guess the fashion industry would be the perfect front."

Cate listened to the cruel accusations knowing they emanated from hurt and, instead of being incensed by them, she felt only immeasurable sadness as the words tripped off Dita's lips, lips that not so long ago had passionately sought hers. Suddenly stopping, Dita looked lost and for a second, Cate saw the pain behind the hard-eyed accusations. She knew she had hurt Dita in the worst possible way. Without thinking, she reached forward to touch her but Dita drew back sharply.

"Dita, please listen to me. Whatever I did, whatever you think you know...you and I, that was *never* a lie. What I felt for you, what I *feel* for you, is real. I'm in love with you."

But Dita wasn't here for two-way conversation. She hadn't driven for hours down the interstate from Boston to listen to excuses or... Bile rose inside her and with it all the memories of her own wretched childhood, of being locked for days in a room while her mother went to other towns looking for *business*, of being left to feed herself on what little she could find, of the other children taunting and avoiding her because of who her mother was. Her childhood had been shredded by rejection and the casual duplicity of a mother for whom she was an inconvenience. If her grandmother hadn't plucked her out of that misery, Dita had no idea how she would have survived.

"Don't try to play on my emotions. I've met people like you before." Dita took perverse pleasure from the fact that she'd actually caught Cate out and placed the manipulative woman off balance. "No, actually I haven't—not exactly like you, for you are pure garbage. You had every advantage and you didn't need to sink so low. Other people aren't as fortunate."

"Dita, you have every right to be angry at me." Cate's voice was ragged and her knuckles were white in the hand that clutched the towel over her heart. Her hair dripped onto her shoulders, spilling in rivulets down the flesh Dita had yearned to touch. "I know I screwed up and I'm terribly sorry for what I did. You have to believe me."

"Give me one reason why I should."

"Because I love you. I was so blind...Dita, please. Can we start again?"

"There's no going back," Dita said simply. "You want to push Seraphim out of business? Well, you've come up against the wrong person because I'm not going to let you destroy everything we've achieved. I'm not afraid of you. I've known adversity in my life and I've always come through it, and I continue to trust myself and my abilities—*honest* abilities—to meet any of life's challenges. You see, Cate," she was whispering now, "I'm better than you. I believe in honor, courage and moral integrity...something you're not familiar with." She leaned in closer. "In case you don't understand me, I'm throwing down the gauntlet. I'll meet you on whatever ground you choose, and I will crush you," she spat the words out viciously. "Because in the end, I believe that good always wins over bad. Now we both know where we stand."

"Dita, don't." Cate's mouth shook so much she had to bite down on her bottom lip to control it. "We're not at war. I don't want to harm you."

Dita had already turned to walk away, but stopped and swung around. "Harm me? It's a bit late to worry about that now." Her eyes glittered like crystal shards. "You know, you made me feel good about myself. Those wonderful days in Italy, you have no idea...*no idea*...how I treasured them. I really thought that here was someone

I loved and who might love me, too. But all you've done is made me feel cheap and used." She paused to wipe at her tears. "I gave you something important, Cate. I gave you my heart, but it meant nothing to you. You threw it away like trash, treated it like something of no value, meaningless."

"Dita, stop." Cate took a few desperate steps toward her. "Please don't leave like this."

Dita looked broken as she gazed back at her, all challenge gone. "Has your heart ever been used? No, I already know the answer. I hope you get what you deserve in life."

She walked out, closing the door quietly behind her. By the time Cate had dragged some clothing on and run out after her, Dita was long gone, as were Cate's dreams.

Chapter Thirteen

Two Years Later

Dita looked out the window to an uninspiring, flaking white-washed brick wall that still bore the fading remains of an old beer advertisement. "Another new customer?" She swiveled her chair to face Leona. "Where on earth do you find these people?"

"Drunk at the Chicago apparel fairs." Leona grinned. "I'm the one who spares them humiliation by carrying them back to their rooms before they shame themselves and cheat on their husbands."

"A fifty thousand dollar order is a nice dividend on a debt of gratitude."

"You know me," the magician's apprentice continued, "always the bearer of glad tidings...I think."

Dita laughed. "You're my lucky charm, and you know it. What are you doing here so late on a Friday evening?"

"Uh...you've been so grumpy no one else would stay," Leona replied cheekily.

There was some truth in the teasing comment. They'd been overwhelmed with work, and Dita hadn't been able to complete her designs for the Fall range they would be showing in New York Fashion Week in just four months' time. It was already October. By now she usually had her preliminary samples in the sewers' hands. She hated falling behind, even if the reasons thrilled her. After almost six years of relentless effort, Seraphim was finally in the black and growing faster than she'd dared to dream. Her next Fashion Week show was going to carry them to a new level, but at this rate she would be lucky to bring together a coherent collection.

Dita's mood was foul today and she'd been unforgiving to her employees, the complete opposite of the way she normally managed the place, with a gentle hand on the tiller. The only one who dared to challenge her was Leona. The young woman knew her worth. She'd only been at Seraphim for two years, but in that time she'd brought in new customers almost every month.

"Earth to boss," Leona prompted and Dita realized she'd been asked a question.

"I'm sorry, what did you say?"

"I said you were cranky this time last year, too. And the year before."

"I was?" Dita arched one eyebrow.

"Oh, yeah. Everyone's making the sign of the cross before they come in here, same as last year."

"How on earth can you remember that?" Dita asked.

"It's my anniversary…you know, the anniversary of when you took pity on me and gave me a job." Mischief glowed in the young woman's eyes.

Dita sighed. This time two years ago she'd just returned from Amalfi after making the worst mistake of her life. She hadn't realized how much that miserable experience still affected her mood every time she worked on Fall designs. "I'll lighten up," she promised. "Now go home. Have a life. You've earned it."

Dita continued working for another hour or two after Leona left, until she'd made headway with her final designs. It was after ten when she gathered her stuff to go home. Rolling her neck to ease the knots, she switched off the lights and took the stairs down to ground level. It was raining but the walk to Seraphim's parking lot was short. They'd expanded their building six months earlier and now shared parking with a legal firm a block away.

Dita reached deep into her coat pocket to find her keys, jangling them reassuringly as she quickened her pace. The narrow alleyway she usually cut through to reach her car looked innocent enough during the day, but she avoided it at this time of night. Dita hesitated as she approached it, then decided only fools or work addicts would be out in this weather. She took the shortcut, striding confidently, her keys in her hand. She didn't see the man until he stepped out in front of her and demanded money. Shocked, she didn't move at first.

"Hand it over, bitch," he yelled, making a grab for her purse.

Dita wrenched herself free, shoving him off-balance. She tried to make a run for it, turning back the way she came. But he was too quick, and with lightning speed threw himself at her. She caught the glint of a metal blade as light bounced off it from the street lamp a few yards away. Forced backward, with his elbow and arm pushed tight against her throat, she was slammed up against a wall and felt him push hard against her, this time into her chest. Then, quite miraculously, he stepped back and released her.

Maybe it was the look in his eyes that made Dita glance down and see the hilt of the knife protruding from her chest. How strange, for other than the rough shove, Dita hadn't felt the knife go in. She stared at him, realizing how young he was, and her assailant's eyes grew wide and frightened.

It must have dawned on him that she might recognize him later, and in slow motion, Dita saw him reach out, painfully extract the knife, then plunge it into her again before he ran off into the night as if the very devil pursued him. Still standing, she watched the rain cutting through the night air, backlit by an arc of light beyond the alley. Then her world grew disproportionate as she slowly slid down the wall to the cold, unaccommodating ground. The pain hit her then and when she reached for the source she felt the awful warm stickiness of her own blood.

She called out and managed to crawl a few steps closer to the street lamp before her body no longer responded. She heard the sound of a car door slamming somewhere not far away, but as she tried to wave her vision blurred and turned pitch black.

❖

Things happen in life that we never forget. For Cate, one of those times was the week her mother died. She remembered how she'd been emotionally overwhelmed, and how empty she'd felt inside. Nothing around her had brought any comfort. Unable to eat or sleep, she'd spent those dreadful days walking in a sea of anxiety, crying and fretting for the loved mother she would never see again. She'd relived that helpless despair again the day Caroline died. The loss, and her guilt that she'd been the one driving, had been hellish enough, but even worse was the recognition she'd been robbed of something precious, the bond between two sisters who should have grown up and gotten old together. Cate had thought they would always be there for each other. She'd been wrong.

Now, faced with the news of Dita's attack and her tenuous hold on life, all Cate's worst fears were back. Whoever would have thought that Dita would be stabbed in a Boston alleyway, walking to her car. The horrifying news had spread like wildfire through the fashion community. No one knew if she was going to survive. Cate couldn't begin to envisage a life without Dita, without knowing that she would occasionally glimpse her at some event or other, from a distance. Of course, she'd given up any hope that she would ever feel her touch again, or caress, or kiss. She would never be able to reclaim the intimacy they'd shared. She was Dita's past. A bad memory. Yet she still felt connected to her.

Cate hadn't stopped to think before she caught the first plane to Boston and rushed to the hospital. She was turned away by a nurse who all but escorted her from the building, explaining that Dita was in critical care and no visitors were allowed. Only immediate family. Maybe it was a coping mechanism that drew her to the narrow, tall Seraphim building. Unable to be with Dita, Cate frantically sought an avenue where she might be useful. Someone would have to keep things moving at the fashion house until Dita was able to take over again. Good man though Marcus was, he was not a designer. He'd been hired years ago by her mother to handle the administration and manage client relationships. He would be able to hold the company together for a few weeks, but time didn't stand still. By now, Dita was probably working her way through samples and color swatches, modifying her designs for the Fall collection she would show in New York early next year.

Memories assailed Cate with every step as she entered the building. Fifteen years had passed since she'd last set foot in these familiar rooms. Where had all that time gone? She wondered if she shouldn't just turn and run, instead of interfering where she most definitely wasn't welcome. But she wasn't doing this for herself, she was doing this for the woman she loved.

She found Marcus sitting at his desk and raised her hands in a gesture of peace as he looked up. "I know, I know. I shouldn't be here, but I need an answer from someone. How bad is she?"

Marcus had been good to her when she was a kid, even after hearing about her supposed delinquent behavior. To his credit, he didn't pole-vault his desk now and throw her bodily out of the building. "The knife missed her heart, but she lost a lot of blood."

Fear crushed the air from Cate's lungs. Feeling lightheaded, she asked, "Is there anything I can do?"

"You shouldn't be here, Miss Canton." Marcus made his allegiance clear. "We're not looking for a replacement if that's what you're hoping for, especially one who tried to put us out of business. Dita's injured, but she's not dead."

She smiled sagely. "You know, Marcus, if I could turn back time, I truly would. I'd love to wipe away all the harm I've done, but I guess if I could do that, I'd be selling some kind of commodity, wouldn't I?"

Marcus's expression remained polite but distant. "How can I help you?" he asked, obviously wanting to move things along and have her leave.

"Actually, I wanted to know if I could help *you*? I know you'll doubt this, and you have every reason to, but I know the Fall collection must be at a critical stage right now and that without Dita…" Cate trod carefully. "I'd like to help complete the work if I can."

Marcus raised eyes filled with astonishment. "Even if your offer made sense, your father would never allow you to be involved, not after all you've done."

Damn it. Cate had hoped irrationally that the full extent of her treachery wasn't known to anyone but Dita. She should have guessed that anyone who really mattered in Seraphim knew everything. "I'll leave, Marcus, but one final question." She carefully chose her words. "If you were ever able to trust me, if you could believe that I really wanted to help Dita despite what I've done…if I somehow managed to get my father's permission to be here, would you be able to work with me?"

Poor Marcus. He didn't try to hide his astonishment at the ludicrous question.

"Bit of a long shot, huh?" She couldn't fail to see the humor in the request.

He shook his head. "I suppose if miracles were ever to happen… I personally have nothing against you, though I have to say your behavior has been—"

"Reprehensible," Cate finished honestly.

"Yes." His straightforward response only added to her discomfort. When he spoke again, his anxiety was apparent. "I guess we could do with whatever help we can get right now." The minute he'd confessed, he obviously regretted it, adding, "Not that I'm suggesting you—"

"It's okay, Marcus, our secret. I promise," she whispered. "Thank you for not throwing me out. You had every right."

She nodded amiably, and left his office. She had another visit to make—one even more unpleasant.

❖

"Cate…" The word hung in the air as William found himself at a loss for what to say. He knew her at first glimpse, the slim, well-dressed woman standing over by the window, silhouetted in the light. He saw the same daughter he remembered all those years ago, but now grown to full adulthood, her face that of an attractive woman and very much her mother's daughter. Instantly emotional, he had to fight to regulate his breathing, realizing the truth in the saying that someone could take one's breath away.

At first, she said nothing, and they stood still, taking stock of each other. William saw the minutest twitch around her left eye, a reassuring movement, for he recalled how it had always betrayed a young Cate's nervousness. Some things never changed. "It's been awhile," he said, closing the door quietly behind him. How much love could infuse a simple statement? He didn't know but with every ounce of his being, he'd poured it into his tone.

"Yes, it has." Polite and cool. Cate's inscrutable features gave nothing away.

"I'm sorry I kept you waiting." Reconciled that one day this reunion had been bound to happen, William had rehearsed for years what he would say when he saw Cate again. He would tell her how sorry he was, how he should have stood by her all those years ago, that he regretted everything and that he begged her forgiveness. He would tell her that he loved her. But instead, today frozen with shock, his mind went blank and he found himself reverting to the comfort of business speak on meeting a new client. He was mildly comforted to see she was having much the same problem.

"I understand. I should have made an appointment." There was no malice or subtext in Cate's response, merely an acknowledgment that by turning up unexpectedly, she'd had to wait to see him. Very civil, very unemotional.

"You never have to make an appointment, Cate." He spoke softly, praying some telepathic family connection would communicate his affection. Years ago they'd both been so close they had joked about possessing the ability to read each other's minds. But now?

"Thank you. That's good to know."

William didn't miss the lack of any personal chord and it saddened him. Quite how he thought she'd act toward him, he didn't know. Maybe he'd expected anger, open loathing, but this cordial, civilized stranger who offered no emotion at all left him aching inside.

"Coffee?" he offered.

"Thank you, no. I don't plan to be here long."

Ah, so that's the way of it. No hope today then of building bridges.
"You don't mind if I do?" William was struggling to maintain composure at seeing her again after all this time. The pouring of coffee allowed him to postpone things a while, to gather his thoughts and emotions. As he lifted the pot he noticed the slight tremor in his hand and was grateful when Cate spoke.

"The office hasn't changed much."

William glanced around at the old-fashioned wood paneled walls and an array of aging high-backed, green leather armchairs. And, of course, there was his much loved oak desk. "I've never been one for office décor. I suppose I like the familiarity of all this. Maybe if I leave it long enough, it'll become fashionable again."

He'd hoped his small attempt at humor might garner a response, but it fell fallow and Cate looked like she was having second thoughts about her visit. He gazed at her warmly, needing her to know there was no animosity from him, not anymore. He knew what she'd done to create Seraphim's apparent run of bad luck, and it had been a shock to discover that his daughter thirsted for revenge. But he would not be drawn into blame and reproach. He owed her that.

"I'm sure my taste in décor isn't what you're here to talk about, is it, Cate?" he said finally. It was time to get the agenda out into the open and put them both out of their misery.

Cate actually allowed herself a half-smile, appreciating his ability to stay calm and professional. She knew he was struggling, for she'd heard the tremor in his voice and seen the slight shaking of his hand as he poured the coffee he then left untouched. He was nervous. She hadn't expected that. Neither had she expected her own reactions. She'd thought she might be tense and ill at ease, more affected when confronting her father for the first time since that angry conversation in Italy fifteen years ago. It seemed, however, that time had exhausted those emotions, leaving only a residue of apathy. It was time for her to come to the point. This reunion was already too long.

"I won't insult your intelligence and pretend you aren't fully informed of what I've been doing with regard to Mother's business. Nor my conduct toward Dita Newton."

William didn't need reminding. Every little detail was burned into him—and he understood her motives only too well. What he didn't understand was why she was here now, after all this time. Uncompromising blue eyes bored into him, and he was grateful again for the coffee as a distraction.

Cate continued, her tone softening. "I never expected to like her, but I did. The more I got to know her, the more uncomfortable I felt with what I was doing."

"It didn't stop you wrecking the Nordstrom contract," William pointed out.

"I tried to terminate the deal, but yes…I messed up. You see, even though she didn't know who I was at that time, we became…friends. That may seem strange to you, and it certainly surprised me, but Dita's very difficult to not like…don't you think?"

William leaned back into the seat, intrigued. Maybe it was the way she spoke Dita's name or the tenderness that crept into her eyes, but he knew there was affection present. "I agree, naturally. We're all very fond of her, and we're hoping for the best. Meanwhile, I'm left wondering what brings you here."

His eyes were kinder than Cate remembered, and a confliction of wisdom and sorrow played in their depths, a recognition that she wasn't here to see him, but was compelled to come to him because she wanted something. The look made her feel an emotion she couldn't explain. "I know what I did in Italy was wrong, and that I hurt Dita considerably, both professionally...and personally, but I want to make up for it. The only way I know how is to help her while she's in hospital."

Her father's eyes narrowed. "What do you have in mind?"

"I know how much Seraphim means to Dita. But she could be unable to work for months. That's a long time in fashion."

"We have a talented team." A defensive note entered William's voice and Cate warmed to him because of it. "They'll do whatever it takes."

She understood his message, that Dita had loyal staff who could not be won over by a usurper, especially one who had tried to damage their label. But she had to deliver a reality check. "You don't have anyone who can complete the collection for Fashion Week. No one is capable of working with her creativity and vision...but I am." She paused, allowing him to absorb the unexpected twist in direction. "I need you to allow me access to Seraphim. I'll finish Dita's collection for her."

William choked and had to put his cup down. "I'll say this for you, when you choose to surprise someone, you really do it beautifully. Let me get this right. You expect me to just let you walk into the business under the ruse of wanting to help? I can't believe you're even suggesting this, Cate. It's unethical."

"Yes." What else could she say? "I know it's a difficult leap of faith for you to make, but think about it. The design process for the next collection is at a crucial stage. If it's not done well, you could destroy Dita's reputation and kill the company."

"Dita's got a young girl who works closely with her..."

"Leona? Yes, I sent her."

Shock registered on her father's face, then a guarded, creeping suspicion replaced it. "What do you mean?"

"I wanted to make up for Nordstrom. So I sent my best designer, one I was personally grooming. Through Leona, I've been drip-feeding Dita new business, to make up for the loss." She paused. "Dita doesn't know, and I'd like to keep it that way."

William shook his head, stunned. "I can't do this. For Dita's sake."

"No, for Dita's sake you must. I know her designs inside and out. Every color, every cut, every fabric. And I've watched her process firsthand. I know how she thinks. Marcus must have told you that she doesn't put half of her ideas on paper. Most of it is in her head."

William grimaced. "That's a big help."

"Please," Cate urged quietly. "It's too late to bring someone else in and even if you did find anyone, they wouldn't do her designs justice. But I can." William wasn't answering but she could see he was at least considering her proposal. She tossed a few nuggets in to try and swing the decision. "Dita would never have to know. Besides you, it would just be Marcus, Leona, and me. I'd keep very much in the background. But together, I know we can meet the deadlines and complete her collection. Please let me do this for her. Can't you trust me this once?"

William's eyes shot up sharply to meet hers. What a loaded set of options she'd placed before him. *Can't you trust me this once?* He'd denied her his trust all those years ago. Was he going to deny it again? Every fiber in his body warned him against handing her the opportunity to preside over the utter destruction of Seraphim. How wickedly glorious it would be to deceive her father, who had once let her down, into playing his own significant role in the coup de grâce. How would he face Dita?

William had no doubt that Cate spoke the truth about no one else being able to finish Dita's collection. And what if her intentions were genuine? If he turned her down, one thing was for sure, he would never see her again…she really would be lost to him forever. Could he handle that? In the end, he felt it was inconsequential whether she was making him a pawn in some clever master plan against his own interests. He *owed* her. He had to do this.

With the deepest sigh, and a step into dangerous waters, he said, "Okay. I'll make the necessary arrangements with Marcus."

"Thank you." It was the first civil comment she'd made to him in years. Her business apparently over, her aim achieved, she started to leave. "I'll give my contact details to your secretary. Please let me know when I can start."

"Wait." William's voice rose. He felt vulnerable and desperate. She couldn't leave, not yet. He'd not seen her for so long. She couldn't just walk out after all this time, he was hungry to simply look at her. Besides, there was so much to be said, much he needed to let her know. He bargained for time, focusing on the practicalities. "You'll need somewhere to stay. This is going to be a lot of hard work and you can't keep commuting back and forth between here and…New York."

Marcus had told him where she lived. He watched her exit slow as she contemplated his words.

"I'll find somewhere." Usually a meticulous planner, she hadn't considered accommodation. Her thoughts had been too preoccupied with Dita.

William cringed. This was such a dispassionate discussion to be having with his estranged daughter. Far more serious things sat between them. "You'd be welcome to stay with me at home." He regretted his stupid idea even before he suggested it. Cate would *never* consider this an option, and no surprise, he watched her eyes darken. "Or there's the *Catalina*. She's still moored down at the harbor."

"You still have her?" *After all these years?* Cate was shocked. When her mother had been alive, the family had spent glorious summers aboard her, vacations that now seemed a lifetime away.

"Well, she's still afloat and livable, though I doubt she's seaworthy anymore, but I've never been able to part with her. Too many memories."

"Is that why you kept Seraphim?" Cate asked without thinking. She'd had often wondered why he kept pouring good money after bad on what had been, until Dita, an unprofitable business.

"No, Cate," he said flatly. "I kept Seraphim for you. It should have been yours all along, but for my stupidity. But it's still there waiting for you when you're ready."

No roll of drums, no flash of lightning, but the impact was gargantuan. Cate clasped her hands to stop them from shaking. He'd kept the business for *her*? She knew he wasn't lying. He'd been nothing but truthful in all his dealings with her—a man of honor. What pathetic irony. To discover that the business she'd tried so hard to destroy and make hers, had always been hers. And now she was trying to rebuild it for someone else. Could anything be more asinine?

But her head reigned supreme over her heart and she gave nothing away, no sign that he'd caught her out and temporarily rocked her foundations. Steeling herself against emotion that might weaken her, she said, "The *Catalina*'s a great idea, better than a boring hotel room."

Years ago, she and Caroline would run down from the house across the extensive, manicured lawns, through the wooded glen at the bottom and across the little dirt track that led to the private harbor. Even when the vessel had been going nowhere, they'd often picnicked on its deck and sunbathed.

"Consider her your home for as long as you need her," William said. "I'll arrange for a set of keys to be ready for collection from the harbor office."

Cate hesitated a few seconds but then tipped her head in acknowledgment. This arrangement would give her more time to work on Dita's collection. It would do. "Thanks. I'll get to work."

William wanted nothing more than to open his arms and pull her to him before she walked out the door, but one look at her told him she would never allow this. She was a stranger before him now, and content to be that. William's heart ached. In a bid to establish some common ground, he blurted, "Cate, both you and I have made our mistakes, ones we wish we could take back. I want you to know I'm sorry. And I love you."

Cate heard the emotion but it didn't register in the parts of her closed off to him, and she didn't know if it ever would. Perhaps the damage was done. "I have to go," she said, avoiding the disappointment in his eyes. "They wouldn't let me see Dita at the hospital. I'm going back."

He walked her to the door and Cate offered her hand, to avoid the awkwardness of having to rebuff an unwanted hug. Her father seemed to understand. After their formal handshake, he said, "Good luck."

Cate made the one concession she could. "I'll stay in touch."

As she strolled to her rental car, she couldn't stop marveling that her father had kept the business all these years, waiting for her return. She'd wasted all that time, lost in anger, sending back the letters he wrote her and plotting to make Seraphim hers…when it always had been. She should have felt overjoyed with the outcome and discoveries of this day. Why, then, did she feel like a loser?

CHAPTER FOURTEEN

Dita surfaced from sleep and immediately wished she hadn't. The last time she'd been conscious, the pain had been bearable, but now it radiated through her. She clenched her teeth together, squeezed her eyes shut, and hoped the action might bring relief. It did not.

"Hey there, you." A voice like syrup flowed and she tried to wake up fully, but couldn't. She was aware of someone in her room and was comforted by the presence. Hospitals were not a place to feel alone.

"You're here," she mumbled, feeling stupid the minute the words left her mouth. Her insides felt as though they were on fire and every part of her ached. "I feel like shit," she declared.

Soft laughter took her away to a sunnier place, where the ocean glittered and the soft, discordant clatter of boat masts soothed her. She was floating again, almost in a dream. A hand held hers. Soft lips brushed her forehead. She smiled, then began to frown. Even when drugged, she dreamt of Cate. Love wasn't something one could flick off with a switch and say "well, that's over now," and disconnect. How was she supposed to recover from that?

"Damn you," she mumbled.

Cate leaned in to hear better, but she couldn't make out the words Dita kept repeating. She glanced toward the door, torn between stealing all the precious time she could and summoning a nurse because Dita was suddenly restless. Cate hated hospitals. People died in them. People she loved died in them.

Though memories of Caroline assaulted her and every brain cell she possessed told her this was a bad idea, she'd found it impossible to stay away. Her name was not on the list of authorized visitors—why did that not surprise her? At first she'd reasoned with a nurse who seemed friendly and told her to wait while she checked to see if Dita could have a brief visit with her. When the nurse returned, she was far less friendly and in a terse manner informed Cate that the patient did not want to see her.

All Cate wanted was to *see* Dita, with her own eyes. Maybe then, the panic that consumed her would ease and she would be able to think about something else. She'd tried to explain, but the nurse said that if she continued to be a nuisance, both patient and hospital would view it as harassment.

Cate had forlornly accepted this but asked the nurse to pass a message to Dita that she cared and hoped she'd be well soon. Cate needed Dita to know she loved her and that she missed her desperately, but one look at the nurse's dour, unforgiving face told her this was a message unlikely to be delivered. She would have to wait until Dita was discharged before she'd get an opportunity to say such things.

Desolate, Cate had left the nursing station and taken the elevator to another level. After gathering herself, she returned to the ward and crept around, systematically checking each room until she found Dita. She didn't want to disturb her or upset her, so she'd lingered just inside the door for several minutes watching her sleep. When Dita became restless, Cate had moved to her bedside to soothe her. For a short while it seemed to work, but the drugs were starting to wear off and Cate knew Dita was in pain.

She was about to call for the nurse when a pair of hazy blue eyes looked up at her and Dita started to cry. "Go away," she muttered weakly. "I don't want you here."

Cate had predicted this outcome, but it still hurt.

"She's radically changed the direction of some of her designs into…" Marcus motioned hopeless confusion, "what I think are a visionary set of ideas."

"But?" Cate targeted his uncertainty.

They were in Dita's office, hovering like vultures over a large table as he briefed her on how far along the design process Dita's new collection was. He wasn't painting a great picture.

"But you see, the late changes mean she hadn't finished capturing them on paper, and everyone is trying to work with half-drawn sketches." Marcus's frustration showed. "You know I've got years in the business and I think I'm intuitive, but—"

"You're not a designer," Cate said sympathetically as she continued to study the drawings in front of her.

"No, I'm not. Look at this." He stabbed a finger at an incomplete sketch. "I don't know whether she wants buttons, bows, zippers, or padlocks here."

Cate couldn't help smiling at his descriptive evaluation of the problem. Casting her eye quickly over the sketch and others Marcus had laid out in front of her, she could see it was but one dilemma among many. "What about the rest?" she asked, knowing she was only looking at a small selection of Dita's work.

Marcus hesitated, clearly fearful of showing her too much and betraying Dita. Loyalties weren't easily laid aside, and trust was not handed over readily to one who had done so much damage and for so long.

Sensing his ambivalence, Cate touched his arm wanting to make some form of connection, which right now was horribly absent. "If I was in your shoes," she said gently, "I wouldn't trust me either." She sprang into action, grabbing a small sheet of tracing paper and placing it over one of Dita's designs, a pencil rapidly beginning to sketch. "Here's what I'd do. I'd conceal the zipper within the inlay of the pleat. Simple, old fashioned, and damn quick to produce." She smiled up at him and arched a brow. "Flattering to the figure, nice easy lines, and simple to maintain…the customers will love it."

"Dita will never accept your help," Marcus tendered unhelpfully.

"She doesn't have to know, Marcus. I'm not going to tell her, and the only others who know are William and Leona. Trust me, they're not going to say anything. All Dita has to know is that you and Leona worked like honeybees to bring her collection together."

"You don't think she's going to be suspicious?"

It wasn't so much a question, more a statement of the obvious, but Cate wasn't listening. She'd soon complete what she'd set out to do, it was unlikely to become an issue. In less than a week, she would walk away as if she'd never been here, like a ghost that had been exorcised, never to return. She did feel like a disembodied spirit, for after all didn't they haunt places because something tied them there, because they didn't want to leave? Cate didn't want to leave either, and for too many reasons.

This had been her mother's place, and being here, Cate felt close to her again. The whole concept of "family" had been sadly missing in her life for many years but it was resuscitated here through happy memories. It was also where Dita worked and something about being here felt strangely intimate. Cate would often find herself thinking, *This is the desk she sits at, this is the window she looks out of,* or *this is the phone she touches.* It was unlikely she would ever be close to Dita again, so she treasured these small echoes of the woman she loved.

"Leona's a talented designer," she told Marcus. "And you can tell Dita you got hit by a wave of inspiration."

Marcus frowned, knowing as Cate did that Dita would never fall for that. Inspiration was not a word synonymous with him. Sighing, Cate couldn't budge his misgivings, and those had to go if they were going to work together and save Seraphim. Despite admiring his faithfulness and loyalty toward Dita, now was not the time to let them dominate. She noticed he was giving her another of those questioning stares he'd been casting at her all morning.

She looked him straight in the face. "You want to know why I'm doing this, don't you. Why I'm *really* doing this." She figured the slight widening of his eyes was all the acknowledgment she was going to get. "It's because I might sleep better at night. We give Dita her blaze of glory, bring her designs to life…and I get to sleep better."

Marcus said nothing and walked out of the office, leaving Cate to wonder if this strange partnership was ever going to succeed. It didn't matter what permission her father had given, if Marcus couldn't work with her, the whole venture would die before it began. As her depression built, Marcus re-entered with half a dozen rolled-up sketches in his arms.

"There," he said dourly, throwing them onto the table. "They all need to be finished, and if we're going to have any chance of meeting the deadlines, the sewers need to be working on samples next week."

Trust at last, or at least as much as he was willing to grant. As Cate stared at the missing designs it dawned on her the immensity of the task ahead. So much work and such little time. Could it be done?

With vigor, she sharpened her pencil.

❖

Several weeks later, three "conspirators" were sitting relaxed and slightly drunk having consumed too much champagne. The sound of their laughter echoed down the hallway of Seraphim.

"We've actually done it. We've finished it all," Leona said jubilantly, a wide grin on her pixie, youthful features as she punched the air dramatically.

Cate, who was curled up in an old comfy armchair stuffed in the corner of Marcus's office, shook her head. "I can say it now, Marcus, but when you came into the room with those rolled-up designs, and said how much time we had to get them to the pattern cutter, I honestly thought we weren't going to make it."

"I feel great." It was as if Marcus hadn't heard her at all. He sat behind his desk, elbows firmly on the flat surface, supporting his head in both hands.

"That's because you're drunk!" Leona laughed.

Marcus smiled like an imbecile. Normally a man of moderate behavior, tonight he had let himself go, and Cate, looking fondly at him, couldn't stop herself from joining in Leona's laughter.

"She's going to be thrilled when she gets back," he slurred. "I know she's been worrying about her collection, despite what William and I have told her." He received no immediate response from his companions, who continued to sip their champagne. "I miss her, you know. A very pretty woman...lovely...nature."

Leona made a choking noise. It amused her too to see him like this. "If I didn't know better, Marcus, I'd say you had a little eye for Dita."

"No, no," he denied adamantly. "I'm merely saying that I miss her. Nothing wrong in that, is there?" He was mildly defensive.

Leona shared a glance with Cate. "No, it's perfectly natural to miss her. You've worked closely together."

"I admire your loyalty, Marcus." Cate meant it. "She's very lucky to have someone like you working for her, and I can see what there is to miss." She showed more emotion than she meant to.

Marcus said nothing, but looked across at Cate and a quiet understanding passed between them. She wondered if he *really* knew what had happened between her and Dita in Italy, or was it all guesswork on his part? Sometimes she thought he knew everything.

"Mind you," he blabbered on. "If I was twenty years younger..." He let the sentence hang in the air. "But I'd still never be her type." He stole another look at Cate, no ill will or negativity implied.

Marcus does know, Cate thought, and she might have pursued the thread of conversation but for the fact her two cohorts had suddenly frozen like the mannequins surrounding them. Cate saw the reflection first, in the window. The light of the room portrayed the unexpected image against a backdrop of the night's blackness. Turning her head slowly and barely breathing, she found herself looking at a figure in the frame of the door. *Dita!*

Like an avenging angel, Seraphim's fashion director stared at them, her body motionless yet coiled tight like a spring waiting to ricochet into action. A dangerous and warning stance, but Cate's heart refused to concede it. She immediately reacted and rose to face the one she'd longed to see, her heart beating wildly as her eyes feasted. Dita was thinner, and this made her appear taller, yet her presence verified the remarkable recovery she had made. Cate's eyes searched Dita's, longing to make a connection, smiling as she did, unable to hide her euphoria—her love. It chilled her to the bone when marble eyes eventually focused on her, a silent message that love was not returned. Cate could hear Leona's voice, hammering out some fabrication to explain her presence here.

"Dita! We were celebrating finishing the collection. Cate...Miss Canton unexpectedly called by to ask how you were, to see if we had any news. We offered her a glass, too. That's why she's here."

The excuses weren't cutting it. Who asks an apparent enemy to hang around for champagne?

"It's great to see you," Leona finished lamely, her enthusiastic smile of seconds ago disappearing.

Like an automaton, Dita turned on a heel toward Cate, and made no attempt to disguise her seething resentment. "Get out."

Marcus attempted to intercede, but too drunk, he stumbled back heavily into his chair, making a lot of noise. Still reeling from the caustic power of those two words, Cate tried to steady herself. She'd hoped that time and success would have eased Dita's feelings toward her since that dreadful meeting in the gym, but nothing had changed. Cate felt terrible but realized that this was not the time or the place to try and appeal to Dita's better senses. Though she longed for the opportunity to do just that, she accepted the situation and capitulated to the demand. There were others to think of...poor Marcus and Leona. She dreaded to imagine what would take place when she left. For them, she would leave quickly, and also for Dita. Though she'd had made a remarkable recovery, Cate didn't want to place her under any more stress.

Cate cast Leona a sympathetic glance as she silently grabbed her coat and left the office. As she walked past Dita, she heard the phone ring and caught Marcus saying, "Yes, we know. She's here."

Damn it. Just one more hour and Dita would never have known.

❖

"Rather a cozy scene," Dita barked acidly at Marcus after she heard the outside door close. "Your choice of drinking partner is questionable given what she's done to us. I trust you have a good reason."

Marcus struggled to form his words and he ended up over enunciating everything. "Dita, it's wonderful to see you, and I'm sure I do have a good reason, but...I'm very much afraid I'm drunk. I don't suppose we could discuss this in the morning?"

The tension was so thick, it could have been plaited.

Dita's response was hard. "We'll discuss this now, and please don't assume because I've been ill, I've become gullible. That was far too homey a scene for my liking. How could you let *her* in here? She's tried to destroy us, you know that, and here you are, playing buddies? Are you so stupid to think she won't try any trick in the book to bring this business down?" She watched him pathetically trying to blink himself sober. "If you can't see that, Marcus, I don't see us continuing to work together."

"You can't talk to Marcus like that," Leona protested. "Not after everything he's done for you. He's worked so hard to keep on top of things while you've been away, and… Miss Canton, she wasn't doing any harm. She's been worried sick ever since you were attacked, and only wanted to find out how you were. I know she's not—"

But Leona never had a chance to finish. Dita moved only her head to alter direction from Marcus to her. "You're fired."

"What?" For a second, Leona didn't seem to understand what had just been said.

"You are fired," Dita repeated more slowly.

The young designer's mouth dropped open. "You can't mean that?" Her anger evaporated and her voice was suddenly very young. "But I've done nothing wrong, and I've worked so hard…we both have. You can't fire me, Dita. *Please.*"

"Leave this building now. Get out."

Where was Dita's trademark warmth? Where was the camaraderie that had existed between them almost from the word go? It didn't matter that she had been sent here by Cate, Leona had genuinely taken to Dita and an instant bond had formed between them. She was so shocked, tears flooded her eyes. How could Dita do this? How could she sack her like this when they had laughed together, shared sandwiches, worked late, and talked designs for hours? Leona could hardly believe it but looking at Dita, she saw the same steely resolve her boss had shown only minutes ago when she threw Cate out.

Marcus had somehow managed to get to his feet and seemed to have sobered amazingly quickly given the circumstances. "Leo," he said calmly, all signs of slurring gone, his face deeply serious. "Best go home. I'll be in touch tomorrow. I'll try and sort this out, but…" He arched his eyebrows at her, the silent suggestion that she'd achieve nothing tonight, not with Dita's current frame of mind.

Leona's eyes flicked rapidly between him and Dita, then back to him again, before she finally left in tears.

"Beautifully handled, Dita," he said, not without a good measure of sarcasm. He moved away from his chair and indicated Dita should sit. Regardless of what had just taken place, she would be tired. "It truly is good to have you back, but I wish you'd waited to see what's been going on before you took such a heavy hand."

"I have eyes," she said sharply, not bothering to sit.

He smiled scornfully. "And don't I know it. You shouldn't have done that to Leona. I was the one who invited Cate Canton in for a drink."

"Whose side are you on, Marcus?"

There was a demand to the question, and it instantly infuriated him. "You have to ask? Your side, Dita...*always* your side!"

CHAPTER FIFTEEN

Due to poor weather, passengers are advised that all flights out of Houston this evening are canceled until further notice. Please check with your airline representative for further information."

The unwelcome announcement echoed across the airport terminal. Like a well-rehearsed chorus, the passengers at the gate chanted their disappointment, Dita among them.

After an alarming, bumpy flight into Houston, compliments of the rapidly worsening summer storms, and then the news that her connecting flight to Albuquerque had been canceled until at least tomorrow morning, she'd thought things couldn't get worse. But then her worst nightmare came true. Not only did she spot Cate Canton in the terminal, apparently caught up in the chaos, but later, when she checked into the most convenient airport hotel for the night, who should be in line at the desk but Cate.

Moaning to herself about bad luck and incredible coincidences as she ordered a bottle of wine from the hotel bar, Dita spied Cate tucked into a corner of the room, sitting alone with a glass of wine in front of her. Dita swore to herself, cursing that this really was like some sick joke, to be stuck somewhere she didn't want to be, in a hotel she didn't particularly rate, and too close to someone she wouldn't spit on if they were on fire.

She contemplated making a run for her room once she was served her wine, but Dita was damned if she was going to let Cate's presence negotiate the terms. She was in control now and would let Cate know that she wasn't the slightest bit fazed by her appearance. As the barman returned with her wine, she asked him for an extra glass, and then casually ambled over to where Cate was sitting.

Cate, intensely aware of Dita's presence, had been watching her since she'd entered the bar. She knew Dita had seen her at the airport, both quickly diverting their gaze from one another, but to then end up in the same hotel? *Oh, for crying out loud!* Now she could see Dita moving toward her, like a bloodhound scenting a trail, and Cate wondered what sort of scene was about to unfold. The last time they had met was at the fashion show, and that had not gone well. She counted to five and mentally prepared herself.

In a smart pair of beige trousers and a crisp cream cotton blouse that accentuated her figure, Dita came to a graceful halt at the small round table where Cate was sitting. Cate immediately wished she'd put more effort into her attire that day, suddenly feeling very underdressed in her favorite faded jeans and light cotton sweater.

"What an unexpected *joy* to see you here," Dita declared, purposefully hovering over Cate. Though polite, there was no hiding her unfriendly undertone. "Business?" she probed as she deliberately cast her eyes disdainfully over Cate's appearance.

"No." Cate feigned calm, but her heart turned traitor and started pounding away inside her to some primal beat. "I'm going to an art exhibition in Albuquerque."

"Me, too." Dita appeared surprised. "I assume you're going to the Ketcher exhibition?"

"If we ever get there." Cate raised her eyebrows in surprise. "How did you know—"

"You mentioned once how much you liked his work. You probably don't remember. You would have had *other* things on your mind at the time." The sarcasm flowed like molten lava.

Cate remembered very well, in fact the memory of that conversation had returned vividly when she saw the listing for the exhibition. She had mentioned her love of the artist's work that wonderful evening when they had shared dinner at a small Amalfi restaurant, the same evening she had realized she was in love with Dita. Maybe she had had other things on her mind that night, like desire, though she doubted that was what Dita hinted at.

"Anyway, so many people are raving about him, I decided to see what the fuss is about." Dita placed the bottle down on the table with the two glasses, astounded by the bizarre coincidence that they had both had the same urge at the same time. "I was going to suggest we share a bottle together, but I see you're ahead of me." She glanced at Cate's empty wineglass. "Thought you never drank alone?"

"Things change," Cate said wistfully.

"Yes, they do."

Cate didn't miss the underlying subtext. It made her feel hollow and empty—they had lost so much.

"May I?" Dita didn't wait for an answer and glided gracefully into the seat opposite.

As the supple body moved, Cate couldn't tear her eyes from it. Without warning, she felt her own body react, desperate for the gentle intimacy they'd once shared. It was only her mind that intercepted in time, warning her that this was no longer an option, that their relationship had shifted polarities. Indeed, she sensed that Dita was metaphorically circling her like a hunter after its prey.

Dita began pouring the wine, and Cate found herself fascinated by the brief activity. Her attention was drawn to a delicate wrist and slender fingers that raised the bottle above the glasses to fill them. It was a simple maneuver, but one that produced a complexity of feeling within Cate. She knew she needed to be quick witted but her physical self was so keenly aware of Dita's presence, her senses were fast overtaking rational thought.

She dared a look at Dita's face and she caught her unconsciously running her tongue across her lip in concentration, before the exquisitely shaped red lips formed a pout. How many times had she seen Dita do this, a quirky little characteristic Cate had come to adore? She told herself inwardly to get a grip; she might be in love with Dita, but the sentiment wasn't returned.

"I have to ask, Dita. Why would you want to share a glass of wine with me?" Sometimes it paid to be up front. Cate was learning that there was a place for openness and truth these days.

Those full lips formed a tight little smile. "It would be churlish of me not to offer you a drink at a time like this, don't you think? Both of us stranded and having to kill time?" Her eyes were bereft of affection. "Then of course, there's the old saying."

Cate lifted her eyebrows in confusion.

"Keep your friends close," Dita began.

"...and your enemies, closer," Cate finished somberly, her heart heavy. "I'm not your enemy, Dita."

"Your viewpoint." Calmly Dita pushed a large glass of wine across the table to Cate.

The conversation temporarily ceased as they drank. Anyone observing them might have noticed that they each took more than a generous sip. Perhaps it was a sign that they were equally tense.

Dita spoke first. "Maybe I also want to have a drink with you, just to prove to myself that I can," she said straightforwardly. "That I view you as nothing more than an irritant, a nuisance, and that I really am over you."

Cate watched Dita's lips move as she spoke, and though she heard the words, she wasn't really listening, but that didn't mean she wasn't responding. She could feel herself becoming increasingly aroused and she was aware of her body temperature rising, of color setting on her cheeks. Perhaps, if Dita even noticed, she might think it was the effects of the wine. A part of Cate *wanted* Dita to know it was more than a good bottle of chardonnay. No one could fake the telltale signs of arousal, could they? Dita would see this was genuine?

"And are you...over me?" A voice inside Cate longed to hear she wasn't.

"It would seem so." Dita stared her straight in the face.

"Where does that leave us now?" If she was trying to hide her disappointment, Cate was failing miserably.

Dita saw the look and it pleased her. Any opportunity to get back at Cate was welcome and for the first time that evening, she allowed herself to show some emotion—incredulity. "It leaves us *nowhere*. We're neither friends, associates, nor business acquaintances. I see you as an adversary, nothing more, nothing less...one I have no wish to cross swords with, but if you become a nuisance, I'll deal with you accordingly."

Accordingly?

"Just keep away," she warned Cate politely. "I seem to remember you saying you'd do that." The reference hinged on the detached conversation they'd had after Seraphim's breakthrough runway show five months earlier. Very graciously, Dita raised her glass in a salute and sipped more wine. "I'm sure we'll be able to keep things nice and distant."

Cate drank, welcoming the affect of the alcohol, which was starting to dull the pain of this unexpected reunion. "I hope this isn't poisoned?" she said with a nuance of humor.

"Regrettably, I haven't had the time or opportunity." Half-lidded eyes peered at Cate.

"I'll remember that if we ever share a bottle again." Cate couldn't help smiling. She'd come to the bar tonight to try and calm herself, but she certainly wasn't relaxed now. Maybe it was because Dita was being civil, even if only to make Cate feel uncomfortable. The strategy was working.

She studied the attractive woman opposite her. Regardless of the stone mask Dita wore, she still drew Cate like a magnet, and Cate wondered if she knew the power she had over her. Was she deliberately taunting her with it? Trying to get a grip, Cate took a deep breath in an attempt to compose herself, but instead all she got was an intake of Dita's perfume, which made everything worse. Her senses swung into overdrive and there was little she could do. How could she be turned on by someone who viewed her as an irritant…a mosquito to be swatted? Dita seemed absolutely unmoved by her presence, maintaining that awful plastic politeness, with only the occasional spike of resentment. Reasonable enough, Cate thought.

The drink was beginning to loosen Cate's tongue, and she leaned forward toward Dita. "I've thought of you a lot…wondered how you've been. Your health…no complications, no setbacks?"

There it was again, that caring, concerned Cate one could almost believe was genuine, except Dita knew better. "I'm well, thanks for your interest."

"Did they ever catch him, the man who stabbed you?"

Dita shook her head. She hadn't been prepared for the question and the horror of her attack flooded back and she felt her hands go clammy.

Cate inwardly kicked herself. "I'm sorry. I didn't mean to dredge up bad memories." Genuine regret and compassion threaded the apology.

There was the slightest delay before Dita answered. "Don't be. I'm *used* to them."

It was a hard response and it dawned on Cate that the statement was meant for her, *she* was a bad memory. She tried to ignore the comment. "I really am glad that you're better, Dita. I'd like you to stay that way." There was nothing she could say or do to bring back the *old* Dita and that knowledge caused a depth of sadness in her. "You look…" Cate stopped, afraid to say more.

"I look what?" A brittle challenge rasped in Dita's voice.

Cate raised her eyes again. "You look…just…beautiful." Her heart encased the words. *Beautiful and alive, my love.* The declaration slurred and she accepted that the wine had found its mark. But she didn't care. Sometimes, alcohol gave people the courage to say what they really wanted to, even if it was wasted effort. Cate frowned and tearing her eyes away from Dita, she drained the remnants of her glass. Maybe it was a good thing that the wine was all gone. Dita was getting angry and Cate was hurting more and more inside. She only wanted to get away from Dita now. It was becoming physically painful to be close to her.

They rose together and silently walked out of the bar and into the same elevator. Only when they both went to press the third floor button did they look at each other.

"306," Cate stated.

"312," Dita added.

They said nothing else as the elevator traveled up and they then walked the same way down the carpeted hallway. Cate came to her room first and turned awkwardly toward Dita. "Well, good night then. Thank you for the wine…and company." She knew her eyes were full of longing and regret, a bittersweet good night.

Turning, she swiped her card in the door, then as she moved to put the light on, she felt Dita come up behind her, putting her arms around her and pushing her into the room, closing the door behind them. Once inside Dita pivoted, shoving Cate hard up against the wall by the door and pinning her by the arms as she pressed her body close. Wasting no time, she lowered her head to kiss Cate hard and she felt her struggle beneath her. Dita didn't know whether the kiss was returned or not, she was beyond caring.

All evening Cate had been looking at her…she wasn't supposed to look at her that way, that wasn't in the rules they now played by. But the stolen glances that she'd caught had fueled something inside Dita and she felt driven to act on them. Only breaking the long kiss to come up for air, she lifted her head a little, still holding Cate firmly up against the wall.

"What the hell are you doing?" Cate demanded, breathing heavily and trying to push her off.

"Tell me you don't want this. Tell me this isn't what you've wanted all evening."

Cate's face creased. "I know you don't believe me, but what happened between us in Amalfi, it was real, Dita. It *became* real. But this isn't."

The room lit only by the outside lighting from the parking lot, Dita could still make out Cate's dilated eyes. Though Cate was trying to talk her out of what was about to happen, her body was singing another message. "Worried for my well-being?" Dita taunted mildly. "Concern doesn't become you, Cate."

She bent in for another kiss but Cate turned her face toward the wall, avoiding contact. "Dita, you'll hate yourself for this. You don't love me."

"Why concern yourself over such minor details? You never have before so please don't start now."

Tired of talk, Dita lowered her head again, fired up by an increasing urgency inside her, her body in pursuit of physical release. Forcing her lips against Cate's, she tried to push her tongue into her mouth but met resistance. Cate moved her head to the side but Dita was tenacious and pressed her lips onto Cate's mouth where she gained access into the wet warmth that tasted of wine. As their tongues dueled, Dita felt Cate's resistance weaken, giving in to the kiss and then eagerly seeking more.

"Tell me you want me to stop," Dita breathlessly demanded.

"I can't."

The answer she'd sought. Her breath short and her head pounding, Dita unlocked Cate's arms and let her hands roam over the still-trapped body, coming to rest on small, firm breasts. The sweater Cate wore became annoying as it blocked the sensations Dita craved. She slid her hands under the soft cotton and upward over Cate's shivering flesh to her bra. Rubbing at nipples through silky underwear, Dita smiled as she felt them harden under her fingers. Oh yes, Cate wanted this. She heard her not-so-unwilling lover snatching a breath between moans of excitement. The sounds drove Dita on.

Frustrated by the restrictive clothing, she yanked Cate's sweater up over her head with one swift movement, throwing it to the ground as she reached back to undo and discard the bra. With free access at last, she returned to Cate's nipples where she began kneading them between her fingers, tweaking and pulling. Cate arched in closer, her desire increasing. Sliding a hand south over a firm belly, Dita began to undo the belt and buttons on Cate's black denim jeans. She'd never seen her in them before, and they made her look damn hot. As she'd watched Cate walk toward the elevator, she'd hardly been able to keep her eyes off the way the jeans framed her figure, how the denim showed the curves of the hips, the roundness of the bottom, and the slimness of the legs. It had shocked Dita how powerfully her body had reacted. Now she wanted her out of them, and with the buttons undone, she thrust her hand down the front of the jeans toward the wet junction between Cate's legs.

"Oh, God…" Cate nearly came there and then, but Dita pulled her hand away, pushing her backward onto the bed.

Cate was ready and desperate to be touched again, her body burning with need, aching for release. How could she deny that this was what she wanted too? She let Dita strip away her remaining clothing and lay there naked on the bed.

Hair loose about her face and still clothed, Dita quickly lowered herself down, pushing Cate's legs apart and whispering, "My turn now."

In Italy, she had wanted desperately to return Cate's passionate touch measure for measure. Back then her heart had been full of love and tenderness, but it wasn't like that now. Though her body was aroused, her heart was disengaged and her mind was in full control. Dita's mission was quite simple, to *service* Cate in a dispassionate way, to let her know *she* was being used this time and that no love existed here in this bland, uninviting hotel room. This was payback time, and Dita wanted only to humiliate Cate, to treat her as nothing of value—as Cate had treated her.

Setting her mouth hungrily on Cate's, Dita pushed her thigh up forcefully against the wet apex of Cate's sex, rocking and sliding, feeling triumphant as Cate began to move against, lost and groaning for more. Dita felt the stomach quiver beneath hers and Cate's whole body trembled.

Struggling for breath, Cate was trapped by sexual fever. She caught Dita's eyes just once. They danced with danger, demanding gratification at any expense. Cate tried to pull back, knowing she was being used, but her body ached to be with Dita again, and if this was her only opportunity, she would be like a prisoner on death row, granted one last wish before everything was over forever. For it would be over, Cate was sure. This was not a union of forgiveness, a meeting of hearts—this was vengeance.

Dita moved like someone possessed, caught up in something she couldn't stop. She felt aggressive here with Cate, something she had never been in all her life, and though she didn't understand why, she didn't care. Animal-like and spurred on, she pushed a hand down between them and ran her fingers across Cate's sex. Cate quivered beneath her, wet and ready, panting with desire. Dita found her entrance and plunged forward, not wasting time with delicate foreplay or gentle teasing. Moving her fingers in and out, she set the rhythm, entering deeper, harder, and faster. Her conquest close, she awestruck as Cate's body bucked beneath hers.

As the buildup toward orgasm overpowered Cate, Dita felt her begin to struggle and heard her cry out several times for her to stop. Dita could see her straining, her head pushed back into the pillow, her body arched in orgasm.

"You want me to stop?" she sniped mockingly, but only paused for the briefest second for a reply. She already knew what Cate wanted, she was beyond reason. And as Dita expected, there was no answer—only groans that consented continuance.

A naked breast rose, pushing itself up against Dita's face. She took the offering and sucked at a hardened nipple. Even when Cate stilled, her climax over, Dita continued pumping away as her own orgasm came. Then she stopped, and soaked with perspiration, lay exhausted across Cate's body. The object of her revenge made only one movement, to reach down between her legs and remove Dita's hand, which still rested there.

With Dita still on top of her, Cate turned her head away and stared at the wall. She couldn't let the stranger Dita had become see the tears that silently soaked the pillow beneath her cheek.

❖

Dita waited until she was sure Cate was asleep, then in a final moment of victory, left something for her to find when she awoke. As she slipped out of the room, she felt she'd evened a score, that she had written the final act to some sordid play. Her anger vented, she hoped Cate would feel some of the emotional pain she had since their time in Amalfi. But as Dita walked along the empty corridor to her room, her elation faded, leaving her feeling miserable. No matter how she tried to heal the wounds of Italy, the truth of the matter was that she'd loved Cate.

A wave of shame flooded her for what she'd just done. Who said revenge was sweet? It damn well wasn't. A ghost of herself, she stumbled into the shower wanting to erase every trace of what had just happened. As she reached out to turn the water on, she noticed the blood on her right hand. Confused, she checked for injury, but there was none. With escalating horror the answer hit her hard as she looked at the dress ring that was still on her finger. Though not large, it was irregularly shaped and now covered in blood. A chill rushed through her as she realized that in her driving fury, she'd been so unaware of what was going on around her, she hadn't taken it off. The blood was Cate's.

She started to shake as she remembered Cate's struggles during their most intense intimacy. She'd been agitated and had asked her to stop…several times. Dita had thought the pleas were part of her excitement, the approaching orgasm pushing her over the top. She hadn't listened, and she hadn't stopped.

Grabbing the ring from her finger and throwing it across the floor, she washed the blood off her hand, knowing the damage and hurt she must have inflicted. She had meant to humiliate Cate…never to physically hurt her.

She slid down the cubicle wall and sat motionless as the water cascaded over her. Hadn't she once sworn she would never lower herself to Cate's level? But she had, and worse. How had it come to this? She'd been fueled by anger, and now that the pent-up feelings were released, what was left? The answer frightened Dita. She knew she wasn't over Cate, that behind her anger, love still remained. Useless love that had nowhere to go, feelings she could not turn off.

Dita wept.

❖

Several hours later when Cate awoke, Dita was gone, and she was crippled with pain. She grimaced as she moved fractionally to see the time on the illuminated alarm clock...not even four a.m. yet. Gingerly moving a foot out of the bed in an attempt to sit up, she cried out as pain radiated in her lower abdomen. She half walked, half crawled to the bathroom, and seeing herself in a mirror, saw the reddened beginnings of bruises on her arms and her still swollen lips. But that wasn't what concerned her.

She edged herself slowly into the empty bath and began to run it. Even the movement of turning the faucet was painful. Huddled up and crouched, the only position that eased her discomfort, she let the warm water bring her some relief as she watched it start to turn pink.

Wrapping her arms around her bent legs and shivering, her small voice echoed in the stillness. "Oh Dita, what did I do to you?"

It occurred to her that Dita hadn't even taken her clothes off.

Cate walked slowly back into the bedroom, having cleaned herself up as much as she could. She reached out to put the bedside lamp on and as she did so, she saw it. There on a pillow lay two hundred dollars. The message was clear, the ultimate insult.

"Touché, my darling. Touché," Cate said, grief stricken.

She didn't continue on to the art show in Albuquerque.

CHAPTER SIXTEEN

Dita felt as though she existed in a vacuum. As the realization had hit her regarding what she'd done to Cate, every day since, she'd felt that something terrible was about to happen, that someone was going to suddenly appear and accuse her of horrible crimes, something she knew she was guilty of. But no one came. No one pointed any finger of incrimination. But it didn't stop her conscience from plaguing her with a cross-examination of everything she'd done that night. Cate Canton might have used and treated her as something unimportant and inconsequential, but she had never, *never* resorted to physical violence. Dita recoiled as she thought again of what she'd done. Never in her life had she hurt another human soul.

The experience was something akin to shock therapy, and her anger had completely evaporated that night in Houston, canceled out by dismay and remorse over her own awful act. She was frightened at what she had done, the level she had sunk to. The only thing that had given her some temporary respite was finding out through a few subtle enquiries that Cate was home and working again in New York City. Whatever damage she might have done to her, she had apparently recovered. That information did ease Dita's conscience, but not much.

Thankfully, an event surfaced that took her mind off her guilt trip for a while. The fashion industry was hosting a gala reception, a tribute to honor the aging Madeleine Zobbio in recognition of her services and charitable achievements. The sparrow-like Zobbio had for years worked to smash prostitution and narcotics in Italy, taking young people off the streets and trying to give them a fresh start. Zobbio never gave up on anyone. She had set up safe houses and worked hard with businesses in Italy and abroad, to create second chances for her protégés. The fashion industry had played a big part in this.

Dita had become an ardent admirer of Zobbio, a woman whom she saw as morally courageous and possessing great integrity. When she received an invitation to the New York tribute dinner, she had no hesitation in accepting. All proceeds went to Zobbio's charity.

The evening proved spectacular and the reception was packed to brimming with a who's who of the fashion world. After the formalities, the spotlight came to rest on Zobbio herself, who slowly but gracefully made her way to the stage to thank those who honored her. Though in her eighties, her petite body frail, the years had not touched her energy or spirit, and her intellect was sharp as she responded wittily to the audience, charming them with her humor and warmth. If she was giving a speech, her banter wasn't perceived as such. Her words emanated from her heart as she addressed the gathering as if they were all members of her family or true old friends.

"I look around this room and I see so many faces I know, and of course, many of these faces I knew when, like me, we all looked younger," Zobbio purred lyrically in her attractive Italian accent. "Who would ever have guessed how much talent I would see pass in front of my eyes, in my lifetime, but it has and now I see all that ability, desire, and success here before me in this room."

Zobbio went into more detail about her charitable works, then gestured for the applause to stop. "Ladies and gentlemen, now I crave your indulgence. There are two of you here tonight who I *cannot* ignore, two very special people who have done so much for the charity and yet have never sought recognition. So tonight, because I am old, I am going to use that excuse to beg them to join me up on stage so you will know them. If I am being honored, so must they."

She summoned her first victim, Ermanno Nardini, who started to laugh and waved a hand as if to swat her away. He was a large, round middle-aged man with thick, wavy white hair that lent him an air of sophistication. After he stepped up next to her, Zobbio reminisced for a few minutes about their long friendship, then turned her attention to the other person she wished to honor, declaring, "Now this one is more difficult to catch. She hates the spotlight and shuns publicity, and

I know she is not going to like me making her bow before all of you. I can see her cringing now."

Not pointing out the woman straightaway, she talked about their friendship. A student of hers, the woman had built her own business and started out by employing just one or two lost souls. Then, as the numbers of Zobbio's charitable cases grew, so did her demands on her friend to find them employment.

"But no matter how many times I asked for her help, she never let me down, and so often has told me that the only reason she's been successful is so she can keep up with my appeals."

Only then did she look into the many faces and urge her friend to join her. Dita saw someone hesitantly rise from a table close to the stage, plainly uncomfortable with the attention thrust upon her. Dita felt a sense of compassionate understanding for this faceless stranger who did so much for others less fortunate than herself and yet shunned the limelight. Zobbio thrust her hands forward to grasp her friend's as she stepped up beside her. The way the two pairs of hands locked together left no doubt of the depths of affection between them. It was a touching moment which made Dita smile. Then, as she heard a champagne cork pop somewhere in the distance, her world turned upside down. She couldn't believe what she saw. Zobbio's unsung hero was Cate.

She felt a bolt of fright. Cate was here! How could this staunch supporter of Madeleine's charity, a guardian and protector of the weak, possibly be Cate Canton? Her mind and body responded like an allergic reaction and she felt sick. Unable to join in the applause and barely capable of standing, she clutched the back of her chair as Zobbio and her two favored lieutenants of charity left the stage and wove a path past well-wishers heading straight for her table.

Gripped by a dreadful panic, Dita lowered her head and prayed that Cate would pass by without seeing her. But she looked up again too soon and found herself staring directly into vivid blue eyes. Cate stopped less than three feet away. She looked as shocked as Dita. Neither said anything, but their expressions spoke volumes. There was no recrimination from Cate, no accusation regarding what had happened the last time they were together. It was when Dita felt her eyes start to well up that a look of genuine concern crossed Cate's features, and for a moment she had the strongest sense that Cate was going to reach out to her, to say something.

But her eyes held Dita's for a final moment and then she moved toward where Ermanno Nardini waited for her.

Deadened to everything around her, Dita left the reception as soon as she could and made the long drive back home instead of staying over in Manhattan. When she entered her apartment, she went immediately to her desk and opened a drawer, fumbling toward the back of it before retrieving an envelope that had not been opened but was ripped in two halves. It was the letter that Marcus had given her back in February, the one he'd seen Cate throw away. Rightly or wrongly, he'd retrieved it. Dita had tried to throw it away too, but failed. Now she carefully pieced the two parts of the torn letter together and started to read.

My Darling Dita,

I've tried to write this letter so many times, but the right words don't come, and I expect this is because there are none to excuse what I've done to you. But I beg you to find it in your heart to read this letter before you discard it, because in its own pathetic way, it tries to explain that not everything I did was carved from lies and deceit.

You were right when you accused me of deliberately seeking you out to further my business plans, but what you don't know is that as soon as I met you, my plans became impotent. I won't waste your time with futile excuses, but my actions regarding Seraphim were all because I believed I had good reason. I sought justice, but in pursuit of that I broke the moral and ethical codes that govern decent people out there. I lost my way, and though you won't believe it, I was once a good and noble person, long ago. But the years eroded it all, plunging me into the slime which is, of course, where you found me.

Dita, if you believe nothing else, know that I fell in love with you. How could I not? You were—are—nothing but kindness, so willing to look for the good in people…even me. You broke through my defenses and I was powerless. No one has ever done that. What happened between us in Amalfi was real, electric, and beautiful. I fell in love with you, and

I'm still in love with you. I cherish those blessed days. And now you know who I really am. I so bitterly regret that my actions destroyed the love we had and that I've caused you such pain.

You may call me your enemy, but darling, you are wrong for I will never be that. I cannot hurt what my heart desires. I can only promise you that I will no longer interfere with the success of your business, and I say success because I am supremely confident that Seraphim, without my interference, will continue to blossom under your management and creative direction. I wish you only every success in all you do.

Maybe one day you will find it in your heart to forgive me.

Always yours,
Cate

❖

A few days after the reception, Dita found William in the rose garden at the back of his home, tending the small bushes. As Dita walked over to him, he looked up and gave her the warmest of smiles. They had always been more than mere work associates, granting a level of trust and friendship very early on in the relationship, but of late, especially after Dita's attack, they'd become closer.

"William, I need some answers," Dita said without preamble. "I know that despite Marcus's dedication and Leona's blossoming talent, neither of them had the ability or intuition to put together my unfinished collection for Fashion Week. I think I know who was really responsible. I knew the day I found Cate at Seraphim but I didn't want to believe it."

William studied the small pruning shears in his hand. His silence was telling.

"You lied to me," Dita said.

"No. I just didn't give you all the information."

"Wrap it up any way you want, but it's still deceit," she challenged soberly.

He didn't deny that either. "It was her way of seeking atonement. She wanted to put things right." He paused. "She acted honorably, Dita…and I'm very proud of her."

"How can you say that after everything she's done to you, done to your family?" It was an honest question.

William indicated a wooden bench in the corner of the garden and Dita sat down with him. She wanted to know the truth, the reason behind Cate's actions, and for the first time, she knew William wasn't going to avoid giving answers. There was a time for every purpose under heaven, she thought, remembering a saying of her grandmother's. So now was the time for truth.

"What's brought this to a head?" William asked.

"A letter. A letter from her. Not much in it, just words of apology, but she writes of seeking justice, and there's an implication of something that happened long ago." Dita stretched her legs out. "I don't understand, but I want to."

Slowly, as the late summer sunshine fell on them, William began to tell her about the disintegration of his family and the rejection of his daughter when Cate needed him most. The sadness in his eyes, and the occasional struggle to complete a sentence told her he'd left very little out and had not spared his own feelings.

"Thank you for telling me," she said quietly.

"Now you know the truth, beyond the rumors and gossip."

"You make it sound as if Cate was innocent all those years ago."

"I'm in no doubt of that," William replied without hesitation.

"Why, what's changed?" Dita almost didn't want to hear this. It was challenging the shape and contours of who she thought Cate really was. Was she wrong?

William could see Dita waging a mental war. Cheerlessly he looked down at his hands which were shaking just like they had the day Cate had turned up at his office insisting on making amends. Was this what happened when deep memories were finally allowed to surface. Did the mental exorcism express itself in the physical sense? He'd always considered himself a man in command of his emotions. Well, maybe not today. And maybe he was getting old, he certainly felt it now.

"Oh, there are still questions and mysteries which I doubt will ever be answered, but as far as I've been able to establish the facts, everything Cate told me back then was the truth. At the time, however, all I could see was my apparently drug-taking daughter ignoring rules, and driving illegally, all of which ended up in the death of her sister. I now realize that, for a while, I *hated* Cate for that. I blamed her for the accident." He grew silent. "I've never admitted that before."

Dita covered his firm square hand with her own. "I'm sorry. I know this is painful for you."

William shook his head. "Poor Cate. Everything was spiraling out of control and there was nothing she could do. No one would believe her about the drugs found in her locker at school. I should have, and I should have been a loving, supportive father, standing by her regardless, but I failed. I let her down in the worst possible way. A long time later, the police busted a group of kids buying and selling. They used to hide their drugs in the lockers of classmates to avoid taking the blame if there was a search." William stared at Dita. He looked weary, more than his age. "Any ruthless behavior on my daughter's part toward you and Seraphim has been *my* doing. I put that hatred and bitterness in her. It was never there before."

"Thank you," Dita said again.

"I'm glad you know the truth, I owe you and Cate that. At least you can judge her knowing all the facts."

The facts. Dita wasn't so certain. She could see that William was finally coming to terms with his shortcomings as a parent and she genuinely hoped he would find a way to reconcile with Cate in the process. Her own situation was less clear cut. "Tell me, did you look for Cate when she first disappeared?"

"Yes, of course. I went to Tom Elgin, her supervisor when she worked at the packing factory, and eventually he told me Cate had gone to Italy to study fashion. I knew she must have headed for her mother's old alma mater."

"Did you find her?"

"Yes." He looked uncomfortable. "I didn't handle it well. I told her that I loved her, that I didn't care what she'd done, I *forgave* her. Bad move. I tried to see her again and I wrote to her, but she always returned my letters unopened. Eventually I stopped trying."

"So you absolved yourself of her."

"Not quite. I anonymously paid for her tuition through a third party. She was struggling financially and needed a lift. I had to put something right."

"Very magnanimous." Dita couldn't control her sarcasm. "Knowing this doesn't excuse her treachery."

"Perhaps not, but all came to a searing halt when she met you."

"You think that?" Dita didn't believe him. She didn't want to believe him, for if she did, it would change everything. "I don't. I'm sorry to speak of your daughter like this, but she'll try to get back what she believes is hers—Seraphim. It's only a matter of time. She may be laying low now, but it won't last."

"She won't do that," William said confidently. "There are two reasons why I know she won't do anything."

"Enlighten me."

"When you were in hospital, I told her I'd kept the business going in the hope that one day she'd return and take possession of what was rightly hers."

Startled that he'd never told her about this intention, Dita said, "I can't say I like that arrangement, William. It puts me in a very invidious position." Deadly serious, she added, "I guess my future employment doesn't look too good, does it?"

"You needn't worry, Dita. That isn't going to happen," he reassured her. "Cate is quite adamant that she wants no part of Seraphim now. She's very insistent that I legally hand it over to you."

Dita frowned and the silence in the room grew deafening. *Her mother's business? The company Cate considered hers all these years?* There was no way she could believe that Cate would stop and walk away from everything. Wasn't this another sordid game she was playing at the expense of others?

"Why would she do that?" Dita demanded.

"I keep asking myself the same question."

Dita didn't like where this was all going. Things were coming out, being said that were making her begin to question everything she thought true. "What's the second reason you believe she won't come after Seraphim again?"

"You'll have to work that one out for yourself." There was no gentle teasing in his voice. He was deadly serious.

One more possibility bothered Dita. "Is there any chance she's changed her mind about this?" She couldn't discuss that devastatingly unpleasant encounter in Houston, but she was sure there would be consequences.

William shook his head. "Nothing's changed. She pushed me again to arrange the paperwork only a few days ago."

"I see." Dita's mind spun like a tornado, making her head—and heart—ache. Nothing made sense anymore. Cate's letter, William's account of the past, Zobbio's tribute dinner, Cate's working on *her* designs and apparently giving up her mother's business.

For a while neither of them spoke.

William was the first to break the silence. "Silly, isn't it. I have all this money and yet I can't buy back the love of my daughter."

Dita scowled, surprised by the twist in their conversation. "Love isn't measured by monetary value."

William looked sharply at her. Had her words been judgmental? "No, it isn't. I don't know why I said that, it wasn't what I meant."

Dita looked across at him sympathetically. "I know." She cast him a ghost of a smile.

"You worry me," he said quietly. "You're tense, you always seem on edge lately, and you don't look well. You are all right, aren't you?"

"I'm fine." She answered with as much warmth as she could summon. "You worry too much."

"It's only ten months since you were hurt." She'd grown thinner, William thought, and there were dark shadows beneath her eyes that hadn't been there before. She looked ill, and Marcus's concerns, voiced on the phone almost every week, were valid.

He knew she still saw the specialist for checkups and her doctors thought she'd made a remarkable recovery. But her body wasn't rebuilding its strength as quickly as it ought because she wasn't giving it a chance. Her success demanded all her energy. William wasn't happy with how hard she worked but there was little he could do.

"I'm fine," Dita insisted, but she was lying. She didn't feel fine. How could she after everything that had happened to her? Besides, it was August and she was working once more on another Fall collection. It brought back memories.

"Would you like to stay for dinner?" he asked.

Sensing an anxiety in him, Dita thought she could guess at the cause. He'd been very open with her, and exposed himself to the possible loss of their friendship. She looked at him fondly, wanting to reassure him. "You made some mistakes. We *all* make them."

William detected something deeper in her final comment. What mistakes had she made? It seemed to him that lately something was gnawing away at her, and he had no doubt Cate was involved.

"You're worrying about me again." Dita was grinning at him, a big broad smile on her face, and it warmed him. Maybe they were still friends.

Returning her smile, he said sagely, "I'm at that age. It's what I do."

CHAPTER SEVENTEEN

I s this a bad time?" Cate asked as the front door swung open.
Her father greeted her with an enthusiastic smile. "It's never
a bad time for you." He stepped back, allowing her in out of the cold.
"You'll always be welcome, Cate. To what do I owe the pleasure of this
visit?"

"I was just passing...thought I'd drop in."

This late at night? From Manhattan? He knew better than to
hope for a genuine and personal call—a daughter wanting to see her
father. That would mean love, and there was none from her. They could
now talk civilly to each other, but they were still a million miles away
from anything remotely like a normal father-daughter relationship. He
suspected another reason for the unexpected social call. With Cate there
was always an agenda.

"How's Dita?" Cate asked, following him into the living room.
She stood in front of the fire, warming her hands.

"I'm worried about her," William said. "I don't know what's wrong
but something is bothering her. Maybe it's some delayed psychological
aftermath from her attack." He looked directly at Cate. "You should
visit her."

"This is the woman who threw me out of her office, remember?"
Cate could have mentioned the two hundred bucks on her pillow, but
that would have been in poor taste. The insult still stung six months
later. "She doesn't want to see me."

"I think you're wrong," her father said bluntly. "She got your
letter."

"I've sent her no letter." The only letter Cate had ever written to
Dita, she'd thrown in the trash.

William shrugged. "She mentioned it a few months ago."

Cate didn't argue. Her father was mistaken. No matter. She'd come here to find out how Dita was doing and, to her surprise, she had also felt it was time to check in with her father. They'd edged cautiously closer since they'd worked together over Dita's collection and she felt a certain responsibility for him even though their relationship hadn't improved significantly since then. "You were saying you're worried. Is something wrong with her?"

"Yes, nothing physical, although I don't like her working so hard. It's more mental, like she's fretting about something but she won't talk to anyone. Not to me, not to Marcus."

Cate remembered vividly the look on Dita's face at Zobbio's dinner. It hadn't been the look of a vanquished woman now avenged, it had been something else which Cate hadn't been immediately able to decipher. In the months since, she had come to believe what she'd seen was Dita's bitter disappointment in her. She'd given her love to someone who had turned out to be a fraud.

Far from feeling like the victim in that hotel room, Cate felt at fault because she knew what had happened that night was an aberration, something not in Dita's nature, an uncharacteristic act she'd provoked by her deceit and betrayal. Cate bore no grudge and only needed to know that Dita was fine—which it seemed she wasn't.

"Stay," her father said abruptly. "Christmas is almost here, and… I'd like it very much if you'd spend it with me." There was desperation in his voice as he continued. "I messed it up once a long time ago and I don't want to do that again." He faltered. "We could celebrate someplace else, *anywhere*. As little or whatever time you can spare."

Cate was about to respectfully decline, a trained negative response she'd developed when dealing with him, but this time something in his face made her stop. It took only a few seconds to realize that her animosity toward him, something she'd worn like a heavy overcoat for so long, had lightened. The arctic feeling inside her had thawed a little, and she could see he was desperately trying to reach out to her. The question was, was she ready to reach back? Not sure how she wanted to answer, she did wonder if spending some time with him at Christmas might not be so awful. They both had much to be sorry for. A slither of a decision began.

"I do have business in Boston before Christmas—"

"Then stay up here," he interrupted, trying to seal the deal. "You could stay on the boat again, and *think* about my invitation."

Cate thought how old he seemed and vulnerable. Two things she'd never associated with him before. She couldn't help thinking that revenge and bitterness were like a double-edged sword. Yes, the blade could inflict great injury on its target, but it could turn on the user too with devastating results. She didn't want to live like this anymore— consumed in anger. Look at what it had done to Dita and her.

Was this her chance to at least repair some other part of her life, perhaps a chance to grant her father a small measure of forgiveness? Could she be magnanimous? Was she capable of that?

❖

For a long time Dita sat in her parked car, motionless. Only her eyes moved, scanning the single docked boat some two hundred yards in front of her. It was an old, less-than-seaworthy vessel, a fifty-five-foot yacht that had seen better days, but even bare of its rigging and sails, Dita could see it had been a fine boat once.

The isolated, privately owned little harbor had nothing else around it. There was just a single track down to it, a small copse of trees and rolling hills to one side and a flat expanse of water to the other. It was late, and apart from an eerie light cast from a full moon that bounced off the water and onto the side of the vessel, this would have been the blackest of nights. It was certainly the coldest, and despite the fact that her car engine was running, Dita still felt chilled to the bone. Her car was old, and though reliable, its heating system hardly worked. How she wished she'd worn something warmer, wished she'd slept better last night and, listening to her growling stomach, wished she'd eaten something today. Too late now, for she was here and she wasn't even sure she wanted to be.

The boat looked empty, but she knew it wasn't. The Seraphim gossip mill hadn't stopped working since William casually mentioned that Cate would be spending Christmas with him. Dita stopped the engine and put her hand on the door handle. Was she going to go over to the boat? Was she going to wake the occupant inside by banging on the cabin door? She'd driven out here in terrible weather with that intention, but now she wasn't sure she was doing the right thing. Go back, part of her whispered. *Don't do this.*

As she contemplated her choices, the natural light faded and looking up toward the moon, she saw it was now disappearing behind clouds—snow clouds—and as her mind absorbed this, wisps of snow started to fall.

❖

On the boat, Cate lay naked across the bed with her arms stretched out and a heavy comforter just below her waist as she felt the whisper of cold hit her chest. Half-asleep, she considered she ought to increase the heating on the vessel but instead idly turned over onto her stomach and pulled the bedding higher. As she snuggled into the comfort of the pillow, she heard a loud thud and the sound of someone falling in through the door that separated the main cabin and annex she slept in. With frightening certainty, she knew she was not alone, that there was an intruder onboard.

She sprang into action, jumping from the bed and fumbling in the dark for the bedside lamp. Panic-induced levels of adrenaline made her heart beat wildly, and in the seconds before her fingers made contact with the lamp, she tried without success to identify the shadow of the prowler who was lying prostrate on the cabin deck, trying to get up. When the light came on, she was shocked to see Dita struggling to her feet.

"Jesus Christ!" Cate dragged a blanket around herself. "What are you doing here?"

The "intruder" lifted her eyes to Cate and burbled some lame excuse. "You left the hatch door unlocked. It's starting to snow out there, so I came in. I didn't mean to frighten you."

"Sweet Jesus, Dita." It didn't matter that Cate knew her prowler, she still couldn't stop the automatic response of fear.

Dita reach out a red-mittened hand to try and calm her, a reassuring gesture supposed to let her know she wasn't here to reap bloody revenge by cutting Cate's body into chunks to be thrown overboard— something her foe might have considered a realistic possibility, given their last encounter. But as she touched Cate's shoulder, Cate stepped back apprehensively, as if the proffered hand carried a fatal electrical charge.

Dita understood. The last time she'd touched Cate, she had abused her in the worst possible way and in the flash of a second, her thoughts replayed that dreadful night. Now it was *her* face that contorted in shame. Cate no longer trusted *her.* What a ridiculous reversal of roles. In a split second, her emotions came to the fore and she found herself talking rapidly like bullet fire.

"Oh, Cate, I never meant to hurt you. The hotel, what I did… I'm sorry. I was angry and wanted to humiliate you, make you feel something of what I'd felt, but never like that, not physically. The ring…I didn't know."

Arms by her side, not wanting to upset Cate more, she felt her body shake and wasn't sure whether it was from the bitter cold outside or the awful creeping chill within her. Pain radiated across her ribs from the heavy fall and she clenched her arms about her tightly for warmth. The only thing she did know was that one of the reasons she was standing here was that she needed to apologize to Cate.

Still gripping the bedding to her like protective shielding, Cate wiped the thin cold line of sweat that had suddenly formed above her lip. If it was possible for someone to bodily stammer, Cate pretty much achieved it. Stepping forward with jerky movements, cautious as though she wasn't quite sure she could risk touching or being touched by Dita again, she placed a hand tentatively on Dita's shoulder.

"It's okay…it's okay," she spoke soothingly as she steered Dita over to a chair by the bed. Sitting on the edge of the bed opposite her, Cate said, "My reaction a minute ago, it was just a reflex. I know you'd never deliberately hurt me like that, and I do understand. You were angry that night in Houston and you had every reason to be. You wanted me to see that."

"The ring—"

"Was an accident," Cate insisted.

"I *hurt* you."

"Yes." Cate didn't shy away from the truth. "But it was an accident…I know that." She cocked her head to the side. "However, the two hundred bucks was a nice touch."

Cate's lips curved slightly, but Dita knew it wasn't a smile, it was something far sadder. Clearly her parting message that night had found its target, but she didn't feel like apologizing to Cate for that. The ring incident…even stumbling onto her boat at this late hour and nearly giving her a heart attack…Dita could say sorry for all that. She hadn't intended to cause anxiety. The cash was a different matter, and maybe she still wanted Cate to suffer a little longer.

Suffer a little longer? Dita psychoanalyzed that thought. Interesting, for the underlying assumption was that Cate *did* care, and enough to suffer. If that were true, then the letter Cate had written possibly held some truth. Dita closed her eyes and rubbed her temples. Her head ached. Actually everything ached. Her eyes. Her body. Her heart. What wouldn't she give for a long soak in a hot tub. If she felt better, physically, she might be able to make more sense of what had brought her here on an icy night. Was it to apologize? Yes…but there was more beyond that? She wasn't even sure if she loathed or loved Cate. Ridiculous as that sounded, the latter was still a possibility. If all the mess that surrounded Cate was removed, there was *another* Cate tucked away, deep inside. Perhaps that rarely seen person was the original, the one she could have been all those years ago. Was that the one who had surfaced in Italy, the one Dita had connected with…had fallen in love with?

Cate watched the panoply of emotions flickering across Dita's face. Unable to resist, she cupped the side of Dita's jaw and was shocked to find it ice cold. Dita's eyes opened sharply, and expecting censure, Cate was surprised when none came. She saw only tiredness gazing back at her. Rising to her feet, she realized she was still naked but for the blanket held around her by a hand and divine intervention.

"I'm going to get dressed and make us both a warm drink," she said. "You okay?"

"Yes…sure." Dita coughed, clearing her throat. She'd never felt this exhausted before. It had to be stress.

"Okay, darling, give me a minute." Cate was swift, first seeing to the kettle and then throwing a tracksuit and thick wooly socks on.

All the time, Dita watched her economic movements, unable to believe she'd been called "darling." *Darling.* Such an intimate and possessive word. Used by one who cares for another. Given what had happened between them, would Cate call her "darling" if she didn't mean it? Just one more riddle to solve.

Dita shivered. She really was cold. Why had she sat outside in the car for so long? She closed her eyes again, and only opened them when she felt a warm mug being placed in her still gloved hands. Cate's hands wrapped around hers for a few seconds, a simple action but it disturbed Dita for she was unsure whether she liked it or not.

"Now," Cate said carefully, sitting back once more on the bedside opposite Dita. "Want to tell me what brings you here, creeping around this boat like a ten-gun salute?" The touch of gentle humor did nothing to hide the serious question. "What's wrong?"

Something had to be terribly amiss to bring Dita out in search of *her*—at this time of the year, at night, and in such atrocious weather. Glancing at the clock by the bed, Cate saw it was well past two o'clock in the morning. Christmas Eve, her mind registered.

"I don't know," Dita said in a wooden tone. "I've been sitting outside in the car for hours, trying to work it out."

"You've been out in that? It's freezing." Despite the urge to do so, Cate hadn't followed up when her father and Marcus said they were worried about Dita, how she wasn't taking enough care of herself. She scrutinized the face in front of her more closely. Dita was ashen and there were seriously dark shadows beneath eyes that lacked their usual sparkle.

"Your letter, I read it," Dita said.

There really *was* a letter? Cate was still mystified. "What letter?"

"You threw it away the night of the Seraphim show at Fashion Week, but Marcus...*found* it." Dita didn't explain further. "He gave it to me, and I refused to read it. I didn't open it for a long time after, and when I did, it made no sense. There were more questions than answers." She straightened up, trying to stretch herself into a more alert state. "I went to William, and he told me everything—everything about your past."

Cate's heart plummeted. Though things seemed to be moving forward between her and her father, she feared what he might have told Dita. She didn't want her thinking any worse of her, *if* that was possible.

Confirming her fears, Dita spoke the words Cate dreaded. "I don't need you."

So Dita *did* think worse of her. Emotionally steadying herself, Cate looked for further confirmation in her eyes. Curiously, she saw no condemnation, hearing only the strangely unemotional statement of what she believed was ostensible fact. "Okay." She mustered as much dignity as she could but it was a difficult act when her heart was fragmenting into several hundred pieces.

"At least that's what I thought," Dita added.

Cate's heart stopped disintegrating. Was there hope? She waited for Dita to say more, but she didn't, not until she turned the conversation on a hinge.

"It's cold in here." Catching Cate's concern, Dita went on. "I'm fine, really. I get like this when I'm tired. I guess I shouldn't have driven to New York this morning—yesterday morning—whatever." She shook her head in confusion, her blond hair swishing about her.

"New York?"

"I was looking for you."

"For me?" Cate thought she probably sounded even more confused than she felt.

"Yes."

"I wasn't there."

Dita's response was mildly arrogant. "I *know* that. That's why I ended up driving back up here."

"You've driven all that way in a day, in this weather?" Not waiting for an answer, Cate pressed Dita. "Why were you looking for me?" Her minuscule ray of sunshine, that infinitesimal speck of hope was there again.

Dita laughed heartlessly. "I keep asking myself that." She shivered again. "Can't you turn the heat up?" She crossed her arms over her chest, flinched, and lowered them as she glanced over to where she had fallen. She wondered what she'd hit.

It was anything but cold in this cabin and alarm bells sounded in Cate's head. After coming in from the intense cold, Dita should have been feeling the heat. Her face should have been scarlet by now, not pasty white. This time Cate hopped off the bed and drew the blankets back. "Here," she spoke in a commanding voice. "Get your clothes off."

The look on Dita's face was indecipherable and it made Cate stop in her tracks, embarrassed. "No, not like that. I mean, just get your clothes off, and get into bed. You'll be warmer."

Cate started to undo the buttons on Dita's navy blue overcoat but a mittened hand rose up to stop her.

"I should go home," Dita said, "I shouldn't have come."

I'm glad you did. I miss you. "Maybe. But you're here now, and you need to rest." Cate gazed out of the nearest porthole. "Have you looked outside? There's a blizzard. No one's going anywhere in this."

"Damn." Dita was visibly upset.

"You're frozen, darling," Cate consoled her. "You need to warm up, and you must get some sleep, otherwise you'll make yourself ill. Now please, help me get you into bed."

There's that word again, Dita thought uncomfortably. *Darling.* She felt trapped. Trapped on a boat by her own weariness and the weather, with someone she didn't trust, and having to lie down in her bed.

Cate sighed. "I know you don't want to be here...but you are, and there's little either of us can do about that. But I promise you, you're safe and I'm not going to...abuse these circumstances. Please get some rest. We can talk later."

Removing the scarf and mittens, Cate pushed Dita back onto the bed, covering her with blankets and tucking her in. She then switched the light out and moved to leave the room.

"Where are you going?" Suddenly Dita seemed more alert.

"I'll sleep on the couch next door. Don't worry, it's comfortable."

"No." Several seconds of silence prevailed. "This isn't right. I steal onto your boat and then rob you of your own bed. I'll sleep on the couch."

"Sorry, Dita, you're not going to win this one." There was a sweet force in Cate's voice, she would brook no argument.

"Then you sleep in this bed with me, Cate, or I don't sleep." Dita struggled to sit up. "There's plenty of room here for both of us." She hesitated. "Unless you can't trust me anymore." Memories of the hotel room in Houston played back painfully. "And if that's the case, I *will* sleep on the couch."

Standing halfway between two cabins, Cate realized the futility of quibbling. "This isn't negotiable, is it?"

"No."

Moments later, still in her tracksuit, Cate slid into bed beside Dita and for the next few minutes, she listened to her shivering and tried to ignore it. Though Cate had pretended she had coped with what had happened the last time they'd been in a bed together, she hadn't. She *did* know the ring was an accident, but she couldn't stop remembering the pain and discomfort she'd suffered for weeks after. There was no denying that lying here she felt nervous. So it took some personal courage to do what had to be done next.

"Sorry, I know you don't want this but…" Cate slowly crept closer and pushed up tight behind Dita, molding herself into her back as she gingerly wrapped an arm around the shivering form. "I need to warm you up," she explained, feeling more uncomfortable than she'd ever felt in her life.

For Cate, it was another sign that Dita wasn't well because she didn't resist. Only in the last moment before Dita fell asleep, did Cate hear her whisper, "This doesn't mean anything."

"I know. Go to sleep."

❖

Like a sentinel, Cate lay awake for the next few hours, unable to sleep and listening to the small but regular breaths that came from Dita, feeling the rhythmic movement of her body as lungs filled with air, then exhaled. This was never in the script, she thought as she lay in the dark. How was it possible to meet a woman she was determined not to like, fall for her, then be discovered as a masquerading rat, only to remain in love with her and find herself now loathed? Not even a Hollywood movie could do this scenario justice. Cate wouldn't have believed it if she could have foreseen it.

Her reluctant bed mate stirred but didn't wake, and Cate relaxed. Her initial nervousness fading, she remembered the closeness they'd once shared and recognized how much she'd missed it. If only she could wipe out her inglorious past, but that was impossible.

Cate had reacted to Dita like a flower to sunlight. Though she'd been no stranger to a woman's touch before they met, her relationships had been mostly brief physical trysts. She'd never wanted anything more—anything permanent—for that would have required effort and trust, both of which until recently, she was incapable of giving. Until Dita. Something in her had responded to Dita's softness and she'd seen a chance to live a different life, with someone she could love…and trust. But she'd destroyed the beauty of that, ruined it.

Cate felt Dita stir again, and this time, a voice echoed in the darkness. "You're not asleep."

"No," Cate answered. "But you've slept."

"Yes." A plain response and then Dita shrugged away from her, a sign she didn't want her touch.

Without further instruction, Cate withdrew, but she was still close enough to feel her warmth, to catch her scent. "Feel better?" she asked, trying to ignore the brittleness of rejection.

Dita remained with her back to Cate. "You said you loved me…in the letter. Did you mean it?" The words were blunt, accusatory.

"Yes," Cate whispered. "I still do." She was saddened that Dita had to ask. She wondered if there would ever be a time when she wouldn't love her? She thought she heard a grunt, like her answer hadn't been believed.

Dita was quiet for a minute before continuing. "When I first read your letter, I was insulted. I felt you were toying with me. Then I wondered why you'd bothered to write at all? If all I was to you was an obstacle to be dispassionately trodden on en route to your objectives, why would you waste time writing to me?"

Cate cringed. She had tried so hard to put her heart into that letter, to find some bridge across to Dita, she had failed. "Want to know the truth?"

"It would make a change," Dita bit back sharply.

Cate acknowledged the censure with a thin sigh. "You were just that at the beginning—an obstacle. My sole intention was to follow you to Italy and find out as much as I could about Seraphim and you…this annoying woman who was thwarting my plans."

"But that changed." It wasn't a question.

Again, Cate thought Dita didn't believe her. "Yes, it did." Was she ever going to convince her? "Don't ask me exactly when because I don't know…only that it *did* change." Her face was up against Dita's neck, close but not touching. "You're very difficult to resist, you know." Cate was disappointed when she received no response. "It was never personal, Dita. You got caught in the middle of something, wheels that were already in motion which when I tried to stop them turning, it was too late."

"Nordstrom?" Dita's anger flared. "You got what you wanted and then bolted, flew home to pursue the next chapter of your sordid little plan."

"Got what I wanted?" *No, I lost everything.* "Not quite. But you're right, I did run, though not for the reasons you think. I left because I panicked and couldn't face you." Cate's voice rasped. "Dita, I had fallen in love with you and all my plans changed. Before we made love that day, I'd tried to abort the deal. I couldn't get through to my assistant but I left him a message telling him not to pursue the Nordstrom contract, to stop everything. When I came to your room, I honestly thought I'd succeeded. I was planning to tell you everything the next morning over breakfast, and beg your forgiveness."

"But you didn't do that either, did you?" It was another accusation.

"No. I got back to my room and found a text telling me the deal had already been signed. I panicked, and I ran. I'd left it too late." Her voice cracked. "I realized I'd ruined…destroyed us." She let a few seconds pass. "I've tried to put things right—"

"Sure." Censure laced Dita's words. "You still have the contract."

"If I'd terminated it, they'd have sued me and I'd have had to lay people off. I couldn't do that. Too many people work for me and they deserve more than that."

"How noble." Dita changed direction once more. "I know you helped Marcus last year after I was hurt. I made William tell me the truth."

The air felt heavy and oppressive between them. Cate mumbled an affirmative. There was no point in denying it.

"Why did you do that?"

Hearing suspicion in Dita's tone, Cate snapped, unable to stand it any longer. All the emotions she'd been bottling since Dita had turned up on the boat, exploded. "Why did I do it?" Her voice rose in exasperation. "What do you think? I know you want to twist a simple act of decency around to fit with your need to believe the worst of me, but you are way off base. Let's see…maybe I worked night and day for a competitor because I'm just a fool. And maybe I sacrificed my own collection that year for the sheer hell of it. Did you even notice that the Zabor show was canceled? Didn't you wonder why?"

Dita's stomach churned. She thought back to the Seraphim show, the glamour and congratulations. Would she have received so much attention if Zabor had also presented their collection?

"When are you going to accept that the simplest answer is

probably the truth?" Cate demanded. "I helped you because I love you. I canceled my own show because I needed to spend all my time making yours wonderful, and I didn't want to take any of the limelight away from Seraphim. I thought I owed you that much."

Dita smoothed her hair back from her temples. One more question pricked at the back of her mind, but she felt oddly reluctant to ask about the "other person," perhaps because she found the idea even more unsettling than before. Attempting a lighter tone, she asked, "So, tell me. Any other sordid little secrets I should know about?"

Cate had reached the end of her patience. She had nothing more to lose. "Actually, yes. I sent you my best designer when I got back from Amalfi, undercover of course. Through her I managed to surreptitiously feed you new business opportunities…just enough to stave off disaster until you were able to get on top of the problems *I'd* caused."

"Leona," Dita stammered, clearly surprised.

"Leona," Cate confirmed. "She honestly adored working for you. She loved your work, your designs, and to say she respected you immensely is an understatement."

"I sacked her."

"I know. She was demoralized. She was never happy hiding the truth. She only did it because she knew I was trying to help you."

"What's happened to her?"

Cate heard genuine concern. "I managed to convince her to go work in Florence for awhile. I've got some business there and she's happy with the arrangement…for now."

"Your stupid plan cost that girl."

"It did, but it wasn't such a stupid plan. It worked. Seraphim stayed afloat and she was instrumental in getting your designs completed when you were recuperating."

Dita appeared to have no answer for that and fell quiet. Though all her questions had been loaded with recrimination, Cate wondered if this wasn't a good thing…clearing the air? And Dita must still have *some* feelings for her. Or why would she have bothered turning up here? Cate wished she could see her face but it was too dark for anything other than silhouetted shapes. "Why can't you believe that I love you?" she asked.

The words were barely out of her mouth, when they induced an instant reaction as Dita flung the bedclothes off and sat up. She turned to face Cate, her voice tight and strained. "Because you broke my heart," she cried. "Because no one else ever made me feel like you did. Those last few days, I felt loved, wanted, and special…like I was the only person in the world that mattered to you."

"You were…you are." Cate raised her hands to cup Dita's face but they were pushed away.

"You left me thinking that I'd done something wrong, and do you know how that felt? You left me to find out the worst possible way who you really were—are—to discover the truth. I had to find out that this person I loved and adored wasn't who she appeared to be. No, Cate, these were not the actions of someone who loved me." Unseen tears lay behind the final words. Again, she cried, "You broke my heart!"

Cate reached behind her for the lamp switch, no longer content to talk in the dark. She had to *see* Dita, and the minute she did her heart crumbled. Dita was wretched, shaking, her tears now visible. She had been hurt. She hurt now. Staring at Cate one last time, she then let her head drop, her shoulders sagging as if the energy had drained from her.

Cate gambled. "Then why are you here if you don't believe I love you?"

Dita's head bobbed up and her eyes searched Cate's in desperation, a frown creasing her forehead. She could only whisper, "I don't know."

The air thickened between them and the silence grew heavy.

"Sometimes," Dita said, as if to herself, "I want to hate you."

"But sometimes you don't?" The implication of something positive surprised Cate.

"Give me one good reason why I shouldn't," Dita pleaded gently.

"I can't." It was an apologetic response bathed in sadness.

"No, you can't." Dita's lips quivered. "Maybe you should have let me fall off that mountain ridge…it would have been so much simpler. You'd have got everything you wanted."

"Don't *ever* say that!" Cate pulled Dita to her forcefully, her eyes stinging with tears. "I don't want anything except you. Saving you was the best thing I've done with my life." Her voice failed her. "I'm sorry. I shouldn't have shouted. It's just—"

It's just what? You love her more than yourself? You'd do anything for her, and the thought of her falling to her death on that mountainside fills you with horror? Cate felt empty. Nothing she did or said held power anymore. She couldn't build the bridge that would take her home to Dita.

"I'm sorry I'm not a real superhero, Dita. I wish I had been... for you. I wish I'd been perfect." For an infinitesimal moment Cate thought Dita believed her, but then Dita seemed to fold before her, falling forward in slow motion into her arms. Surprised, Cate caught her, her heart beating wildly. Threading her fingers up through Dita's silken hair, supporting her head, she asked urgently, "What's wrong, darling?"

She thought she heard Dita whisper her name. Then she heard it repeated and Dita added, "I don't feel too good."

Cate felt the warmth of Dita's body but also an unnatural dampness about her skin. Like a bolt of lightning, she drew back to study her. "What do you mean?"

"I can't breathe. My chest hurts." Dita placed a hand on her chest, over the scar from her stabbing. She couldn't hide her fear as she gazed at Cate, the emotion mirrored back. She'd not felt right all day, and had put it down to nerves and exhaustion catching up with her, indigestion caused by lack of food and being behind a steering wheel for too long. Now she feared the painful twinges were none of those things.

Although she was frightened, Dita took solace in the fact that she was with Cate. Whatever the truth about this woman, she was the one who had hauled her off a mountainside and stopped her falling overboard on a ferry. Dita had always been *safe* in her hands. How strange that she should suddenly acknowledge that. As Cate drew her closer, protective and gentle, Dita concentrated on taking shallow breaths, forcing air into her lungs. Limp like a rag doll, somewhere in the distance she could make out the calm authority in Cate's voice as she spoke into her cell phone. She was relaying information as she sought help.

Cate had called William.

CHAPTER EIGHTEEN

It's stopped snowing," William said. The only acknowledgment he drew from Cate was a subtle shift of eye direction, from the cup to him, then back to the cup. He spoke again, still in automatic dialogue mode. "It'll be Christmas Day in a few hours."

This time Cate looked at him, sympathetically recognizing he was as lost as she was. She entered the thus far one-sided conversation. "You got your wish."

"Hmm?"

"We're spending Christmas together."

He canted his head toward her, a slight curl forming on his lips. "Not quite what I had in mind." The smile reached his eyes. "Merry Christmas, Cate."

She nodded wearily. "Merry Christmas."

As soon as the words were out, she wished she'd put more energy into them, regretting how wooden and emotionless they'd sounded. How intriguing, she thought, that she actually wanted to be nice to her father. It was funny how the mind suddenly shifted into a position of forgiveness, often without any real thought process.

"I'm sorry, Cate." In the ugly night silence of the deserted hospital corridor, his soft-spoken voice still ricocheted off the walls. "I should have trusted you."

With a calmness that surprised him, William started to reveal the things he'd shared not so long ago with Dita, the reasons that he *finally* believed in Cate's innocence. Like peeling an orange, he carefully laid bare all the segments of what he knew and now understood. And all the while, he watched Cate watching him…listening. "I won't ask you for forgiveness. I don't deserve it, but…" He brought his confession to a simple end. "I should have been a better father."

Cate inhaled, preparing to say something, but he interrupted her.

"I know none of this matters to you anymore and that you've moved on." He was echoing words she'd once said to him. "But it matters to me, and I at least want you to have this apology." He paused awkwardly. "I regret it's been a long time coming, but it's no less sincere."

The clinical silence returned, broken only by the occasional distant sound of medics going about their duties, the echo of footsteps unseen. A minute passed.

"I was going to say thank you," Cate said quietly.

"Oh." William had expected the usual condemnation, but as he looked at her, there was nothing to suggest that and Cate never camouflaged what she thought of him. There was honor in that. How could he ever have doubted her?

For a while they said nothing further; both weary, both worried about Dita. Then chancing his luck and feeling uncharacteristically brave in his daughter's presence, William broke the silence.

"Can I give you a piece of advice?"

Cate eyed him cautiously. "Let's not get carried away."

Her dry humor moved him to a place where he could speak his mind. "You don't have to take it from a delinquent father. See it more as from some poor soul who has just risked life, limb, and sanity, driving us all to this hospital in the worst snowstorm he's *ever* been in and… who may be permanently snow-blind for the rest of his life." He paused before offering his *real* message. "Don't give up."

Don't give up? She frowned. What was he talking about?

"I know how much you care for Dita. I know you love her. Don't let her push you away." He smiled tentatively, still afraid of rejection. "She still cares for you a lot, you know, I can see it in her eyes."

Cate could have taken his advice negatively, told him it was none of his business, but she recognized that he was trying to help, and in some way, his advice did suggest hope—although she didn't think there was much there. But maybe he saw a different side to Dita, one that was more open, more readable. As yet, Cate couldn't get beneath her anger or pain.

"That said," he sat back and let his head rest against the back of the couch, "I hate hospitals." He sighed heavily.

"Me, too."

William heard the unmistakable tone of one cursed by memories and his heart lurched as he acknowledged what they would be. He turned to face her, and saw how she almost mirrored his position, head back and staring up at the ceiling. But then she moved, a simple twist of her head canted toward him, and in one blinding moment, he was transported back in time and looking into the eyes of the teenage daughter who had once loved and trusted him unreservedly.

They broke the connection at the same time, as though it was something too painful to sustain. And as they continued to sit there, side by side, waiting for news of Dita, Cate's hand fell between them and lay next to her father's, their little fingers just touching. It was such a small insignificant gesture, but profound in its emotion.

William took a deep breath and closed his eyes. Without looking at her, he lifted his hand to cover his daughter's.

Cate let it stay.

❖

Cate quietly entered the bedroom where Dita lay sleeping. The doctor had discharged her with instructions to rest in bed and eat nutritious food for a few days. He said she was exhausted and somewhat anemic and had reminded them—unnecessarily—that only a year ago she had received extensive internal chest damage. Her body was still repairing itself and rebuilding strength. She'd agreed to return to William's house and spend a few days recuperating.

Worried Dita might get cold, Cate gently dragged the comforter higher. Then feeling like a stalker, guilty that she was invading another's privacy, she quietly backed out of the room and returned to her childhood bedroom. Caught in a feeling of inexplicable fear, Cate nervously paced. She studied the photos and the small ornaments on the dressing table, before returning to the bedside once more to check on Dita. She gained a curious strength from simply watching her breathe. Sitting now on the edge of the same bed she'd slept in as a youth, looking around her, Cate wondered if she'd made the right decision coming back here.

Everything in the room was much as she remembered. Her father had changed nothing, and she found herself curiously touched by that. Family photos still hung on the walls, as did many of her drawings, the ones that had whispered the promise of talent to come. They all looked the same but nothing was. The Cate today was very different from the innocent young teenager who'd dreamt her dreams here.

She pushed the palms of her hands against her eyelids, fighting off the competing exhaustion and overwhelming emotions that were surfacing. Earlier, when the three of them had driven back here, she'd had some control over her feelings, occupying her thoughts with the basics of getting something to eat, and then ensuring Dita got to bed to rest. It was interesting that Dita, having spent time recuperating here, clearly felt more at home in this house than Cate did.

Once she was lying down and William had retired, Cate had crept around the house like a burglar who didn't belong there, trying to face her demons, revisiting rooms one by one, and letting the past assault her senses. But she'd insisted on the latter, strangely wanting to claim back a part of what she'd lost all that time ago.

Now, for the next fifteen minutes, all she did was stand looking out of her bedroom window as daylight dissolved into night. She was still terrified to go to sleep, childishly afraid that something dark and sinister waited to claim her if she did. In the darkness, she recalled that her last memories of being in this house had not been good ones. Though the years had passed, her recollections were as vivid as if they'd happened yesterday.

Hearing a noise behind her, Cate turned sharply, her heartbeat at once erratic. But no evil apparition loomed. Instead she saw only beauty as Dita stood in the doorway clutching a comforter about her.

Concern immediately pushed Cate's fear aside and she asked, "Are you okay?"

It amazed her that though Dita had been ill and had a rough few days, she now looked rested and quite wonderful. Cate internally questioned whether she saw her through rose-tinted glasses, but no, Dita was the sort who would probably look like Sleeping Beauty on her deathbed. It lifted Cate's spirits that she appeared better.

"I'm fine," Dita answered softly. "I woke up and couldn't get back to sleep. I heard movement."

"I didn't mean to wake you," Cate whispered, without need for there was no one else in this part of the house.

"You should be sleeping. You and William haven't had much, thanks to me." Dita smiled apologetically, leaning against the door frame, but Cate only laughed lightly.

"I shouldn't be too concerned. Once I nod off I normally sleep like the dead, and as for William, I suspect he'll be living off the story of his drive to the hospital through that blizzard for years to come. I think you've made his day...he feels a bit like a hero." Her voice was full of warmth.

"Yes, well, I'm sorry I've messed up the festive day for both of you." Dita sat down on the edge of the bed.

"So, what's stopping you from sleeping? You should be shattered." Dita had been listening to Cate move around for ages.

"Oh nothing...and I am." Cate flippantly pretended there was no real problem. "Just one of those stupid moments where the body refuses to shut down."

Dita sensed otherwise. "Share your thoughts?" she prompted, an unexpected kindness entering her tone.

Cate played with her thoughts briefly, seeking a starting place. "I suppose I was thinking about the last time I was in this room. I was much younger then," she laughed halfheartedly. "I was a bit of a free spirit. That Cate probably drove her family insane. She was always laughing, and moving around the house like an overdosed chocolate addict. All she could talk about was fashion and she used to drive her sister to despair. Caroline always craved peace and order...the scientific one. You'd have liked her. She was very loving, articulate, and clever, and always so wise...but also terribly serious."

"It must have been wonderful...having a sister."

A smile escaped Cate. "She was going to be a doctor, so she was always dissecting things in her bedroom, which caused enormous trouble with the housekeeper! We would go through the ritual of Father pretending to be angry, but secretly loving every minute of it. Caroline would act slighted and deeply somber."

"And you?"

"I was the one always laughing. They were such happy days, you see?" A moment of intimacy passed between them before Cate sighed.

"But they didn't last." The smile evaporated and was replaced by pure pain. "I don't think a day goes by when I don't think of Caroline."

"You were close?"

"Very. I thought we'd always be there for each other." Cate paused. "I can feel her here."

"Her ghost?" Dita asked, reluctant to interrupt the insight into a usually well-boxed heart.

"Yes," Cate confirmed somberly.

It didn't take much imagination on Dita's part to realize what Cate must be feeling, and though she wanted to reach out and touch her to show support, she couldn't. Too much had happened between them and she still bore the wounds. Instead her mind and heart negotiated a settlement—she could be kind. Now wasn't the time for bitterness or recrimination.

"Maybe there are ghosts here, Cate, but they're nice ones…ghosts who love you, and who know the truth. They don't judge you."

"I hope not." Cate had been stoic as she'd remembered, but she suddenly felt frail. Fighting back tears, she had to look away.

Again, Dita felt compelled to put her arms around her—something she would have done for a person she knew less. But still tied down in confusion, it was something she couldn't do. *Love or loathe.* Dita didn't like her own reticent behavior.

Cate wiped her tears away brusquely and returned to the window. She pointed across the garden to an old, snow-covered oak tree. "My favorite tree," she said fondly. "I used to lie here at night and watch the way the moonlight shone through its branches…like it is now. I've always loved that tree, but I don't know why because it gave me this." She tapped her capped front tooth. "I disturbed a bird. It flew at me and I fell."

When Dita padded across the room to stand near her, Cate pointed to a shed in the far corner. "That's where my mother taught me to make my first snow angel. I was about four." Her eyes crinkled with love as she recalled the memory.

Dita smiled, afraid to say anything in case she broke the spell. It was like she was being offered a rare look inside an old sea chest that had lain undisturbed for years, its contents full of wonderful, sparkling surprises. This sharing was a joy, intimate and golden.

Cate seemed to sense her thoughts. "I just wanted you to know something about me, the Cate I used to be."

"Why now?" Dita queried, no animosity, merely curiosity.

Cate contemplated her answer. Maybe she wanted to offer Dita a glimpse of her past life. A life when she had been gentler, more caring, more capable of feeling…not merely obsessed by achieving business objectives. Perhaps in sharing these things, Cate could show Dita that there was still something worth salvaging inside her, something that might force Dita to reconsider this non-relationship they currently had. Cate wanted something back, no matter how flimsy.

"Whether you choose to believe it or not, Dita, these past months without you have been unbearable. I've missed you so much—all my fault, I know—but I simply can't imagine my life without you in it in some measure, be it ever so small." Cate stayed steady and calm but beneath the composure, she was the opposite. "I've made a lot of mistakes, haven't I, but I've tried to put things right."

"We've all made mistakes, Cate; William, you…*me*." Dita hesitated as she remembered something. "That evening at the gym…I said some *terrible* things to you."

Cate blew her apology away. "Forget it, I have. I deserved them."

"No, you didn't deserve everything I said." Dita dug her heels in. "Without any evidence, I labeled you. I called you something you weren't, just as everybody else did all those years ago. I was wrong and for that, I'm truly sorry. What happened to you was terrible…tragic. To lose two of the most important people in your life and go through it virtually alone with your father blaming you. No one should have to suffer like that. I can't begin to think how you must have felt." It pleased her to see the apology register in Cate's eyes. She finally added, cautiously, "William's bitterly sorry, too."

It was a strange young face that stared back at her before Cate nodded sagely. "I know he is." She shrugged. "But everything is now in the past and we all have to move forward. If not, the past becomes a prison keeper. It's taken me a while to see that." She gazed at Dita plain faced, hoping that there was still a chance of a future between them.

"Is that why you've told William you don't want Seraphim?"

"Oh, lots of reasons, Dita." Cate sighed.

"I'd like to hear them…to understand."

"Not tonight…some other time. All you need to know is that I mean it."

Dita was about to push the conversation forward, not content to let it drop, but the look from Cate told her there would be no further discussion on this—not tonight anyway. So Dita abided by that decision. Instead, she watched a few snowflakes falling and automatically pulled the comforter to her for warmth. "Do you realize every meaningful conversation I've ever had…or felt I've had with you has always been in a bed or bedroom?"

A small contained chuckle rumbled somewhere in Cate's chest, and Dita thought it a lovely sound. When she spoke, Cate's voice was low and husky. "Maybe we should be lovers."

Here eyes were bright and intense. Though Dita wanted to look away, she couldn't and was left unable to reply.

Cate stepped toward her, until she was less than a foot away. She whispered her question. "Could we try again…if I asked for a second chance?"

There was a painful delay in response, and as each second ticked by, Cate realized what the answer would be.

"I can't." As the simple reply fell from her lips, Dita thought her heart was going to tear. They were the hardest words she'd ever had to speak. She'd said them as gently as she could, knowing the effect they would have, but what could she do? This wasn't about getting even, it was about emotional survival. Her heart had been broken by this woman and she had no way of knowing if it wouldn't be broken again. The risk was too great.

The security light outside flicked off, robbing the room of its brightness. Cate thought the sudden darkness symbolic, the end of something short lived and bright. Her heart plummeted.

Dita watched as Cate slowly stepped back from her, only a half step but enough for Dita to know she had indeed hurt her. And it didn't matter that she'd once been hurt by Cate. Torn by the emptiness in Cate's eyes, she tried to soften the blow. "I do believe you when you say you're sorry, Cate…and that you love me…I genuinely do. But it doesn't really change anything. I don't see how I could ever trust you… not after everything that's happened between us."

Cate's world silently imploded. Dita couldn't forgive her, couldn't trust her. It was over then. She wanted to run and hide somewhere and break down but knew she had to be strong for just a moment longer—for Dita. She could cry later.

So she steadied herself and, breathing in deeply, straightened her back. "I guess I expected you to say that, and…I accept your decision." She managed a smile of sympathy, knowing Dita would have hated being the bearer of such bad news…honest news. Aided by the moonlight, she could see that Dita's eyes had pooled. They'd shared something special in Amalfi, and they both knew its loss.

Though not the outcome she'd wanted, Cate respected Dita's candidness and only wanted to make things easier for her now. Cate would accept this rejection with honor and courage. It was the least she could do for the one she loved so much. A growing heaviness cramped in the pit of her stomach. All she wanted now was for Dita to leave her alone. To have her here, so close and yet with no love returned, it was too much to bear.

She tapped Dita lightly on the arm. "You need your sleep, and I think I do now."

Thankfully, Dita took the hint. Their conversation over, she quietly bid Cate good night and left. Only then did Cate lie down on top of her bed, and rather than break down over what she'd lost this night, she let go and something wonderful happened. She fell asleep.

❖

Despite the finality of their agreement, something in the air had cleared and Cate and Dita managed to spend the next two days in amiable, if mildly restrained company.

William had his driver take Dita back to her Boston apartment when she was ready to return to work. She wasn't sure why, but as the car moved down the drive, her feelings grew disturbed and uncomfortable. Only a few nights ago, she had told Cate that it was over between them, that there was nothing left to salvage. She still felt that way, that her decision had been the right one. Why then, when she looked back at Cate, who was pretending to be so strong but who couldn't hide her wretchedness, did Dita feel churned up?

She spent most of the trip in silence, convinced she'd done the right thing for her emotional well-being, but experiencing little of the resolution she'd expected. When they arrived outside her building in

Boston, the driver handed her an envelope. It was from Cate. Dita waited until she was indoors before opening it.

The envelope contained no message, only two hundred dollars.

CHAPTER NINETEEN

I'm glad you could come," William said as he pulled a chair out for Dita. He'd invited her to join him for lunch at the Eagle's Hole, a restaurant at the golf club where he was a member.

"For a nasty minute I thought you were asking me to play," she said with a measure of good-humored sarcasm. "My penance for making golf jokes?"

"Oh yes, but you'll appreciate the food here. It's very good."

After they'd ordered their meals, William asked how business was going.

"Couldn't be better," Dita said lightly. "Spring sold through completely, and after last month's show, we've had incredible press. The Fall collection is looking like a sellout. I'm already thinking about next year."

"Planning something exciting?"

Dita found it sweet that William feigned an interest in the fashion side of the business. He always managed to ask one or two intelligent questions before his eyes glazed over. She'd learned long ago that she needed to keep the finances to the fore and the designer-speak to a minimum. It must have driven him to distraction to have had a wife and young daughter obsessed with all this.

"How is Cate doing?" she asked, as she usually did these days, knowing William enjoyed being able to answer. Still, the question always sparked a pang in her. Cate had left the country only days after Christmas, severing their contact entirely.

Somehow Dita hadn't expected that. She wasn't sure what

she'd envisioned exactly, some kind of friendship? Occasional social encounters where they would act like near strangers? The thought was dispiriting, but the prospect of never seeing Cate at all made her feel even worse, strangely lost in fact. Dita forced herself to make polite small talk over the meal, chatting about the weather, the road works in the city and how much longer it took to drive everywhere.

Eventually, William dropped a large brown envelope in front of her. "I thought you might like to sign this, or take it home to look at… whatever you want."

"What is it?"

"It's the legal documentation that begins the process of turning Seraphim over to you." He sounded perfectly relaxed but Dita's blood pressure skyrocketed.

"You want to do this now?"

"Now's as good a time as any," he replied casually. "It's no good me hanging on to it and I want to know it'll be in the best possible hands…"

Dita stared down at the envelope. "Are you sure?"

"If you're worried about Cate, please don't be. She's the one who put the wheels in motion. This is what she wants."

"It's too much, William."

He dismissed her qualms with a shrug. "You're only getting what you've built." Her set the envelope next to her purse. "Look, read over the fine print at home. Take as much time as you want, there's no hurry. As long as something is settled before I die." He raised his eyebrows jokingly. "But don't be surprised when I leave it to you anyway in my will."

William chuckled but Dita didn't find his comments humorous. She had grown to love this man and the thought of his passing upset her. She wiped a hand across her forehead, feeling hot, and wondered if the air-conditioning was working properly. She stabbed a lettuce leaf aggressively with her fork, not sure how to tell William that she didn't think she could sign these documents. When she looked up again, he was smiling indulgently at her.

"There's no rush. Sign when you're ready."

William noticed her dark look and knew it for what it was. Somewhere along life's road, he'd found a fledgling with clipped wings that had wanted to soar but had never been given a chance. It had filled him with quiet joy to be able to help Dita achieve her dreams, something he'd wished he'd been able to do for Cate. He couldn't deny that he felt blessed that Dita thought so much of him. It was partly because of their bond that he wanted her and Cate a chance to sort themselves out. Each had told him there was no chance of a long-term relationship. They'd settled for some kind of lame truce, as far as he could determine.

Dita must have read his mind. "Has Cate mentioned when she'll come back?" An innocent enough question, she'd thought, asking a father for news of his daughter, but the topic elicited a knowing smile from her lunch companion—as though he'd been expecting it.

"What?" Dita queried.

"Nothing." His smooth, honeyed response irritated her. There had been a lot of soft-spoken subtext since Christmas.

"You can be really maddening at times."

"What have I said?" Innocent brown eyes stared back at her.

"It's what you don't say."

He looked mildly amused as he sipped his wine. Taking time before putting his glass down—deliberately, Dita thought, he tapped her glass, which lay untouched. "Try the wine. It might help you relax."

"Relax?" she reiterated cagily.

Cutting into a succulent piece of steak, William nonchalantly dropped his special nugget of conversation across the table. "I can't remember if I mentioned I had a phone call from Cate last weekend." He eyed her reaction as he guided the fork to his mouth.

Suspicious eyes scrutinized him. "No, you didn't."

He feigned surprise. "Well, she's invited me to Italy to have a look around, see where she lives and so on. Just a week."

"That sounds wonderful." Though she tried hard to convey joy, Dita couldn't contain the slightest flutter of envy.

"Yes, I think so. She obviously thinks enough of our— relationship—to want to build on it, don't you think?"

Still he watched her, his gaze starting to unnerve Dita. If he'd been waiting for an answer, it was one she couldn't give. Her mind could only process the fact that Cate didn't want to rebuild any relationship with *her*. Totally depressed, she hoped his question had been rhetorical. Fortunately, it had.

"Just thought you ought to know," he said, apparently drawing this particular thread of conversation to a close.

❖

Dita bought herself a new car. This was the moment where it all sank in, that she was a success and that Seraphim was a prosperous business. She no longer felt that work was an uphill battle merely to survive. Her days of having to go out and search to find interested retailers were in the past. They came to *her* now, in their dozens.

It was wonderful to be able to face the world from a secure footing, and not a day went by that she didn't thank her lucky stars. Her health had returned and with it a rich vein of creativity. It seemed that every thought she had morphed into successful designs, which in turn saw the ever-attentive fashion press gushing and fawning. She had even taken on two young college students.

Professionally, everything was raining golden nuggets. Why then wasn't she happy?

Dita had tried hard since Christmas to try and move on with her personal life but it wasn't that easy. She had turned down Cate's plea for a second chance and thought that would bring closure. However, when Cate had left for Italy, her decision had unsettled Dita more than she'd believed possible. Her sense of loss was overwhelming—and this was someone she could live without?

What did she want? That question had driven her to the yacht at a time when she'd still harbored the embers of anger. But now that they were extinguished, the truths she'd learned about Cate were beginning to resonate inside her, quietly altering her frame of mind—and her heart.

Dita couldn't help replaying over in her head that last Christmas at William's house. Cate's behavior over that period had been exemplary. There had been no unpleasant scenes, no bitter recrimination. At a time when she would have been hurting like hell, she had made sure Dita wanted for nothing. Dita no longer had any doubt that that Cate's feelings for her were very real. Even the way she'd returned the two hundred dollars to Dita was devoid of spite and vindictive words. Dita no longer had any doubt that that Cate's feelings for her were very real.

She winced when she thought of what she'd said to Cate long before she'd known who she really was, of the comments about her relationship with William being more like that of a father and daughter. She'd mentioned that both he and Marcus considered her designs like Helena's. Then there had been Dita's ridiculous comments about feeling Helena's spiritual presence. Although unintentional, she might as well have driven a stake through Cate's heart.

With clarity she saw that she'd been punishing Cate for her *own* mother's sins. It had been easy for Dita to transfer the mantle of her mother's faults and betrayal onto the only other woman in her life she'd taken risks to love. Much of Dita's repressed bitterness and mistrust had resurfaced to latch onto Cate. It had taken her a long time to separate her own childhood hurt from the present.

And then came the deeds for the transfer of Seraphim, immediately proving her wrong in her determined suspicion that Cate had a destructive secret agenda that could unfold at any moment.

Distracted by these thoughts, Dita stopped at the deli on the same block as Seraphim to get coffee and fresh fruit for breakfast as she did every morning.

She was a regular and greeted the owner, a dark-haired guy in his fifties, cheerfully. "How are things?"

"I got some news," he said as he poured her coffee. "I'm selling."

"Oh, no." Dita hoped he hadn't fallen casualty to the economic downturn that had already claimed several small businesses around their locale.

He quickly allayed her concerns. "I've done okay and it's time for a change."

"What are you going to do?"

"I'm moving to Florida. My sister, she runs a flower shop there. I'm going to help her out…do some fishing…kick back."

"That sounds great," Dita said. "Do you have children there?"

"No, I don't have kids…never married." His eyes softened. "I had the chance. There was someone special, but I blew it."

A little taken aback by his straightforwardness, Dita said, "I'm sorry."

She wasn't looking for a full confession, but he gave her the details anyway. "She made a mistake. We're all human, know what I mean? I had my pride, so I played the hurt guy and dumped her…the only woman I really loved."

"What happened to her?"

"Oh, years later, I'm downtown and there she is with her kids. Beautiful. It was like we'd never been apart." He sounded surprised as he said that, and pained. "Funny thing, I never could get it out of my mind that those kids could have been mine. We could have had all those years. Been happy." He stopped reminiscing and refilled Dita's coffee. "But hey, you make the call as you see it. So long as you can live with the consequences…so be it. Guess I made a bad call."

So long as you can live with the consequences.

His words remained with Dita, haunting her.

CHAPTER TWENTY

Cate arrived late for her father's birthday dinner. The other guests were already seated, chatting away at the chic, expensive restaurant that specialized in Mediterranean cuisine. Moving forward into the more secluded part of the restaurant, she came to an abrupt halt as she spotted Dita, who was still unaware of her entrance. With her blond hair down and flowing, Cate thought she looked as dazzling as any of her dreams constantly reminded her, and she couldn't stop the smile radiating on her face nor the warmth of emotion flowing through her. Cate loved this woman and always would, but a sharp little pain in her heart reminded her that Dita was unobtainable.

She should have expected to see her here, she supposed. Naturally her father would have invited the woman who ran his fashion house. Cate had known when she left Italy that she was bound to encounter Dita somewhere. She'd thought about that eventuality before agreeing to her father's request to join him for the small dinner he was having to "celebrate living so long." But stupidly, she hadn't anticipated seeing her tonight, and her father hadn't mentioned she would be present, though he'd gone into some detail as to who else would be.

Cate could guess why he'd failed to mention Dita to her. He knew that relationship was strained, to say the least, and wouldn't have wanted to discourage Cate from coming. He hadn't so much asked her to come home as begged her, saying that if necessary, he would hop on a plane and physically come and get her. She had a feeling he would have, too. She had to admit he was really trying to put things right between them, and maybe something was working because she'd felt bad leaving after Christmas, when they were just beginning to reestablish their relationship.

Cate had intended to come back soon anyway. Even though it was possible to run the business from abroad and Saul continued to do a first-class job, she missed the U.S. fashion scene and the buzz Manhattan always gave her. She'd suffered withdrawal symptoms not attending New York Fashion Week, despite receiving almost hourly bulletins from Saul and various members of her team.

Of course, her return now had *nothing* to do with her pining for Dita. Those feelings remained painfully unchanged; she was still hopelessly in love with her. Each day, her waking thoughts and those before she fell asleep at night were always of Dita. Hell, she even dreamed of her most nights. She tried to take consolation in that fact that she'd made the right decision. She had to let Dita go, and that unfortunately meant keeping a distance between them.

Still, Cate wasn't a fool. Even though Dita had told her in so many words that it was over between them, she knew Dita's heart was still involved, albeit betrayed and bleeding. The sensible decision to end it all had come from Dita's head. It was a survival move. She needed closure and Cate respected that. All she could do now was be honorable and avoid Dita as much as she could. If she'd remained in New York that would have been almost impossible as they moved in the same professional arena.

Honor and fairness! Cate scoffed silently. When had she ever been that where Dita and Seraphim were concerned? Love changes everything, she thought. Just too late. A twinge of anxiety added to her emotional cocktail as she wondered if Dita knew she'd be here. However, that was before she saw Dita sense her presence and look up, casting a reserved smile. It appeared she knew. Cate was relieved. At least her appearance hadn't thrown Dita into a state of panic or annoyance.

Tipping her head in acknowledgment, Cate forced her eyes away from Dita and scanned her father's other guests. She had no doubt that her father had carefully chosen his fellow diners, ones he could trust to put her at ease. He had chosen well. They were all faces from her past, her youth. Buzz Coulter, her father's longtime attorney. Tom O'Kelly, a retired banker, who stood as she approached the table. The glint in his eye held affection. Next to him stood Ele, her father's long-standing and recently retired secretary, who had always been more family than employee, especially after Cate's mother died. Cate felt a lump rise in her throat as she traded glances with the beaming older woman. It was Ele who had taken quiet care of her father in the office after Helena's death and who had also become a sounding board for Cate and Caroline when they fretted about their remaining parent.

Ele tugged at Cate's hand and wrapped her arms around her, whispering in her ear. "It's *so* good to see you again." She gently squeezed Cate to her. "Before this evening is out, I want you to talk to me, tell me everything you've been doing and what your plans are. Promise me!"

"I promise."

But Cate had no idea how to answer those questions. Her past, especially with regard to Dita, didn't seem too glorious, and as for future plans? Staying as far away from Dita as she could get...for Dita's sake...for both their sakes. She glanced across at her uncertainly. Dita seemed content to remain in the background and Cate didn't question why—she didn't need to. The answer was apparent in the faintly apprehensive gaze she returned, and in her stiffening posture as Cate greeted everyone.

Mildly self-conscious and a little overwhelmed at the enthusiastic hugs from Tom and Buzz, Cate said, "I guess this means you remember me." She laughed. "At least I hope you do, otherwise we have two guys here with a big social problem."

Finally, her father stepped forward and gave her a cautious embrace, daring to place a kiss on her cheek. It seemed he was growing bold. Their hug still had a stiffness to it, but Cate was glad to see him looking so happy. As she sat down, Cate deliberately looked across at Dita again and waited until their eyes met.

To Dita it seemed the unspoken message conveyed in Cate's stare was one of understanding, as though she sensed Dita's discomfort. Again, they bowed heads civilly, and although the brief contact should have made Dita feel better, it didn't. All she wanted to do was tell Cate that she'd missed her. She also realized how much she envied the others who had embraced her. Dita knew this was probably the first time Cate had seen any of these people since she left Boston all those years ago.

What must be going through her mind? As they'd gone up to greet her, Dita's heart had sung for Cate, who needed this—who deserved it. And although she'd wanted to join in, she knew she wasn't a part of this.

She wanted to say something to Cate, to show her she was truly glad to see her again, but she felt unsure of the reception she might receive. She'd spent the past few months examining and re-examining the strange saga of their relationship, if it could be called that, and could only conclude that Cate needed distance between them, which was obviously the reason she'd left the country to work in Italy.

It was futile to think she hadn't broken Cate's heart by rejecting her at Christmas. Cate's life had been full of rejections and Dita knew she had added to them. She would be the last person that Cate would want a hug from now, and her presence here was probably making Cate feel awkward. And yet she looked so genuinely pleased to see her, Dita had thought for a moment that their connection was still alive. The promise she'd felt in Amalfi had flooded back when her eyes first met Cate's, stealing her breath away. She had no way of knowing if Cate felt the same rush of wonder and hope that settled on her in that instant. Dita felt the prickle of tears and looked away.

Cate saw a strain on Dita's face that hadn't been there when she'd entered and felt deep regret. Dita was the only one who hadn't welcomed her, not even a handshake. Understandable but bitterly disappointing no less, and how her heart felt that loss. Again she wondered if her father had made a mistake having the two of them here together. Dita wouldn't have wanted to turn down her father's invitation. What a mess. But if they could both play a courteous game for the next couple of hours, it would soon be over, and at least there was some physical distance between them. Cate was seated between her father and Buzz whilst Dita sat on the other side, next to Tom. Safe and uncomplicated, Cate thought gratefully. Dita wouldn't have to worry about making polite inane conversation with someone she had no desire to talk to.

Appetizers came, wine was served, conversation was made, and Cate remained hyperaware of Dita's presence. With secretive glances, she could hardly tear her eyes off her. Dita was stunning, dressed in a sleeveless pink satin square-necked dress that showed off a swanlike neck and delicate collarbones. Cate remembered kissing her way down that neck and beyond, she remembered the taste and feel of that smooth skin. This was going to be a long night.

Dita soon became deeply embroiled in conversation with Tom, clearly a comfortable discussion, for every now and then the two erupted in laughter. How envious Cate felt when Dita reached out and placed a hand on Tom's shoulder whilst making some point. At that moment she wanted the earth to open up and swallow her. Losing something precious was bad enough when she'd played no part in it, as was the case with her mother, but when it was entirely her own doing?

"A penny for them," her father whispered, leaned toward her.

Shunted out of her thoughts, she looked at him with an empty gaze.

"I said, 'a penny for them'…for your thoughts," he repeated. Cate shrugged and smiled back but his face took on a knowing look. "Don't worry, I think I know what's on your mind."

"Oh, I doubt it," she replied, sucking in air.

"Never underestimate someone who has been alive as long as me."

It might have sounded like a gentle joke but the look on his face was one Cate remembered from her past, the look that showed he really had understood. It had been a long time since she'd seen it. Was this evening going to move entirely around sad memories, of things past? Pushing her gloom to the side, and sensing the moment was as good as any, Cate reached into her purse and pulled out a small package. Handing it to her father, she said, "Happy Birthday," with an emotional energy she really didn't feel.

"Can I open it now?" he asked.

She couldn't help but smile at his surprise. "It's your birthday, knock yourself out."

Discarding the wrapper, he examined the blue leather box. He slowly removed the lid, and visibly froze. There inside was a beautiful set of cufflinks, almost identical to a pair her mother had given him many years ago.

"I promised you once I'd buy you those when I became successful," Cate volunteered quietly, wondering if she needed to remind him but as he looked at her, she could see it had been unnecessary. Something unsaid passed between them and they shared a poignant moment, possibly the moment of a daughter's willingness to forgive and move forward and a father's desperate need for absolution. Only time would see if things worked out.

Her father had been devastated at Christmas when she'd told him she was returning to Italy, and although she'd been insistent that it was only a temporary arrangement, she'd seen the panic in his eyes. She knew he feared that the barriers between them would return and that their fragile new father-daughter relationship would crumble. Even now she wasn't sure how she really felt about him, but she cared enough to not want any more hurt or distance between them. If she was ever going to get her personal life together and move forward, she had to learn to let the past go. Forgiving was part of that.

So the proverbial ball lay in her court as far as her father was concerned, and he was getting older. The one thing Cate *did* know was that she genuinely wanted to rebuild some form of relationship with him and the only way to find out what shape that would take was to spend time with him and see where emotions led.

Studying the fine detail on the cufflinks, he said, "Cate…thank you."

Cate allowed the smallest measure of affection to creep into her voice when she said, "I hope you like them."

Fearful that he might turn emotional, she retreated into the back of her chair, not ready for a father's demonstrative embrace, if indeed he'd been capable of giving it. The gift had truly overwhelmed him and she watched him fighting his emotions, not wanting to break down. He distracted himself by replacing the cufflinks he wore with the new ones.

Cate quickly turned to Buzz, desperate to avoid anything too familiar, too intimate. Although she had offered a twig of peace and was willing to build on their present cautious overtures, it would be a long time, if ever, before she could allow this man permission to embrace her fully as a daughter again. She caught Dita watching her once more, and the intensity of the gaze sent an unexpected surge of heat through her body.

"So, how's Italy?" Buzz unintentionally came to her rescue.

What should have been a simple question between the two of them instantly wasn't. Everyone at the table stopped talking and turned to listen. It seemed they were all interested in her answer and Cate unwillingly found herself the center of attention when all she really wanted to do was blend in with the rest. Acknowledging that she was trapped, and with false bravado, she attempted to brush the topic away. "The coffee is to die for."

William tutted loudly. "Sorry, Cate, but you're going to have to do better than that. I had to change my birthday celebration from lunch to dinner to fit in with your flight times. Details, Cate…details!" He knocked the table with a knuckle for effect.

She noticed Dita smiling at her—affectionately. Resigned to the inevitable, Cate spread her hands in a theatrical show of defeat and spent the next few minutes sharing anecdotes and bitchy fashion gossip from Europe.

Buzz declared her a lunatic for working in such a bizarre industry. "Why don't you take up a decent pursuit, like golf?"

A wave of soft laughter rippled round the table and Dita leaned forward into the group, eyebrows arched. "I realize we designers are up against the establishment here," her eyes lighted on Cate, "but why would any intelligent person want to spend a good part of their day walking around trying to hit a small ball into a ridiculously sized hole with a stick?" Her eyes flashed again toward Cate, who allowed herself a half grin and tilted her head to acknowledge the unexpected support.

"You're wasting your time, Buzz," William moaned. "They don't hear the call of the green and the flapping of the flag, the gentle breeze rustling through one's hair. They've never felt the pure joy of swinging a five iron."

"Oh, please." Dita scoffed.

"Sad," Buzz said with dramatic gravitas.

"Bitterly so," William playfully added.

"And with that deep disappointment, I'm going to retire to the bathroom to vent my emotions in private before the entrées arrive!" Buzz rose from the table, making a play of throwing his napkin down before he smiled contagiously and left. Ele and Dita took the opportunity to excuse themselves too.

With Dita temporarily gone, Cate had a chance to draw breath and relax a little. She'd thought this evening might be emotionally unsettling, and that was *before* she'd known Dita was going to be here. How could anything be so fantastic yet so awful at the same time? But Cate didn't regret being here. Any opportunity to see Dita again and stock up on new memories meant everything to her—they were all she had.

Turning as the seat next to her was occupied once more, Cate started in shock when she found herself almost nose to nose with Dita, whose wolf-like eyes were locked on her intensely. Catching her perfume, Cate instinctively pulled back as if the vapor might paralyze her. She saw a slight smile rise on Dita's lips, the quiet recognition of the affect her close proximity had.

"I thought I'd try a change of scenery," Dita said, her voice casual and lilting, not at all restrained as it had been during their last real conversation in Cate's childhood bedroom. Indeed, Dita was the epitome of relaxation now. *She's found her closure.* "Actually, Buzz wanted to chat with Ele so we decided to swap places," Dita explained. "You don't mind, do you?"

"Why would I mind?" Cate replied more intimately than she'd meant to. Though an automatic response, it was true nonetheless, and since they both understood the rules of their new arrangement—that feelings ran deep but nowhere—they could at least be honest with one another.

Nothing is ever simple, is it? I have a father on one side who's looking to embrace me...which I really don't want. On the other side is someone I adore but who has made it very clear our relationship is over...who keeps getting too close. Cate repositioned herself on the pretext of turning into the conversation better. In truth she was trying to edge as far to the other side of her chair as she could. Dita's too-close proximity was having an unsettling effect on her.

"How was your flight?" Dita was obviously keeping to polite, safe conversation. This from two people who had once, even if short lived, been lovers.

"As boring as ever." Glancing down at her watch, Cate calculated that they might have to continue making bland conversation for two depressing hours. She smiled back courteously at Dita. *Keep smiling, Cate, it's as difficult for her as it is for you. Make an effort.*

Dita watched the rather sophisticated way Cate swirled the contents of the glass in her hand before drinking. *She's so tranquil and calm, completely unlike me...a bag of nerves.* She'd asked Buzz to change places with her, claiming she wanted to catch up on a few things with Cate, making it sound like old buddies wanting to talk...girl talk. But it was nothing like that. The minute she'd seen Cate again, she was desperate to be closer to her. Stupid really, since she was the one who'd insisted there could be no *them* anymore.

Her heart had sunk when Cate drew back from her a moment ago. *She doesn't want me here.* Dita also hadn't failed to notice that Cate had even glanced down at her watch, obviously counting the minutes till she could make a polite exit. She knew Cate loved her, but perhaps she'd found her own closure in the five months since Christmas. Had Cate moved on? That thought depressed her. Was it really possible that Dita had failed to extinguish her feelings, but Cate had been more successful?

Not ready to accept this, Dita decided to disprove it. "So, what brings you back home?" *Say me, please.*

Cate put her glass down and regarded Dita with resigned amusement. "Work and play."

Play? Dita glued a smile to her lips. Had Cate not just moved on, but found someone else? Dita felt wretched. She'd not heard the answer she wanted…she hadn't received *any* answer. Surely if there was anything left between them, this might have been the opportunity to hint that there was something they could work on? A pair of mesmerizing blue eyes settled on her warmly. Cate was still smiling inanely at her, no irritation, no emotion…just a look of contentment, like she knew something Dita didn't.

"I suppose lots of things brought me back," Cate said more seriously. "I need to sort out a few business matters. Then, of course, there was Father's birthday."

Not me, then. "Yes, of course, the birthday." Dita couldn't hide her disappointment. Her cheeks ached maintaining a smile, forcing bravado and false happiness when all she wanted to do was blurt out to Cate how much she missed her, that she'd been wrong. Foolish. Afraid. Why, then, didn't she say something? Maybe it was because she feared the answer—that she really had lost Cate. At least this way she could still hope. "He's missed you, you know…William."

Cate regarded her fingers as they played with the napkin in her lap. William was chatting with Ele but she still lowered her voice so he wouldn't hear. "Yes, I know, and we're working on it…both of us, but these things take time and can't be rushed."

Dita noticed that Cate had just called William "Father," and it warmed her. She hoped these two special people in her life were finally moving toward a safe haven, some place where they could draw breath and rebuild bridges. It pleased her that their relationship was improving. If only hers and Cate's was as simple. "You sound optimistic."

"Do I?" Cate lifted her eyes to Dita's. "Well, maybe. Time can heal a lot of things if we're prepared to give it a chance."

Time can heal a lot of things if we're prepared to give it a chance. The words weren't lost on Dita and she heard the deli owner's voice again... *So long as you can live with the consequences.* She stared at Cate and thought, *I didn't give you a chance.* Dita's smile faded, she no longer had the heart to wear it. She felt vulnerable and awkward.

A glint of concern surfaced in Cate's eyes. "How's your health? Everything okay now?"

Behind that look, Dita caught the genuine fondness. "Much better, Cate. Thank you...I'm stronger now, back to how I was before."

"Good."

It was only a simple word but Dita thought she heard so much behind it. She was unable to take her eyes off Cate and when her look was returned with the same intensity, Dita questioned herself. Had she got it wrong? Did something still pulse between them? She sensed Cate move and for one glorious moment thought she was about to reach out and touch her forearm. But though Cate's hand rose, nothing happened. The loss of that touch—its anticipation, hit Dita ridiculously hard and she felt her eyes cloud over.

"I'm glad you're here this evening," Dita said with ridiculous formality, just trying to hold herself together.

"Yes." Cate cringed at her newly inadequate conversational skills. Everything was so stilted between them where once it had flowed.

Dita's heart ached. *Such empty words between us that speak only of loss.* For her, the realization that she was still in love hadn't come as a sudden revelation, it was more like a door slowly opening to throw light on her feelings. As time passed, that opening had widened and with it the acknowledgment that she loved Cate and wanted her in her life. She looked at the napkin clutched in Cate's hand. How she longed to be able to reach out and take that hand. *Lucky napkin.* But it was too late. She had lost everything.

"Damn it, this is so difficult," she said in frustration more to herself than to Cate, but her words were heard and misunderstood.

"I won't be here long," Cate murmured, obviously imagining Dita was uncomfortable around her.

"No, I'm glad you're back," Dita blurted out, causing Cate to look at her strangely as if she didn't believe her. Dita sensed it. She was making such a mess of things. "I *am* glad you're back, *honestly*. You left very abruptly for Italy."

"Did I?"

"Yes."

"I saw no reason to hang around." Cate had difficulty smiling.

Dita heard her strain. She needed to say something to change that, but what? "Cate, I—" She couldn't finish her sentence, for a dish of steaming vegetables suddenly hovered between them. A somber-looking waiter stood at her side asking which ones she wanted.

With Dita's attention diverted, Cate quickly pivoted toward her father. She grabbed him by his arm, speaking with urgency. "Don't ask why, just change places."

"What?"

"Change places," she repeated quickly.

"Now?" He couldn't hide his surprise.

"Now." She eyed him sharply.

William promptly did as he was instructed and changed seating with his daughter, who muttered something about wanting to "catch up" with Ele. Did she think he was born yesterday?

Cate had no option. The longer she and Dita sat next to each other, the more agitated Dita seemed to become. Eventually the evening came to its inevitable conclusion and everyone started to get up from the table. Cate was the first to leave it as she went to retrieve her coat and phone for a cab, leaving the others chatting. As she made her way back toward them to say good night, the group had moved away from the table and stood near the central kitchen rotunda where guests could watch the preparation of their food.

What happened next was like a scene from an old black-and-white movie. Dita was standing on the periphery of the main group with her back to the central kitchen, rifling in her handbag. One of the chefs— an Italian—appeared flustered and raising his voice, stepped out from behind the rotunda moving absently in Dita's direction. Hearing his elevated voice, Dita turned to see what all the fuss was about, only to find herself inches away from a long kitchen knife. In the flash of a second, the blood drained from her face and her terrified gaze was riveted on the knife pointing in her direction. The bag in her hands fell and the contents spilled across the floor as her legs began to buckle.

Before she could fall, Cate rushed to grab her, standing in between her and the knife, enfolding her tightly in her arms. "It's okay, Dita... it's all right. He's not trying to hurt you."

The chef immediately began talking in bullet-speed Italian, summoning a kitchen hand to take the offending knife and mopping his face in embarrassment.

Leaning into Cate, Dita felt a protective hand on the back of her head. She hadn't a clue as to what was being said by the chef, but by the time he'd stopped talking some of her composure had returned. Speaking into Cate's neck, she asked what had been said.

Cate eased back slightly to look at her, her eyes tender. She cast a quirky half grin. "He says he's sorry and something about spinach."

"Is that all?"

"He also says you're very pretty." There was no hiding the affection that radiated from Cate, and Dita automatically fell forward into her arms again.

"Oh, Cate," she whispered, realizing she was at last where she'd wanted to be all evening and that she never wanted to leave this woman's embrace again.

But then she heard William's voice and the others around her, flapping and making a fuss. Coldness swept over her as Cate released her and stepped back to allow the others to come forward and console her. By the time Dita had placated them *and* the chef, Cate was nowhere to be seen. She had vanished...again.

❖

Dita managed to drive herself home. There the events of the evening continued to unsettle her and though tired, there was no way she could sleep. Sitting at her desk, she switched her computer on and waited for it to boot up, drumming her fingers on the plain wooden desk to some silent beat. She reached down into a drawer and extracted a photo. It was the one she'd furtively taken of Cate at the Herculaneum. Never able to throw it away, even in her angriest moments, Dita stared at it for the thousandth time.

She loved this photo. It had captured Cate in a rare moment, relaxed and unaware the shot was being snapped. There was a certain look on her face, one that surfaced when she let down her shield and discarded all the defensive paraphernalia that usually surrounded her. It was a youthful and innocent face. Dita was drawn to it. She'd seen the same look in the early hours of Christmas morning when Cate had pulled her to a bedroom window to show her a picture-perfect winter scene of a snow-covered oak tree lit by a full moon. It had been a special moment. Dita hated that she'd batted her away. Were the two of them destined to remain out of sync with each other forever?

The computer came online but Dita no longer had any interest in checking her e-mail. She turned it off and made her way to bed, taking Cate's photo with her.

So long as you can live with the consequences.

She knew she couldn't.

CHAPTER TWENTY-ONE

They're both beautiful fabrics," Dita said as she stood in the large warehouse of a textile supplier located outside Providence. She'd made the trip planning to see Cate in Manhattan. According to William she wasn't leaving for Italy for at least a week.

Dita was thankful, suspecting it would take more than a couple of lunch dates to convince her to give them another chance. She concentrated again on the two different materials in her hands, unsure of which one she preferred. They were both attractive patterns but she only needed one.

A familiar warm husky voice suddenly spoke from behind her. "Buy the one in your left hand. It's softer and the weave is closer. It'll be stronger, last longer."

Dita's heart missed a beat as she turned to face Cate, unable to hide her surprise or the smile that automatically lit her face. "You're here! What a coincidence." Her eyes took only a second to run the entire length of Cate, who looked casual and relaxed, dressed for business.

"Not entirely," Cate said. "I phoned your office and they said you were here."

"You phoned?"

"I wondered how you're feeling?" Her tone was light and friendly, as though they were just two business acquaintances who'd bumped into each other unexpectedly. But their eyes rested on each other for too long. "It's good to see you again, Dita."

Cate meant every word. She might have said something else but was interrupted by the salesman who returned to her with paperwork to sign. It didn't stop her having to force her eyes away from Dita to deal with the matter at hand. Signing quickly, she gave the man some final instructions and hoped her voice sounded calm, for she certainly didn't feel it. Seeing Dita, even though she'd intentionally tracked her down, still stunned her.

As Cate turned back to Dita she found she was still being scrutinized and couldn't stop swallowing hard, for it wasn't a simple look, where someone watched another casually. Dita's gaze was loaded with emotional intensity. Cate could only acknowledge that her suspicions were right; Dita's heart was still involved even if her head instructed otherwise. Robbed of any ability to make small talk, Cate let herself feast her eyes and draw pleasure from being in the presence of the one she loved.

A quiet cough and Dita was reminded that the sales assistant was still waiting for *her* decision regarding the fabrics she continued to hold. She turned and apologized, and with no more thought, pushed the material in her left hand forward. "This one, please." She ordered the rolls she wanted. Then, turning back to acknowledge that she'd chosen the material Cate had suggested, Dita found her gone. Panic engulfed her for a split second until she heard that voice again, a few yards away. Cate was talking to someone she knew.

Watching her, Dita felt a sense of wild anticipation. Somewhere between one glass of wine and another, last night, she'd decided to take action. She knew she'd made a mistake at Christmas and she hoped she wouldn't be too late to salvage something. She had to try. She was going to claw her way back to Cate if it wasn't too late.

Perhaps it was the manner in which Dita approached, Cate thought, the way she now stood facing her with those incredible eyes moving over her body. Cate knew something had shifted.

"You called me?" Dita prompted.

"Yes. I thought last night was awkward…well, I felt awkward, maybe you didn't. But I thought we could have dinner one night before I leave." Cate had vacillated before she finally picked up the phone, but her thoughts kept coming back to that moment when she first saw Dita in the restaurant and felt the heady power of their connection. "Don't worry if you're busy or don't want to."

"No," Dita said hastily. "I'd like to…very much."

Cate felt the faint damp of Dita's breath fall across her face. It was all she could do not to lean closer and kiss those unforgettable lips. "Good. I'll call you."

Dita reached out and caught her by the hand. "Cate...don't go."

"Okay." Cate's awful state of apprehension was calming. She had asked for the date, and Dita had accepted. She coughed uncomfortably, clearing her throat of what seemed like dry rocks wedged there.

Dita glided gracefully closer, leaving barely six inches between them. "I want to ask you something."

Cate was powerless and couldn't take her eyes off her—hell, she couldn't even blink. *I'm done for.* "Yes?"

"Have you moved on?"

Cate's face was a mosaic of mystification. Dita felt only compassion. She knew her question had thrown Cate off balance, which for someone who always liked to be in control, would be disturbing. Cate's tension was tangible. Not that Dita felt any better. She was breeding a butterfly farm in her stomach and was fighting to not lose her nerve and go to pieces. Her question was such a calculated risk. All the fine words she'd rehearsed and perfected, planning what she would say to Cate on those hoped-for lunch dates, now seemed like noise. Excuses. Justifications. Calculations. Waiting for Cate's answer, only one thing mattered—the future they could have if only Cate felt as she did.

Dita put her hopes into words. "I'm asking because I love you. I made a mistake at Christmas. I was afraid. But Cate, I'm tired of looking back. I want to build a future with you."

Shocked, Cate stared around the rolls and bales of fabric stacked high around them. This was such an unlikely place to hear the words she'd longed for that she almost laughed. And yet, what could be more appropriate than two fashion designers having this conversation in a textile warehouse? She took the longest time to study her companion, trying to make sense of what was happening. A questioning, quirky half grin set on her face. "This is...unexpected."

"I can see how it might be."

Cate placed her hands on her hips and arched a brow. "You have a habit of doing this, of surprising me."

"I hope that's a good thing."

"Mostly...yes."

They unashamedly stared at each other. For too long, they'd missed one another and like starving people, they soaked in the nourishing vision of the other. Cate's heart, desperate for the fairy tale, pounded with hope. She placed a hand on Dita's waist. "Let's continue this discussion somewhere else."

Dita welcomed the feel of the hand and wished she'd not worn her jacket. How she wanted to feel Cate's touch on her skin. As Cate guided her out the door, Dita said, "I thought I could live without you…I can't. I still love you and I want you to know that." Their steps didn't falter. "I hate you being over there in Italy, so far from me, and I loathe the way everything was left between us at Christmas…the way *I* left things. Cate, I don't want to lose you."

Cate stopped. In her wildest dreams, she'd never thought to hear this, and still not convinced that she was hearing correctly—that Dita was doing a complete one hundred and eighty degree reversal. Cate remained, at least on the surface, a picture of composure and tranquility. She drew a deep breath. "What's made you change your mind?"

Dita faced her, one hand moving up and over her hair like she was trying to smooth it back into place. Nerves…for Dita's appearance was immaculate. "If I have to settle for occasional acquaintance or distant friendship, I will, but that isn't what I want. I want to try and get back *us* again. Now…your turn. Why are you really here? Just to ask me out on a date?"

"Yes. Although I hoped for more."

The answer intrigued Dita, the unspoken implication of more made her ache. There was a raw brutal honesty wrapped in something quite desperate—a whisper of vulnerability. "I thought you were avoiding me."

"I was only trying to make things more comfortable for you," Cate replied.

"Well, you didn't. It's been miserable without you." Sadness wrote itself on Dita's face as she added, "And at the dinner…I thought you'd moved on."

The seriousness of Dita's answer hit Cate hard. Her voice sank to its huskiest level, tenderness engrained in the tone. "Darling, where would I *move on* to?"

"You've gone back to Italy."

"You made your intentions very clear at Christmas and I had to honor them."

Dita nervously shifted her feet. Other things needed to be said.

"You should never have asked me for a second chance that night, Cate. I was tired, not feeling good, and I had this stupid connection in my head that linked you and my mother."

"Your mother?"

"It's a long story. She had a drug problem and virtually abandoned me."

Cate instinctively edged closer to her, placing her other hand over Dita's in quiet support. "I'm sorry."

"I *know* you've never done drugs, Cate, and I knew that at Christmas, but for whatever reason, it didn't stop me from feeling insecure." She laughed soullessly. "We all have our issues and I guess those are mine. It was so easy for me to blame you for my mother's sins." She dipped her head, studying their linked hands. "I'm sorry."

"All that matters is you're here now, and so am I." Love shone from Cate.

"But it shows how our pasts thread forward into our present *and* future, doesn't it." Dita could see how each of them had been caught in the trap of their childhoods, it was something else they had in common. "I see it all clearly now...but retrospectively." A solitary tear trailed down her cheek. "I just want you to want me again."

Cate pulled Dita into her arms. "You think I've ever stopped?" She felt Dita push in close to her, locking arms around her waist. "How could I ever let you think that?" Cate whispered softly in her ear. "I want what you want, Dita. I want *us* back again, too. I still want that second chance." Then, the gentlest touch of humor came. "Is *now* a good time to ask? And for pity's sake, tell me if it isn't."

Dita drew back and rested her hands on Cate's shoulders, adoring the way she was being regarded, with love and eyes that spoke of possibilities. "It's the perfect time. And I want that second chance to start right now."

"That could be arranged." Cate kissed her with deep tenderness. "I love you, Dita."

"I love you, too," Dita murmured. "Let's go home."

❖

They stood naked before each other; the only intrusion of the external world into the inner sanctum of Cate's bedroom was the sound of distant city traffic. They'd been intimate before, but this time was different. Neither spoke as they entered a solemn ritual created from deep, profound meaning.

Cate stepped closer to Dita, not touching but sensing the electricity in her, as the hair on her arms tingled with an expectancy of what was to come. "Have we got it right this time?" she whispered in the dusky half-light, and she felt the breath of a "yes" whisper across her face like a kiss. She breathed in, intoxicated.

A moment's grace, no more, and Dita dipped her head, her lips searching for Cate's and in the last fragmentation of a second, she saw the haze of love in Cate's eyes. Their lips touched like butterfly wings before Dita skipped her way down Cate's neck, then trailed upward to let a slow, tantalizingly breath caress her ear.

"I love you," Cate responded, letting her head tilt to a side, granting Dita access, trust implicit.

Dita ran the back of her fingers lightly down Cate's arms, feeling her tremble beneath her touch. "Time is ours," she whispered into Cate's ear. "Time to nurture love and to heal our wounds. Let time be our servant."

They moved in synergy toward the bed, lying down and facing one another. At first neither moved, content to absorb the life rhythm of the other, to listen to the regularity and cadence of each breath as it filled the silence of the room. The half-light allowed each the quiet observance of the shape and curves of the other. In time, inquisitive hands reached out to gently explore subtle, enticing arcs and bends, and fingers ran across the plains of stomachs and the rolling hills of breasts. They moved closer together until their lips met again, full and ready, beginning a slow exchange of chaste kisses. Each time their lips touched, their bodies moved infinitely nearer until thighs, breasts, and stomachs became indistinguishable. A leg slipped between two thighs. Heartbeats increased. The assured regularity of breathing disappeared, replaced by a more erratic tempo as body temperatures rose.

Silently, Cate touched Dita's breast but as her hand made contact, Dita stopped its progress, instead tracing feather-like fingers across the soft skin of Cate's cheek, then the neck and clavicle before moving downward and pausing on a rising breast. There, she circled a lone finger around a pebbled summit, moving across the tip and occasionally pinching it gently until she felt it harden in response. All the time, she pushed her long lean leg higher against the center of Cate's sex, rocking gently.

Hearing the increase in her lover's breathing, Dita carefully turned her onto her back and splayed her legs open, placing herself between them. Her full length over Cate, she pushed herself up onto her elbows, letting her hair fall across Cate's nakedness. She dipped to kiss her again, all the time drawing her own body slowly up and down Cate's, provocatively thrusting her sex closer. The moment of chasteness gone, she pushed her tongue into the warm mouth that welcomed her.

The body beneath hers hungry, Dita responded, slipping lower, kissing her way down damp skin. She stopped to caress a nipple, sucking, biting, and teasing before continuing her journey south, her tongue moving like a slippery snake to rest on Cate's quivering stomach. In no rush to reach her destination, she circled the salty milieu of a firm abdomen, while her hands played again with nipples, lest they felt neglected. Ensuring their pert, erect state, satisfied they were happy, Dita kissed her way over the hairline of the pubic bone and down further. At the clitoris, she swept her tongue from side to side as she felt Cate squirm beneath her, the slow teasing pushing her limits.

But Dita would not be hurried, and pushing Cate's legs over her shoulders, she continued her nurturing, one hand placed low on Cate's abdomen barely above the hairline, while the other moved tauntingly lower. Several times she gently pushed on the abdomen and trailed her hand across Cate's sex, each time feeling the crescendo in Cate build. She circled the opening in ever-tighter sweeps until Cate pushed up and moaned. Feeling the welcoming wetness awaiting her, Dita was ready.

Slowly, she eased a single finger inside her lover and immediately felt the body beneath hers buck again. With careful attention, one finger became several as she pushed ever deeper in a progressive ritual of withdrawal, hesitation, then re-entry. Her rhythm grew quicker and more frenzied as Cate's body demanded more, pushing down on Dita's hand and arching itself up and off the bed, rocking the two of them like hot dancers locked in a tango.

Cate's irregular breathing spurred Dita on, the fast panting of her lover's arousal building her own sexual excitement, until together they moved as one.

"Don't stop," Cate gasped, sounding like a runner in the final stage of a marathon. A heartbeat later, she climaxed, arching so high Dita had to hang on tightly.

Eventually Cate fell exhausted, and creeping back up to her, Dita nuzzled her face into the nape of her neck, kissing her there just once, tasting the salt before collapsing worn out at her side.

"Thank you, my love."

It was the way Cate said it, the inflection of *my love*, Dita thought her heart was going to burst with pure joy. This was her pleasure, the pleasure of giving to the one she loved and knowing how much she loved Cate. She felt a hand caress her face and hair, and in utter contentment, she closed her eyes and allowed weariness to claim her.

Cate listened to Dita's breathing as it calmed. She sensed no movement. "Are you falling asleep on me?"

"I think I might be," Dita replied dreamily.

Warmth oozed back. "Sleep, my darling."

Darling. That beautiful word again, said in that husky tone. Dita could no longer keep her eyes open. "I'm sorry…"

"Don't be." Cate kissed her forehead. "Close your eyes. I'll still be here when you wake."

"Don't let me sleep too long," Dita whispered. "I have an important date with someone I love."

A voice lilting and soft spoke, called out, speaking that it was time.

The angel took courage and, rising to a knee, stretched first one, then the other wing, extending them out as far as was possible.

It felt the light nurture and feed it.

Now standing, its strength returned, in one fluid graceful movement, the angel arched its neck and looking upward, flew.

It was going home.

EPILOGUE

Bernard Bressinger stood in the large hall where the runway show had just ended and awaited his chance to pounce on potential interview material. Contemplating, as always, the articles he could run in a bumper edition, he thought how fast things changed and moved on in the fashion world. For the past few years, he'd attended similar shows and listened to gossip about the unfriendly rivalry between the fashion houses of Seraphim and Zabor. Everyone had a story to tell about the personal unpleasantness between the competing designers. Now the two arch-rivals had just stunned the fashion industry by announcing the merger of their two houses. Not that Bernard was completely surprised. If there was one thing he'd learned in this business, it was that no one could ever predict who their friends would be from one season to the next.

Catching sight of the ever-elusive Cate Canton, he rushed up to her and dared to ask for an interview, but one hard glare confirmed she was never going to grant him what he wanted. Some things never changed.

"Mr. Bressinger, I don't do—"

"I know, I know," he interrupted her with a tone of resignation. "You never give interviews and I should talk to your manager, Saul de Charlier, who'll be happy to address my questions." He couldn't hide the world-weary tone of his voice, and as he glanced back at her, expecting to see her moving away from him. He was surprised to find her looking at him, grinning.

"No," she said in that seductive voice of hers, "I was going to suggest you talk to my partner, Dita Newton. She's the one with the charismatic personality, and quite why I'll never understand, but she seems to like the media." Her deep blue eyes sparkled with humor.

Cordiality? This from the woman with all the personal warmth of an ice cube? Bernard felt his right brow rise automatically as his ever-present masculinity moved into overdrive. Maybe she was thawing. Was his charm beginning to have an effect? He certainly did have a way with women, but then when a man was as suave and sophisticated as he, it wasn't difficult to understand why the opposite sex melted in his presence. Yet this particular woman had never found him her type and he knew the reason why.

What a shame, he thought, as he watched her stroll over to Dita Newton, and then witnessed the intimate look that passed between them, the hand placed on a back and the effect it had on the recipient. Of course, there were *different* rumors now, delicious hints that the new partnership was far more than purely business. For once, he didn't doubt the rumors.

Pondering a few tastefully suggestive headlines for the Dita Newton exclusive, he was startled when Cate Canton cast a backward glance in his direction and a warm smile. Bernard was so taken aback he found himself doing something completely out of character. He smiled back at her in open friendship.

"Damn," he muttered to himself. "And such great legs. What a loss."

About the Author

I. Beacham grew up in the heart of England, a green and pleasant land, mainly because it rains so much. This is probably why she ran away to sea, to search for dry places. Over the years, and during long periods away from home constantly traveling to faraway places, she has balanced the rigidity of her professional life with her need and love to write. Blessed with a wicked sense of humor (not all agree), she is a lover of all things water, a dreadful jogger and cook, a hopeless romantic who roams antique stores, an addict of old black-and-white movies, and an adorer of science fiction. In her opinion, a perfect life.

The author would love to hear from readers and can be reached at brit.beacham@yahoo.com.

Books Available From Bold Strokes Books

The Lure by Felice Picano. When Noel Cummings is recruited by the police to go undercover to find a killer, his life will never be the same. (978-1-60282-076-0)

Death of a Dying Man by J.M. Redmann. Mickey Knight, Private Eye and partner of Dr. Cordelia James, doesn't need a drop-dead gorgeous assistant—not until nature steps in. (978-1-60282-075-3)

Justice for All by Radclyffe. Dell Mitchell goes undercover to expose a human traffic ring and ends up in the middle of an even deadlier conspiracy. (978-1-60282-074-6)

Sanctuary by I. Beacham. Cate Canton faces one major obstacle to her goal of crushing her business rival, Dita Newton—her uncontrollable attraction to Dita. (978-1-60282-055-5)

The Sublime and Spirited Voyage of Original Sin by Colette Moody. Pirate Gayle Malvern finds the presence of an abducted seamstress, Celia Pierce, a welcome distraction until the captive comes to mean more to her than is wise. (978-1-60282-054-8)

Suspect Passions by VK Powell. Can two women, a city attorney and a beat cop, put aside their differences long enough to see that they're perfect for each other? (978-1-60282-053-1)

Just Business by Julie Cannon. Two women who come together—each for her own selfish needs—discover that love can never be as simple as a business transaction. (978-1-60282-052-4)

Sistine Heresy by Justine Saracen. Adrianna Borgia, survivor of the Borgia court, presents Michelangelo with the greatest temptations of his life while struggling with soul-threatening desires for the painter Raphaela. (978-1-60282-051-7)

Radical Encounters by Radclyffe. An out-of-bounds, outside-the-lines collection of provocative, superheated erotica by award-winning romance and erotica author Radclyffe. (978-1-60282-050-0)

Thief of Always by Kim Baldwin & Xenia Alexiou. Stealing a diamond to save the world should be easy for Elite Operative Mishael Taylor, but she didn't figure on love getting in the way. (978-1-60282-049-4)

X by JD Glass. When X-hacker Charlie Riven is framed for a crime she didn't commit, she accepts help from an unlikely source—sexy Treasury Agent Elaine Harper. (978-1-60282-048-7)

The Middle of Somewhere by Clifford Henderson. Eadie T. Pratt sets out on a road trip in search of a new life and ends up in the middle of somewhere she never expected. (978-1-60282-047-0)

Paybacks by Gabrielle Goldsby. Cameron Howard wants to avoid her old nemesis Mackenzie Brandt but their high school reunion brings up more than just memories. (978-1-60282-046-3)

Uncross My Heart by Andrews & Austin. When a radio talk show diva sets out to interview a female priest, the two women end up at odds and neither heaven nor earth is safe from their feelings. (978-1-60282-045-6)

Fireside by Cate Culpepper. Mac, a therapist, and Abby, a nurse, fall in love against the backdrop of friendship, healing, and defending one's own within the Fireside shelter. (978-1-60282-044-9)

Green Eyed Monster by Gill McKnight. Mickey Rapowski believes her former boss has cheated her out of a small fortune, so she kidnaps the girlfriend and demands compensation—just a straightforward abduction that goes so wrong when Mickey falls for her captive. (978-1-60282-042-5)

Blind Faith by Diane and Jacob Anderson-Minshall. When private investigator Yoshi Yakamota and the Blind Eye Detective Agency are hired to find a woman's missing sister, the assignment seems fairly mundane—but in the detective business, the ordinary can quickly become deadly. (978-1-60282-041-8)

A Pirate's Heart by Catherine Friend. When rare book librarian Emma Boyd searches for a long-lost treasure map, she learns the hard way that pirates still exist in today's world—some modern pirates steal maps, others steal hearts. (978-1-60282-040-1)

Trails Merge by Rachel Spangler. Parker Riley escapes the high-powered world of politics to Campbell Carson's ski resort—and their mutual attraction produces anything but smooth running. (978-1-60282-039-5)

Dreams of Bali by C.J. Harte. Madison Barnes worships work, power, and success, and she's never allowed anyone to interfere—that is, until she runs into Karlie Henderson Stockard. Aeros EBook (978-1-60282-070-8)

The Limits of Justice by John Morgan Wilson. Benjamin Justice and reporter Alexandra Templeton search for a killer in a mysterious compound in the remote California desert. (978-1-60282-060-9)

Designed for Love by Erin Dutton. Jillian Sealy and Wil Johnson don't much like each other, but they do have to work together—and what they desire most is not what either of them had planned. (978-1-60282-038-8)

Calling the Dead by Ali Vali. Six months after Hurricane Katrina, NOLA Detective Sept Savoie is a cop who thinks making a relationship work is harder than catching a serial killer—but her current case may prove her wrong. (978-1-60282-037-1)

Shots Fired by MJ Williamz. Kyla and Echo seem to have the perfect relationship and the perfect life until someone shoots at Kyla—and Echo is the most likely suspect. (978-1-60282-035-7)

truelesbianlove.com by Carsen Taite. Mackenzie Lewis and Dr. Jordan Wagner have very different ideas about love, but they discover that truelesbianlove is closer than a click away. Aeros EBook (978-1-60282-069-2)

Justice at Risk by John Morgan Wilson. Benjamin Justice's blind date leads to a rare opportunity for legitimate work, but a reckless risk changes his life forever. (978-1-60282-059-3)

Run to Me by Lisa Girolami. Burned by the four-letter word called love, the only thing Beth Standish wants to do is run for—or maybe from—her life. (978-1-60282-034-0)

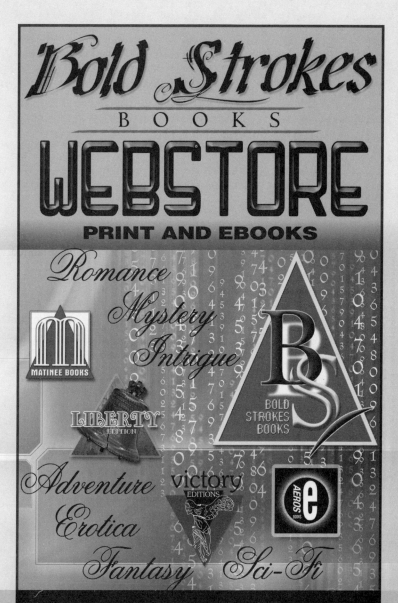

"But you're wrong," Van-See said. "I was in prison, too, I . . ."

"Sure," Block said, "your stooge, the phoney chairman pulled a fast one, double-crossed you. He kept Nick and Adinah on ice, just in case he tripped up, had to prove he didn't kill anyone. But you were the brains behind it all, Van-See."

Van-See half turned, dug into his pocket.

The gun was half out when the girl shot him.

Block said, "You'd've gotten the Nick Siscoe part back too. Had it all along, in fact. Just hearing you talk was a dead giveaway. That XI tape you were fed loused up the erasure. But here's a crash course if you want it."

Block reached into his pocket, handed me a round object wrapped in a black hanky.

"What is it?"

"Your XI tape."

I looked at it. "I was a bastard," I said, "and so was the Chairman."

"You're okay, Nick."

"You think so?"

"Sure. We both are."

"I hope so."

"I'm betting on it. After all, you and I still have a whole galaxy to straighten out."

About the Author

ISIDORE HAIBLUM was born in Brooklyn, New York. He attended CCNY, edited the college humor magazine, *Mercury*, took honors in Yiddish, and graduated with a BA in English and social science. He has published nine science fiction novels including *The Mutants Are Coming, Interwood*, and *The Tsaddik of the Seven Wonders*. He was also co-author on a book about the golden age of radio. His many articles dealing with Yiddish, humor, and popular culture have appeared in such publications as *The Village Voice, Twilight Zone* Magazine, and *Moment*. He lives in New York City.